This novel contains content that might be triggering, for a list of possible triggers please visit:
https://www.abbeyfox.com/the-wicked-kingdom-trigger-warnings

World map design and emblem: aaguirreart
Chapter headers and ink illustrations: Heather Soulliere
Character and Cover Illustrations: www.camiladavila.com

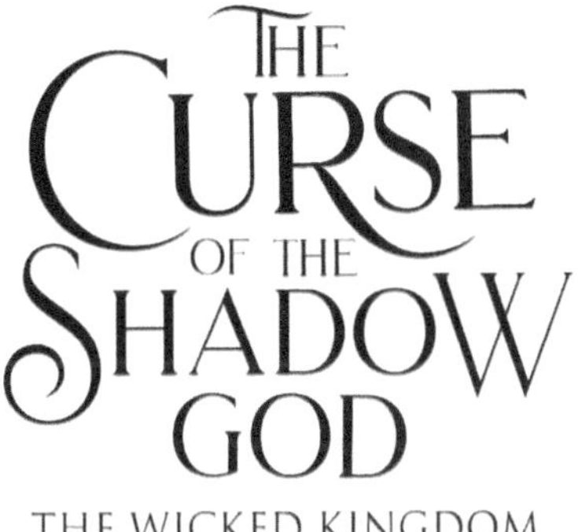

THE CURSE OF THE SHADOW GOD
THE WICKED KINGDOM

The Kingdo[m]
Obsidian City
Sable Forest
Iron Kingdom
Plume City
Leona Sea
Iron City
Rama Sea
Tatum Ocean
Pearl Island
Grey Island
Seems
City
Titian
Willowbrook
Arnin

OF CASZTIAN
ALVER MOUNTAINS
CITY OF CASTI
BOLD KINGDOM
CITY OF BOLD
ENDER DESERT
OCHRE CITY
EROS OCEAN
CITY OF MILANIA
RIVER
ILIAN TOWN
SUN FOREST
PPER
SKY CITY
KINGDOM
SILVER KINGDOM
CITY OF SILVER
RUST ISLAND
BRIAR CITY
N

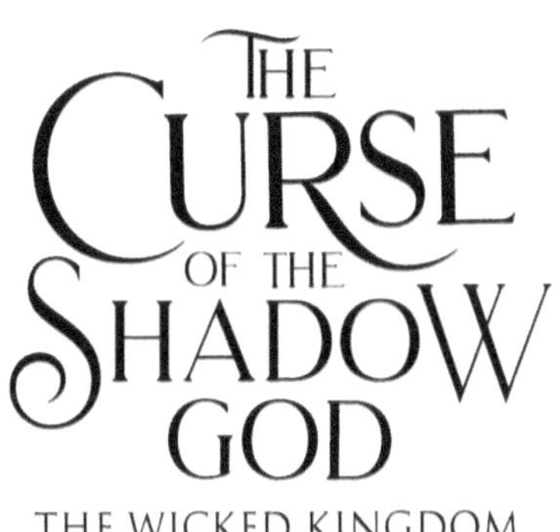

THE CURSE
OF THE
SHADOW GOD

THE WICKED KINGDOM

Society of Crows

To Cora Elder, sorceress of the second order, also known as Violet Elder,

We've matched you to Gavin Luna, healer of the Valdor Assembly. Failure to proceed with this command will cause prosecution by the laws of the Iron Kingdom and our gods. This letter is binding and final; from the moment of its delivery, you and Mr. Luna shall be one unit. A dissolution will be considered if there is a failure to produce the 'child'.
Ceremony to be held in a fortnight and to be witnessed by the Valdor Commander Julius Coventry, and society members Vera Rosenest and Haerion C. Windsboe.

Signed,

Marcus Elm

The Society of Crows guarantor

1

VIOLET

THE WHISKEY BURNED AS IT WENT DOWN HER THROAT, tasting bitter like betrayal. Drops of amber liquid trickled down her cheeks and neck, cooling her skin, but they failed to ease the ache that had settled in her chest like a growing sickness which took over her every thought.

No matter how much she drank, the memories kept on coming.

Fugitive.

Lowlife.

Deserter.

She should have known better than to trust that people would side with her. No one would turn against the Crown, which demanded that magical humans marry only for procreation, for the preservation of magic.

The parchment she held in one hand crumpled in her tightening fist, the neat penmanship disappearing behind crisp folds, hiding the name she had long since memorized.

Gavin Luna, her groom.

Warmth spread through her gut, part liquor, part boiling anger. She slammed the empty glass on the worn surface of the table.

"Another!" she growled in Obsidian, hoping her accent wouldn't mark her as an outsider to the people of this mountain. Blending in was imperative to her escape. Her voice, though loud, was almost drowned out by the instrument playing in the background—a guitar strummed poorly by a drunken man. The bartender at the end of the room glanced back at her with a frown. He wiped his hands over a spotted apron that wrapped tight over his round stomach.

He grunted loud enough that she could hear his displeasure despite the noise. His dark copper skin—a similar shade to hers—glistened under the light of the lanterns as he walked back toward the bar, presumably to fetch her drink.

Perhaps shouting orders was odd here in the mountains. It was common in the Iron City's taverns. She'd done it often enough when she'd gone out with her assembly after a tough assignment. Not that she cared if this man was offended by her manners, or lack thereof. Trying to please others was one of the many reasons that she was in trouble to start with.

She scrunched her nose at the mess she'd made when slamming her empty glass on the table. Her dinner lay spilled before her. The lentil soup had still been lukewarm, too, even though it had sat untouched the entire evening. Now she regretted her impulsive outburst. She had little coin left, and wasting food was idiotic if she intended to survive a week, let alone cross the mountain range.

Her trip across the Obsidian mountains would be considered unwise by most in her shoes. But she had to see her family one last time before she had to leave the kingdom for good. They were the only wholesome thing she had left.

"Bad day?" a woman wearing red slurred from the table next to hers. The scent of chewed tobacco and tooth rot plumed out of her thin, cracked lips. Violet jumped at the newcomer's sudden appearance. She could have sworn she'd been alone in this part of the room.

The skin on her arms pebbled, and her gut twisted as she studied the old woman carefully, taking in her frail bones and thin frame. Not an obvious threat, but in a world of magic she couldn't take a risk, no matter how harmless the person or creature looked.

She didn't linger on her haggard neighbor's form, quickly moving her gaze back to the entrance of the tavern. Keeping an eye on your escape route could mean the difference between freedom or capture, and she hadn't traveled this far to get caught again.

"It's not a good day for me either," the woman continued, tapping her long fingers against her clay mug. She had the thick knuckles of someone who worked with her hands and spotted skin that had once been fair, but which had been deepened by the sun. Most likely a traveler, worn down by the unforgiving mountains of the Iron Kingdom. "I'm Luelle."

"Violet." She forced the word out past stiff lips. It wasn't her true given name, but a nickname her little sister had given her, as her eyes were purple, like the flowers. That had been long before the Crown had ripped her away from the shelter of her family's arms. It was the name she'd always used with her closest friends in the assembly. Friends—hah. Treacherous vipers, the lot of them.

"Are you new in town?" Luelle asked. At first, Violet had assumed Luelle's voice was distorted by liquor, but it was a thick accent from another land. The woman didn't wait for a response before taking a healthy swig of her drink and wiping the drips that trailed down her chin away with her wrist. Her eyes, hazy with age, flitted toward the door. "You must be. The Iron City clothes give you away. I must admit, I wasn't expecting to find a fallen soldier when I was sent here."

A fallen soldier... What a nice way to describe what she truly was. A deserter. The scum of this land, in the eyes of the Crown's army.

Violet leaned away. Her limbs felt too heavy, weighed down by the alcohol running through her blood. She pressed her lips together and buried the condemning letter inside her coat's pocket. Her first mistake had been to drink this heavily when she needed to be alert and ready. She cursed her stupidity as the lights of the room danced above her head.

Desperation wasn't a good look on anyone, and she was teetering on the edge of a precipice. Her escape was only a breath away from failing.

The bartender's large shape loomed over her as he placed a tall glass on the table. "Next time get the drink yourself, princess…" He frowned at her spilled dinner. The corners of his lips twitched, and Violet witnessed the moment something shifted in his eyes. "I don't clean up other people's messes. You shall have to pay me for my trouble." His gaze trailed down the curves of her breasts.

She slammed the gold coin on the table, forcing him to meet her eyes. "Your cleaning is not my problem."

He twirled the gold coin with two fingers, and his dark tongue traced his bottom lip. "This won't cover your bill."

"It's what my first drink cost."

"Too bad, prices just went up." He brought his hand over his dirty apron, hooking a finger on the fabric belt. "It'll be five gold coins for the drink and the cleaning."

Her scowl deepened. "I won't be paying you five pieces of gold for mediocre whiskey." Not when that alone would pay for breakfast in the morning.

"That's the price, princess." He leaned over the table, which groaned under his considerable weight. "But you can pay me out back."

She scoffed and pushed the glass away from her, fingertips tingling with a warning of her awakened power. "I don't want the drink. I haven't touched it, and I won't be washing dishes for something I didn't have."

It would have been a lie if she'd claimed his shifty gaze didn't bother her, not when the place was full of people who seemed keen to ignore what was happening. "You won't be washing dishes. You'll be on your knees, putting that smart mouth to use."

He stepped forward, and her blood raced through her. The alcohol left her body as it ignited like dry kindling, her magic answering in kind as she lifted a hand and the light of a spell bloomed from her palm. "Please lead the way," she said. "I bite, and I would love to take a souvenir."

The bartender staggered back, his eyes wide as they stuck to the gray swirls of her power which hovered over her skin.

It was a normal reaction for a non-magic-wielder when they saw the beginning of a spell for the first time. His lips flapped open and closed, and he muttered something that was lost beneath the screeching of the singer on the stage, who was still playing his guitar like the end of the world was near. The bartender stormed away, glancing back every few seconds as if she might follow him to the counter.

Luelle hummed next to her. Violet had almost forgotten she was there. "That was quite the display you put on there."

Violet felt her cheeks heat. Making a show of her power in front of humans was not a smart move for a fugitive, but alcohol and anger made for a poor mix.

"It's hard to travel this part of the world alone as a dame," Luelle said.

"I do all right." The wind howled through the crevices of the windows, calling her attention outside where a blizzard raged. "This can't be. It wasn't snowing when I got here."

"It's a spell." Luelle grimaced before she sighed. "It signals that an emissary has arrived."

Violet's throat tightened, and she gripped the edge of the table until she couldn't feel her fingers anymore. Cold crawled up her back, seizing her lungs as her mind caught up with Luelle's words. "Emissaries don't exist." Even though she intended to sound confident, her words rang like those of a scared child. Sweat covered her skin, and the memories she had wanted to forget for years came crashing down on her.

"We both know what this means, dear. I was called here today by destiny to deliver the message." Luelle leaned forward, resting her arms on the table.

Violet held her breath as past and present collided. Her worst nightmare had returned. An ambassador of the gods, no longer human nor fae. Luelle wasn't the first she'd encountered in her lifetime, and she wouldn't be the last if the first message she'd received was true. The old woman's skin glowed with a reddish tint of magic that made Violet's nose itch. The scent wafted around them, familiar like the parchment pages of an old book.

"You are doing this now, in the middle of this

place?" Violet's voice shook as she tried to stand up from her seat.

Luelle's silver hair billowed around her head, and the sound of the tavern died down around them. "Your ancestor called upon Dargan, the God of Shadows, for a soul to be spared. The price of a soul can only be paid with another of the same blood. He shall have your firstborn, and your debt shall be repaid."

Tears welled up in Violet's eyes, blurring her vision. The same words that had been spoken to her three years ago, come to haunt her again. Two different emissaries had hunted her down in her most vulnerable moments. The air thinned and the weight of her limbs sank deeper into the calf-skin chair she sat on.

"The God of Shadows will be delighted if I send his messenger back in pieces." Violet lunged out of her seat, grabbing the knife from her belt, and pressed the sharp blade against the sagging skin of Luelle's neck. "He can have my future child over my dead body."

"He will get the soul." Luelle's steady voice shouldn't belong to someone whose blood was beading along the edge of a blade, but her face didn't show a trace of pain or fear. "I'm not afraid of dying. I have lived enough for ten of you. If you can kill me, do so with a clear conscience. You will release me from this torment."

Violet hissed and pulled the knife away. She stared at the small cut on the emissary's throat. It closed in front of her like it had never been there.

There were very few things in this world that could

shock her into silence, but her ties to the Shadow God would forever be one of them. The God of Shadows wanted her child—and so did the Iron Crown. It was why she had to run away from her groom.

No matter her desires, a marriage with the expectation of procreation meant a baby. One that would be born to be taken away by the Crown or by a god.

Violet lifted her chin, and her lip trembled. "What will happen if I don't have any children for him to take?"

"The deal was for Dargan to receive the second magical child born of your bloodline. You, being the first, were spared, but if you cannot produce an heir, he will take you instead."

Silence descended upon them. Dimly, Violet registered music still playing in the background. Luelle's lips tightened into a thin line. She appeared just as unhappy with the news she was forced to give.

"How long do I have?"

"We are four emissaries. You've already met Cullen, who saved you from drowning in the Hulten lake."

He could go straight to the shadow world himself and get flayed alive for all she cared. The bastard had tricked her into believing he was a friend, when all along he'd been trying to get her to fall for him, and to give Dargan what the god wanted from her. Her child. The fae were usually cunning creatures, but he had taken it too far.

"Did he save me so Dargan wouldn't lose his chance of claiming his soul?" Violet wished she could control the bitterness in her tone, but she had cared far too much for this man who had seen her as nothing but a task.

"We are bound to keep you safe within reason until he claims the debt he is owed, yes." Luelle cleared her throat, and Violet got the impression that her relationship with Cullen, however short and messy, wasn't a secret.

"Are you all under orders to sleep with me and get me pregnant, too?"

Luelle looked down at the table, clearly ashamed. "That was... his choice. Dargan never instructed us to do such a thing."

Violet had suspected as much and doubted Luelle was up to the task either way. But she'd been surprised before. "Who else is coming then?"

"You'll be visited by two other emissaries before he comes to collect."

"Cullen used his magic to alter what I saw, to trick me. Do you also have the gift to alter visions?"

Luelle hummed, taking her time to give her an answer. Violet suspected she was trying to decide whether the information would hurt or help her position. "We all have a particular gift that makes us desirable to our god. Rare and coveted amongst the powerful. But no, I'm not an illusionist."

So that was what Cullen was... The emissary answered one question and two more appeared.

"What gift is he expecting my child to have?" Violet had known Dargan had his eyes on her ever since

Cullen's arrival, not that the last emissary had shared much about the particulars. Instead, he had distracted her with his attempts to seduce her.

Twenty-year-old Violet had been an idiot.

The heaviness was back in her chest, constricting her breathing. No longer did she mourn the so-called friends who had slammed their doors in her face when she'd sought refuge. Now the reality sank in. She would never outrun fate, and even if she did so, it would come at the cost of being denied what she craved the most. A family of her own, like the one she'd been stolen from —those that she loved most.

"That is not for you to know... yet."

"Well, fuck that! Why does it have to be me?" She slammed her hand on the table again. She doubted anyone cared. "I already have the Iron Crown trailing my steps. They forced me to wed, and they also want my future child."

Hers and Gavin's, but he wasn't here to plead his case.

Luelle nodded like none of this was news to her. "It's an unfair world, but it wasn't always this way. To answer your question, your bloodline was very power- ful. A special magical trait lingers dormant in your cells —however no magic has been granted to the Elders for many generations."

"Why does he even care about that? He is a god."

Luelle opened her mouth, but the chime of a bell rang in the distance, and the flames of the lanterns flickered with a current of icy wind blasting through the front door. A man entered the room and stomped the snow from his boots.

Violet straightened in her chair. The strain in her jaw echoed all the way down her neck and shoulders. She recognized his regalia. The Iron City's traveling coat was made from thick gray fabric, and the kingdom's emblem shimmered, neatly stitched, on the right side in golden thread.

How had he found her? Was he alone? She hadn't told a soul what road she was taking, and the Obsidian mountains were unforgiving, especially when traveling alone. Known to house mostly non-magic-wielders, they should have assumed it would be the last place she'd head for.

Her gaze drifted toward Luelle, who was reclining in her chair. Her worn eyes fixed on the newcomer, her frown easing. "Your future has been in motion for quite some time. A gift from me to you, Violet: you have been betrayed and betrothed, and you will escape Dargan's claim over you by the end of this journey, but it won't be what you hope for. You can find a way back to her in the old libraries of the world."

Who did Luelle mean by her? And how could she not want to be out of this mess? Could this mean that the old woman was a soothsayer?

Cullen, the illusionist. Luelle, the soothsayer... Who would be the next emissary?

The man had not seen her yet. If Violet was stealthy enough, she could escape out the back. She couldn't stay, and yet she hesitated to leave.

"Will I see you again?" Her eyes trailed the sorcerer from the Crown across to the bar, where the bartender was cleaning a glass with his dirty apron.

"No," Luelle said.

Violet swallowed as sweat dripped down the side of her face. She inched out of her chair, grasping the hilt of her knife tightly enough that her knuckles ached. "How do I break the hold he has on me?"

"You can't avoid him."

"But can I evade him?"

Luelle's thin lips tilted down. She turned her clay mug with both hands, and the scrapping of its porous texture over the wood surface of the table set Violet's already frazzled nerves on fire. "There is an artifact that can help those who seek to escape—for a time. The Stone of Clemency."

A stone, really? Were all these undying bastards insane?

The man turned around, searching for someone in the crowd before pulling the hood of his coat from his head. She met his gaze from across the room, taking him in: his almond skin, the long shaggy hair that fell in loose waves over his russet eyes.

Her heart lodged in her throat, making it hard to breathe, listen, or focus on anything else. She jumped from her seat, instantly forgetting the Shadow God and his claim on her future. All she could focus on was him, as he towered over the rest of the bar.

Gavin Luna was not a bastard she would soon forget. She would recognize him anywhere. The way his eyes lit up when he found her amongst these people, like he had found a prize he would collect. The mark on the sharp edge of his jaw, where her blade had nicked him and the cut was still visible under the shadow of a day's old beard.

She would never admit out loud that occasionally she wondered how his whiskers would burn her most sensitive skin if he rubbed them against her in ways she was not allowed to dream of.

He was hers, and she was his. And if the damn paper she held inside her pocket had anything to say, he was here to bring her back home.

2
VIOLET

Screams erupted around the tavern as Violet's magic poured from her every pore in a billowing wave that pushed the table against the nearest wooden column. The rooftop thundered with the impact, and it rained dust and debris over the fleeing patrons.

"Violet!" Gavin's voice thundered over the commotion, but she was already halfway down the narrow corridor toward the back door. Her rasping breaths drowned out the creaking of the worn floors under her pounding feet. She pushed past the heavy door and met a wall of frigid air.

Snow piled over wooden crates and baskets of waste. It reeked of piss even in the storm, and only the magic swirling around her limbs warmed her skin against the bite of the cold.

The sun had taken refuge behind the shingle rooftops long ago, and gusts of wind blew the snow sideways, clouding her already limited vision.

Had Gavin come alone, or were there more soldiers waiting to ambush her behind every crate she stole past? Violet tightened her grip around her knife's handle, her heart thundering as she looked around, expecting someone to jump out of a dark corner. The shadows extended from every direction, closing in on her.

Inches of fresh snow hid her footprints, and snowflakes stuck to her wool coat and the tight curls of her hair. The end of the alley spilled into the center of town. The establishments that lined the path glowed in orange tones while plumes of smoke billowed out of their uneven iron-pipe chimneys.

Before she could step out into the street, a black shape blocked her path, silhouetted against the snow-brightened night sky. She attacked without preamble, though her movements were reluctant at best as she avoided truly hurting him. She aimed low, not to kill him, but only to debilitate him enough so she could escape. The shadowed figure dodged the initial slash of her blade, as if it were anticipating her moves.

Violet swiped across again. She was blinded by the storm, and the spicy scent of his magic flooded her senses. Whatever spell he was casting pushed her back like a warm bubble that pricked her skin. She slid over the fresh snow that had accumulated on the ground and fell too fast to react. Her own blade slid into her like her body was butter, and her scream pierced the air and echoed down the cramped alley.

Time froze as red hot pain extended from the side of

her hip and warm blood trickled down her leg. The claws of the surrounding chill froze her movements. Violet hissed and pulled out the knife with a loud squelch.

"Dammit, Violet!" Gavin leaned forward, all tanned skin and messy brown hair that fell over the angles of his face. His agility should be forbidden in this cold, and yet he moved as if he were unhindered by his heavy coat and the freezing weather. He reached for her with steady hands, but she kicked him away with both legs, ignoring the sharp bite of her wound.

Gavin grabbed her leg before it hit his ribs, though the force of the impact vibrated up his arm, and the side of his body collided with the building next to him. Still, he didn't let go of her. "Stop. You're hurt."

"I should have killed you!" she shouted, and his gloved hand tightened around her ankle. His grip was rough enough that it distracted her from the wound in her hip.

"You tried to kill me before." His lips rolled back, showing straight white teeth, and anger flared in his eyes.

It wasn't entirely true. She hadn't wanted him dead that day just like she didn't tonight, but she wouldn't correct him on the matter. When she'd thrown her knife at his commander, Gavin had jumped into the crossfire in a foolish display of bravery. She swallowed the knot in her throat as she studied the ragged cut on his jaw, visible even in the gray light of the stormy night.

"Let go of me." Violet kicked again, but the adrenaline running through her body was dwindling, and the sharp pain up her hip and lower back was becoming unbearable. She stiffened in her spot. "Where are the rest of the lackeys?"

"Who?"

"Your assembly. I presume they joined you to hunt me down?"

She blinked rapidly to clear her vision as the ground spun around her. The mixture of alcohol, pain, and magic use had depleted her. Her limbs sank deeper into the snow, and frozen water soaked the back of her clothes. Gavin sat back, giving her some space. Perhaps he sensed that she'd lost the energy to fight him.

"It's just me. I need to know how bad your wound is." He raised both hands, as if she was a wounded animal ready to bite. From this close, every detail of his face was visible: his bushy brows, and his straight nose. He attempted to lift the side of her coat to examine her wound, but it stuck to her, wet with blood. Violet gasped as a wave of pain rushed through her, making her body run cold and hot.

"Stop." She clung onto his shoulder, her fingers dug like claws into the fabric of his coat. "I don't need your help."

Their breaths mingled, and they stared at each other while snowflakes peppered them in white. When had they moved so close to one another? He smelled of freshly picked herbs and the ocean. This was the first time she had noticed it.

Violet had known that Gavin was her match days before their wedding, but even then, he'd not been a stranger. She'd never admit it, but reading his name in her letter had sent her into a panicked frenzy that felt remarkably like exhilaration. A numbing, tingling sensation that extended to the very ends of her finger-tips—a feeling of pure want.

Gavin was the healer of the Valdor Assembly, led by Julius Coventry, not her old commander. But hers and his had worked together for years. Watching him from afar had long since given her a foolish sense of safety. He had shown no interest in her, and she maintained a distance with men she felt drawn to so she wouldn't form any attachments.

Gavin pressed his lips into a thin line. "I need to close your wound and get you warm."

Her teeth rattled, and she grabbed his hand to prevent him from touching her. "I'm not your patient. Don't touching me or—"

"You will kill me? Not tonight." Gavin shook his head and reached for the knife she'd dropped. "May I remind you that you were the one that reached for me just now?" She scowled, but he continued, undeterred, "Other than to examine your wound, I won't be touching you, but you have to let me see it. I can tell it's deep because you've lost a lot of blood."

"Stop being nice. I know what you're doing, and it's not going to work. You won't take me back." She pushed away from him, biting the inside of her cheeks to stave off the pain. He watched her wobble to her feet in silence, rubbing his fingers together. Violet held onto the side of the building, gasping for air as the ground shifted beneath her.

Gavin's eyes picked up the blade from the ground, studying the bloodstained silver metal. He frowned with a resigned expression. "Do you want me to leave you here? Maybe you will make it through the night."

Violet hesitated. It might have been the cold or the fact that something about his words rang true. Getting hurt in a place like the Obsidian mountain town of Scoria wasn't ideal. The chances of finding a magical healer were slim, and waiting for her body to do its job without the aid of magic meant staying here for a long time. That meant capture.

"Are you here to take me back?"

"Yes." His voice came barely above a whisper, but she shook her head and instantly attempted to step away. Her power flickered in and out, giving her strength and dulling her pain. "Stop, Violet. I will not force you to return with me, but we need to talk about it after I heal you. You need rest and sutures." He made a disapproving noise and pulled at the satchel that wrapped around his stomach, rummaging through its contents.

"I don't want to talk. In case you don't remember, I tried to escape when I saw you."

Gavin sent her a stern look and brought out a rolled piece of gauze, holding the edge of it between his teeth so he could tear off a long piece. He was quick with his hands and worked in silence as he wrapped it around her leg, right above the cut. Then he dug through his bag and passed something shiny to her. "Drink this. It will ease your pain."

The vial flew into the air as she shoved his hand away. "You think I'd drink anything you give me? It's probably a sedative so you can take me back to the Iron City while I'm asleep."

Gavin sighed and raised his face to the sky. "Gods, give me patience."

"Ha!" Acid burned her tongue. "The gods won't give you anything, in case you've forgotten they just left us in the hands of The Society of Crows."

Flurries melted against his shocked face. Maybe her outburst had nothing to do with their previous line of conversation, but her hatred for the gods burned bright right now. Especially when the storm raging around them was caused by a god's emissary.

"That's it. I've had it with this nonsense." Her heart jolted as he strode toward her, faster than she could track in her current state. He lifted her with one arm under her knees and hooked the other one behind her back.

"What do you think you are doing?" Her adrenaline spiked, but she wrapped her arms around his neck regardless, and they stepped out into the raging blizzard. The crisp air bit at her skin, but Gavin carried her as if she weighed no more than a child.

"I'm taking you somewhere warm and dry." It was hard to see anything in the night, especially in the middle of the storm, and yet she could make out the light amber ring that rounded his pupils. It was the same color as her mother's skin. The snowflakes stuck to his dark lashes. If he noticed her staring, he didn't say a word about it.

Her stomach twisted with a sudden desire that tugged at every part of her, much like it had on the day they'd been pronounced husband and wife. When had someone's appearance alone made her weak at the knees? Or perhaps she was growing delirious from her wound. He was too pretty and that reminded her too much of Cullen, who'd played with her like a cat with a rodent that it intended to kill but not eat.

"I told you if you touched me, I would have to kill you." There was no heat behind her words. She'd still escape, but later. At least Gavin didn't seem keen to drag her away from here tonight in the middle of this storm.

He glanced down at her, and his lips twitched. "I've known you'd be the death of me ever since I got that letter. Might as well make you comfortable before you do it."

"That forsaken letter came to ruin us both—you probably didn't even know who they'd forced into your life when you got it."

He brought her closer to his body, his jaw clenching as he looked toward the lights shimmering through layers of wind and ice.

"No, I knew who you were."

Violet swallowed and ignored the fluttering in her stomach. She needed to heal fast and escape him and this place as soon as possible. Not because she hated him, but because he was her worst nightmare. She liked him too much for this interaction to be safe. He had cracked her defenses, destroyed her carefully crafted plan of never allowing herself to be interested in a man again. To truly want intimacy, both in body and mind. At least she wasn't dreaming about a family yet, because that was something she couldn't have.

Unless she found her soulmate. She was one of those fools who still believed those existed, and maybe if she found hers, Dargan wouldn't be able to claim the debt she owed him.

Alas, her time ran out, and while Gavin wasn't her soulmate, he was the only man she had this attraction to. Her arranged marriage didn't feel like a farce when her body heated with his nearness. She wanted his touch; she craved him, and that was dangerous.

She focused on the scar she'd caused, and remorse stirred in her chest. Her fingers itched to trace the pink edges, to soothe them by way of apology.

Damn him.

3

VIOLET

They entered the inn through its vast doors, carved from cedar and fortified with rusty iron inlays. Statues made from the same materials framed the entrance on either side. One depicted a sculpted beast, half wolf, half human. Stuck mid-shift, its massive hands formed the shape of a triangle, the universal symbol of peace.

The other sculpture was of a man. The heavy cloak draped over his shoulders reminded Violet of what she'd seen people wear around the town earlier in the day. The man stood proudly, a good head and a half shorter than the wolf beside him. His hands formed the same triangle symbol.

But a glint of silver, the only known poison that could kill a shifter during the full moon, hung from the sculpture's belt like a warning hidden under the guise of partnership. If only Violet had been as good at reading signs before now... Perhaps her friends' betrayal wouldn't have devastated her so.

She allowed her nose to dip into the fabric of Gavin's coat and closed her eyes. Everything spun around her, weakness threatening to pull her into a slumber. Her body was failing, her mind numb, but she couldn't let herself fall asleep, or she might lose it all again. She had to stay awake. Had to keep plotting her next move.

If werewolves inhabited these mountains, she could use that to her advantage. They usually worked against the Society of Crows and would be an excellent ally to have on her side. However, they were also expensive, and she didn't have enough coin to pay for safe passage across the mountains.

The warmth of the inn's receiving room seeped through her numb skin. The doorbell's chime alerted the innkeeper of their arrival, and soon a stout lady rushed toward them. Her tangerine-colored dress billowed in the air with her quick steps.

Hopefully, Gavin would avoid talking with her. Non-magical humans were often curious about sorcerers, and Gavin's gray aura must have given them away as soon as they entered. But Violet couldn't find it within herself to ask him to stop using magic, not when the spell he was casting was keeping them warm.

His steps slowed as the innkeeper reached them. She studied Violet's face first, then the curve of her bleeding body and the frozen layers of her coat. Her small hands covered her red-stained lips, muffling a shocked gasp that made Violet roll her eyes. "Gods, what happened to her? Is she all right?" She spoke loudly enough to draw the attention of the entire room.

Why couldn't Violet escape people and their false interest in her wellbeing? They acted like they cared, but when the tides turned they always shut their doors in her face, shouting insults while hiding in the safety of their seemingly perfect lives.

Truth was, they lived in the same broken world as she did. They simply denied it.

The ones who acted the nicest in public always stabbed you in the back when the time was right. "It's none of your business, and leave the gods out of this." Her voice came out with less of a bite than she intended. Damn, but she was weak.

The innkeeper's rosy cheeks lost all color, and her pale, almost non-existent brows dipped, covering her round eyes.

Gavin's hands tightened around Violet's ribs, warning her to keep quiet. "My wife and I have been out in the cold for a while, and she had a terrible fall and is hurting. I hope you'll forgive us for dirtying your space."

Wife. This was the first time she'd ever heard that word from his lips. The way her heart sped was unacceptable, and it darkened her surly mood further. Violet narrowed her eyes. Whatever game he was playing to have her succumb to his trickery, it would not work.

Blushing, the woman brought her hand to her chest, evidently another display of false concern. "Was it the storm? Harley, our maid, came back not long before you two walked in. She said she nearly broke her back by slipping on the ice right outside the inn."

Violet closed her eyes. If only she'd hit her head during the fall. Then she wouldn't have to suffer through this small talk. An icy sensation crawled up from her wound, dulling her senses further. Was she the one who whimpered? Surely not.

Gavin stiffened at the sound, pulling her closer and inhaling deeply. "We have to get going. Please send extra towels and something warm to eat to my room. I need them immediately." His tone was clipped. Was she imagining the concern in it?

Just as the icy grip of pain came again, something warm chased it away. Healing magic radiated outwards from every point he touched her. Her eyes fluttered open. When had she closed them? Gavin's jaw was clenched tight, and sweat beaded over his face, droplets trailing down his tanned skin.

He must be exhausting every resource he possessed to keep her awake and comfortable. Why?

"We will send some right away. Do you need me to call the healer?" The innkeeper's skin turned green as she looked at the floor. "She is losing an awful lot of blood."

The room kept spinning. Her eyes felt so heavy.

"That won't be necessary. I'm a healer. I'll take care of her."

Violet glanced back over Gavin's shoulder at a group of patrons sitting by the fire. They were talking in hushed tones, their eyes following them as Gavin headed for the stairs. Her heart sped, and she looked away just as quickly, the prickle of their stares heavy on her all through the room.

"Put me down now. I can walk by myself and get my own room." Her frozen feet might not hold her up, and she had serious concerns about ridiculing herself if she tried to walk, but she couldn't allow him to do everything for her. There were only two plausible reasons he'd heal her after what she'd done to him. One, he was waiting for her to collapse so he could take her back to the Iron City without a true fight. He'd already admitted that was his goal. With her present, he could demand the contract of marriage be dissolved because of her actions and be rid of her forever.

Which would be fine by her, right? It would. What had her gut twisting was what the Society of Crows would do to her if that happened. It had nothing to do with him.

Or two, he was trying to fool her into trusting him. Then, later, he'd betray her like all the other people she'd cared for.

She wiggled in his arms, pushing away from his chest and ignoring the flare of pain. "Put me down. Now. Next time I say it, I won't be so nice."

Had the cold frozen her brain alongside her toes? Was she insane for asking him to put her on the ground when injured? To demand her own room when she needed to save her coin to work with the werewolves?

"Was that you being nice?" His brows arched, and she glared at him, at the smirk that curved his thick lips. "There's no need to be difficult. Would you be able to walk to the third floor on your own?" Violet tightened her lips into a fine line. "I thought so."

"You can't seriously consider this. We aren't friends, and here you are calling me your wife, claiming you want to heal me. We both know this is not real."

The wooden steps creaked under their weight. Violet held onto the sound to keep herself from fading back into her exhaustion. Truth was, the idea that she could help herself right now was the lie, much though she hated to admit it

"It's not a lie," he breathed. His arms shook with the strain of carrying her for so long. "We are married, regardless of whether you and I had anything to say about it. In fact, I distinctly remember that neither of us spoke during the ceremony."

Memories of that day flooded Violet when she closed her eyes. The way Gavin and her had stood in silence while spells and binding magic were cast on them by the magistrate and witnessed by Gavin's commander and two members of the Society of Crows, Morgan and Vera. The warmth in his russet eyes had grounded her then, promising that everything would be all right, and for a moment she'd been naïve enough to believe it.

"Do you understand the nature of a healer? Of how it works?" Gavin continued. "When the magic comes to us, we are called to heal people. It's a need I can't explain, and it has nothing to do with who you are to me. I saw the amount of blood you lost back in that alley. Trust me, you'd be unconscious by now if it weren't for the spell I've been casting on you this entire time."

"Fine, so you're called to heal me with your oh-so-special magic. But it's a lie that we are wed, because we didn't lie with each other." What a ridiculous joke. She instantly wished she could take the words back.

Gavin's breath skimmed over her lashes, and his gaze seemed to burn right into her soul, picking apart the flimsy wall she had built against him. "I was there, Violet. I know full well how much I got to touch you."

She swallowed as his voice dropped low, melting her insides. It almost made her forget she was hurting. He cleared his throat as he strode on, taking them down a short corridor, past several doors. "We shouldn't talk about this out here, or we'll have a murder of Crows coming for us by morning."

If the Society of Crows worried him, that meant he'd come here by himself. Not that this made her less suspicious of his intentions. She had to keep reminding herself that although he was acting like an ally, he could still be a wolf in sheep's clothing.

4

VIOLET

THE ROOM WAS SURPRISINGLY LARGE, WITH A MEDIUM SIZE bed pushed against the far wall and a narrow table, carved from the same orange wood on the other side of the room. Violet tightened her fist around the lapels of Gavin's coat, and her mouth went dry and gritty.

She might be half drunk, lightheaded, and cold, but she had enough sense to know she couldn't lie down in the same bed as her groom.

"Calm down, there's no need to get so stiff. The bed is yours. I've no ambitions to turn this into our official wedding night. "

Her frozen cheeks would have warmed if it weren't for the blood loss. "I said nothing..."

He laid her on the bed; the dark linens wrapped around her body as she sank into the feather bed. After sleeping on hay and fur beds for the last month, the softness beneath her was a pleasant surprise.

"Your body language says it all." Gavin pushed her

coat down her shoulders, his brows pinching with concentration. She only caught up to the fact that he was undressing her when she was pulling her arms out of the frozen sleeves.

"What do you think you're doing?"

Gavin didn't stop as he dragged the offending piece of clothing out from underneath her. "We have to remove all your wet clothes to prevent cold sickness. It might be too late for that." His eyes traced her body, and settled on the curve of her hips, where the wrappings he'd tied around her leg back in the alleyway were now drenched in red. "I'll have to cut your pants to get access to your wound."

"No." She paused, collecting her scattered thoughts. She couldn't stop trembling. "I'd rather take them off myself if I have to." Ruining her only pair of pants was not on the cards tonight, even if they were bloody, wet, and dirty.

Gavin pressed his lips into a thin line and stepped away from her. He muttered something inaudible under his breath and dropped his satchel on the table at the end of the room. It creaked and wobbled with the substantial weight of its load before tipping over. The contents spilled out in a mess of gauze, herbs, and jars full of potions. Orange flames blazed alive inside the lantern that rested on the tabletop.

Gavin shrugged off his wet coat. "Very well, if you insist on doing it yourself, do so quickly. Hypothermia isn't my only concern. You're losing an awful lot of blood, Violet. More than I would expect with the way you fell into your blade." He rolled up the sleeves of his gray shirt, revealing tanned skin over toned arms.

She shifted on the mattress, trying not to wince or hold her breath in any way that might make him turn back around and undress her like she was a damsel in distress—which she was not. It had taken her years to gain respect from men like him in the assemblies, and she wasn't about to lose that now.

The bed sank beneath the weight of her body as she awkwardly untied the strings that held her woolen pants together. She hissed, her movements floundering when pain ripped through her, no longer dulled by his healing touch. Her numb fingers fumbled as she tried but failed to push the garment past the curves of her hips. Taking a deep breath, she reached for the tourniquet. She'd have to undo it to take off her pants. But how long until she passed out from blood loss?

Gavin wouldn't let it get that far, not when he'd done so much to keep her conscious.

She glanced up at the sound of approaching steps. Gavin was mid stride, only a few feet away from her. "Do you need help?"

"Sure, I'm feeling frail. Why don't you come here and lend me a hand?"

"You really don't want my help, do you?"

"I'm a soldier, like you. I've been hurt plenty of times, so let's skip the coddling. I can take my damn pants off on my own."

"You'll die without coddling right now. Let me at least do this." And before she knew what he was doing, he'd grabbed the pants right above the tourniquet, and ripped them open. "There. Don't take off the wrapping until I'm back." Gavin headed for the door, pausing before he crossed the threshold. "Everyone needs to be taken care of at one point or another, Violet. Even the fiercest of warriors."

And he was gone.

It took her embarrassingly long to strip away the rest of her pants. The wind slammed into the thin glass windows, and her breath billowed out of her chapped lips into the chill air of the room.

Her skin looked gray against the pale fabric of her undergarments. She shouldn't be so cold anymore after removing her wettest clothes, right?

Blood and murky water stained her plain cotton drawers, and while she shouldn't care that her husband would lay eyes on her body for the first time in this manner, it was enough to light a new fire within her. She needed to get underneath the heavy wool blanket —not only to get warm, but to hide her figure from him.

The task proved difficult with her dwindling energy and the pain that pulsed up her leg. Steady and unyielding, she pulled the fabric from underneath herself. Worry pricked the back of her mind as she took a deep breath to stay awake. She hadn't been lying to Gavin when she'd said this was not her first time being injured. Violet had been cut plenty of times—had been cold before too—but never like this.

This felt different, like her energy was being drawn

from her like a vampire drew blood; her limbs were heavy, and her fingers felt sluggish. She rasped a breath past stiff lips and tried to sit up, draping the wool blanket over her shoulders. The blanket itched against her skin, but she welcomed the small warmth it gave her. Gavin entered the room. The steaming pitcher of water he held in one of his hands sloshed over the floor. Had he been gone for a minute or an hour?

"Why did you get under the covers?" His harsh tone wasn't one she'd heard before. He was by her side in the blink of an eye, dropping to his knees and placing the pitcher of water on the floor. His pewter shirt strained over his wide shoulders, marking just how fit he truly was underneath his unassuming healer clothes.

Violet opened her lips to explain but nothing came out. A line wrinkled Gavin's brow while his wide hand pulled the covers off her body. "Stay still."

"I'm cold," she forced past chattering teeth, swatting his hand away. It wasn't even about her idiotic worries of nudity. Her body needed to stay warm and awake. She needed the blanket. Why couldn't he see that?

"I want you to keep it on." His eyes dug into hers, and the silhouette of his body blurred around the edges. He allowed her to push his hand away from the blanket. "But your drawers are wet. You need to take those off as well."

"You'd like that, wouldn't you?" Violet lay back, and wrapped the blanket over her torso like a cocoon that smelled of dust and wet hair. She closed her eyes, but her body wouldn't stop shivering. She just needed to rest for a while, regain her energy, and then she could cast a spell and dry her clothes. No problem.

"Not like this. Not while you dread my touch," he whispered. "I will start stitching your leg, then we can talk about the wet clothes. Violet? Are you awake?"

She was so tired and heavy. Her body seemed to keep sinking into the mattress like an anchor dropped in the ocean.

"Don't fall asleep."

The prick of a needle cut through the layers of her torn flesh. His blazing fingers seared her icy skin. She breathed past the grogginess of her thoughts. "D-don't tell me what to do."

"Stay awake, and I won't have to."

Was she imagining the panic behind his words? Was she really dying from a stupid knife cut, and her lack of proper winter attire? The edges of her vision blackened around the halo of the burning lantern, and she was pulled under the dark blanket of sleep.

5

VIOLET

Three weeks ago

It was the beginning of the end, and she'd run out of time. The bell clanged in the background, making the building tremble with each beat. Dust fell around her. One, two, three chimes left her ears ringing with a high-pitched screech which lingered.

It was the signal that a ceremony was about to start down at City Hall. It could have been a sentencing, a commemoration—but in this case, it was her wedding. Today, Violet would be forced to marry a man she couldn't have. Not that she wanted to.

She was only in this mess because she had entrusted her intentions to her chamber-mates, all of whom she had considered friends a week ago. She wouldn't make that idiotic mistake again.

The tight curls of her hair bounced as she tried but failed to tuck a section behind her ear. She reached for the edge of the ornate mirror in front of her before taking a deep breath to calm her rattled nerves.

The silver pins she held fell to the tabletop, bouncing with a click before rolling off onto the shaggy fur beneath her feet. Making herself presentable for her nuptials felt a lot like giving up, and she wasn't ready to do that yet.

Her body sank into the uneven cushion of her stool, and she slumped forward, burying her face in her sweaty palms. The scent of lavender oil clung to her skin, worsening the steady throbbing in her skull.

When Violet straightened again, she met the cool, calculating gaze of her chaperone in the mirror.

Vera Rosenest was the Society of Crows member who had come to collect her a week ago. Vera had kicked the door of Violet's chambers from its hinges and issued her with a binding letter condemning her to her fate. She had also forced her into this room, where she would have to wait, alone, until she was married.

Violet cleared her throat and continued fixing her hair, hating the cold, watchful gaze of her guard as she pressed a flower-shaped pearl pin into the puff of her curls.

"You have a visitor." The corners of Vera's lips tilted downward, and she moved aside to allow a man into the room. At nearly six and a half feet tall, Terrance Horn was rumored to be the son of shifters. It wasn't uncommon to hear of a child born from a union of human and werewolves or other shape-shifting beasts, although many people denied they took place.

A lie surely spun by the Society of Crows to prevent

sorcerers from wedding other species, since shifters from Caztian followed their own set of rules.

Terrance walked toward her, holding a white and pink arrangement of flowers that had wilted in the frigid air outside. His bald head shone, but his messy red beard looked freshly trimmed and oiled. He was wearing a tunic decorated with gold medals and a gaudy embroidered ribbon.

"I didn't think you were allowed to visit me."

"Aye—I couldn't until today. You look… nice." He shifted on his feet, avoiding her eyes as he studied every corner of the room instead as if the spiderwebs that decorated them were more interesting than her. "I figured it would be good to come and see you before the ceremony."

She trailed her fingertips over the corset that embraced her curves; the softest silk she had ever touched. Shimmery thread made a flower pattern that contrasted with a brighter shade of pearlescent white.

"You didn't have to bring flowers. This isn't something I want to celebrate," Violet whispered, after she was sure she wouldn't crack under the pressure building within her.

"Violet, saying that kind of thing is what got you into this mess." Terrance's voice had turned bitter. She'd heard him use this tone before, with those outside their assembly. Never with her.

His words weren't the truth either, and he knew that. He was well acquainted with the vipers who had called themselves her chamber-mates, and he'd probably suspected that Violet wouldn't stick around to be matched.

Terrance hunched his shoulders as he wandered around the small chamber. His wide hands, scarred and callused, *stood in sharp relief against the delicate petals of the daisies and white peonies he held. "See this as a good outcome. Your groom is filthy rich. Isn't that what all women like?"*

Violet narrowed her eyes. "I thought you knew me better than that."

Terrance's lips flattened, but he said nothing. Maybe he wasn't looking for an argument. She didn't want to get into a fight, either. However prickly, Terrance was all she had left.

Violet reached for the bouquet and buried her nose in the petals. The scent was pleasant enough, and their texture like velvet.

She wasn't into things that men like Terrance thought women liked. But she had to admit flowers were different. Her little sister, Thalea, said Violet's eyes looked the color of the flowers. It was where her nickname had come from. Violet.

The people in the army had adopted the nickname, and it always reminded her of the best parts of her life. A past with a family that cherished her.

The bells resumed their ringing, and her stomach clenched.

The time was near. She could almost smell the frankincense in the air.

Trembling with a cold she couldn't shake, she followed Terrance as he walked toward the dressing table and picked up the parchment letter that bound her to Gavin. The paper was wrinkled, leaving the neat penmanship unrecognizable to all but her. She'd memorized it a long time ago.

"I would rather your husband was less—I don't know...

pretty? Someone who could keep your fire in check." He grunted and dropped the offending paper on the bed.

"Stop that."

"They should have picked one of us. Not someone from the Valdor Assembly and their pompous rich boys. Those men don't know how to treat a woman like you." Her commander hooked his fingers around his leather belt and walked toward the window. He peeled the gauzy curtain away, letting the light of the early morning sun bathe his wide, scarred face. "Particularly Julius—he is a special trouble with the way he treats women..."

"I wish they would leave me alone." Violet dropped the bouquet on the bed and took a deep breath, wiping her sweaty palms on her dress.

She had spent most of the week trying to escape her fate. And yet, after three years without any intimacy, it was easy to fantasize over a passionate wedding night with an attractive man. However unlikely it was to happen.

Her throat grew dry at the thought. Fidgeting, she sat on the edge of the bed.

"I've heard Luna is decent in battle." Terrance's words brought her back from her reverie.

Terrance pushed away from the wall. Right. She'd almost forgotten. He'd come to take her into the city hall, like most commanders did when weddings took place.

"Are we leaving now?" She glanced toward the door, which stood ajar. She wasn't supposed to be left alone in a closed chamber with a man, but her chaperone was nowhere to be seen.

"About that. I won't be taking you there today."

Violet blinked away her confusion. The flower crown he'd brought with him, and then his polished attire. Terrance had come ready for the ceremony. What had made him change his mind?

She frowned. "Why not?"

"Don't make this more difficult than it needs to be…"

"You are dressed for the occasion. Tell me why."

He groaned and glanced at the ceiling. "There's no need for me to be present. The Crow will take you there in my place."

That sounded like someone had convinced him to step down. Violet didn't like it.

It was customary for the commanders of both assemblies to be present at the arranged ceremonies. Julius would be there, after all, representing Gavin's assembly. Terrance should be there for her.

"I still don't understand. It's expected for my commander to be there."

Terrance's hard eyes pinned her. He dragged his hand over his bald head. "You haven't made this easy for me, Cora. You made a mess with the wrong people, and the Crows got involved."

Since when did he call her by her given name? "What's difficult for you here? You're not the one being forced to marry."

Terrance wasn't much older than her, in his thirties at most, and still unmarried. He wouldn't know what it was like to be thrown into a union with no say in the matter. Most people could form attachments with other sorcerers and plead their case to the Crown. But that wasn't what had happened with Gavin and her.

"What did you expect would happen when you go around flapping your mouth about your escape plans?"

The withering look she sent him didn't seem to affect him. "I had no intention of actually doing it." That wasn't true, of course. Violet had revealed her intentions to her chamber-mates in a haze of drunkenness. She'd never expected her friends to run and tell on her the very next day. Lesson learned.

Terrance moved toward the door, his massive body obscuring the sight of the hallway beyond. He turned back to her when he reached the threshold. "The reason I won't come to your ceremony is because I've been told you haven't been a member of my assembly since you received your letter. You were transferred to the Valdor's that very night the Crow took you. You will fight for the Crown alongside your groom. Under Julius. Not me."

"What? No!"

"The Society has issued an order, and in spite of your constant insubordination, I'm heeding their command."

"I don't want to leave our assembly or be forced to serve under that man." Julius, a lech who had wandering hands. She stepped toward Terrance but stopped when she noticed movement outside. Her chaperone was back and listening.

Another friend who was pushing her aside like nothing. She followed him toward the hallway. His expression was now masked with an indifference that hadn't been there before. Fire lit up his eyes as he lifted his chin and paused by the door.

"You have shamed us by plotting to become a deserter. Pull yourself together, Cora, and don't force them to hunt you down. For once, heed an order from your commander."

"You said you weren't my commander any longer, so why would I follow your spineless orders?" She forced the words through gritted teeth, failing to hide the tremble in her voice.

Vera stood by the door, casting a more threatening shadow than the giant next to her. With her graying hair pulled back into a high bun and a black and blue costume, it was Vera, not Terrance, who kept Violet locked in her gilded cage.

Vera. The Crow. She was clearly giving them a moment of privacy because she knew that Terrance had to hand her over to Julius. Had Terrance just found out about the change today?

"I guess you'll be someone else's problem now." Terrance's expression might have shown a trace of remorse. Did it matter? He was still leaving her in the hands of a monster.

Violet's blood turned to ice, and she stepped forward to slap the smirk off his face. She didn't care if the spell locking her in this room would hurt her if she crossed the threshold. It would be worth it.

"Commander." Vera's croaky voice befitted her withered face. Her eyes narrowed in disdain as Terrance sketched a mocking bow and flashed one last look at Violet before he disappeared down the corridor.

Violet stormed to the bed and picked up the flower crown he had brought her. They wrinkled beneath her tight-

ening fist. She threw the wreath from the open window with all her strength, hoping it would hit him on his way out.

Vera hummed, clearly amused. "Pull yourself together, girl. Or your new commander will find a reason to teach you a lesson, and you don't want to be a woman who steps out of line in his assembly." Her pale lips twisted in a sinister smile that sent a crawling sensation up the back of Violet's neck.

"You enjoy watching your own gender suffer at the hands of a powerful man?" Violet's words dripped with poison.

"I believe those who seek to desert our gods, those who dread serving our people and our country, deserve to be taught a lesson. You aren't a woman that commands respect. You are a peasant, a deserter, the scum of this land. And you won't be a runaway bride if I have any say in the matter."

Violet lifted her chin, straightening her back to hide the fear that weighed down her chest, sending a pulsing ache through her body. She wouldn't waste her words on a woman who believed so blindly in gods and a kingdom corrupted by greed. Those who didn't respect the sacred bond between a child and their parents were evil in Violet's eyes, and she loathed the Crows just as much as she hated the gods that had forsaken them all.

"I'll walk you to the ceremony shortly," Vera said. "Morgan will be there as well. We expect you to be presentable. So fix your hair, unless you want further trouble." And she turned on her heel and shut the door behind her.

If these fools thought she would go down without a fight,

they were mistaken. Violet opened the doors of her closet wide and pulled out her woolen coat. She couldn't thank the evil gods for luck, not when this was her fate—but at least it was winter. While the Crows had stripped her of her visible weapons, they hadn't checked every fold of fabric.

Tearing the lining open, she reached for the knife she had sewn into a hidden pocket months ago. The bone handle was cool inside her grasp, a contrast to the leather that protected the blade. A parting gift from her father when she'd been taken from her home at the age of eleven.

It was small enough to hide in the under-layers of her coat. Sharpened to a deadly point, it could be lethal when used right. Tonight, those bastards would learn not to mess with Violet Elder.

6

VIOLET

SHE CRACKED HER EYES OPEN, STILL SLUGGISH FROM HER dream. She'd expected to be back in the bridal chambers, and her heart was stumbling too fast in her chest. The warm air that caressed the side of her neck sent goosebumps across her back, and a blanket of seawater and peppermint wrapped her in an embrace that chased away the lingering panic from her limbs.

She inched back, stretching toward the furnace behind her, trying to bury herself deep in its embers to melt the cold that wracked her bones. The chattering of her teeth registered in her mind as large fingers trailed over the flimsy fabric of her chemise. The palm of a wide hand flattened over her belly and pulled her back toward a rigid torso that was all male. Butterflies flew in her stomach, and her skin tingled with a sudden awareness as she pressed the curve of her ass against him.

His breath stuttered, and his hand—still resting on her stomach—held her in place. Even with the pain throbbing in her hip, her body longed for more than it should have.

Was she awake or stuck in a haze of delusion? Surely Gavin wouldn't be so bold as to lie with her.

"Are you really here?" Violet whispered. She didn't want him to go. Instead, she craved more, for him to pull her back and press himself where she wanted to feel him.

He shifted away from her. "I'm just here for body heat. I'll be gone once your temperature is stable."

Gavin was trying to save her, and she couldn't fight him over it. But that didn't mean she'd like that she was now indebted to him. Magic came at a price, and if they used their power without rest wielders like themselves always had a breaking point. Gavin was surely nearing his, since he'd been healing her for hours. He had to be spent by now.

Violet sighed while magic continued to heal her from within, thawing the ice in her blood. Before long, she'd gone somewhere that even dreams couldn't haunt her. Somewhere pleasant. Darkness.

When she next blinked her eyes open, she flinched with the bright sun that spilled over her and the unfamiliar room. She sat slowly, catching the woolen blanket that draped over her chest, letting the cold of the room nip at her skin. A wave of nausea crawled up her gut, and she covered her face with her icy hands, breathing in the iron tang of blood clinging to her skin.

"Easy there." Gavin's voice startled her, and she tried to jump out of bed. In her weakened state, the blanket caught on her legs. She cursed and stumbled, but large hands held her before she could tumble to the floor.

Her breath caught in her throat, as pain surged through her healing wound whenever she moved. She'd searched for his warmth during the night—exactly the opposite of what she was supposed to do.

"I'm fine," she said, and pushed his hands off her body as fragments of the previous night came back to her in her daze. "I can do this."

"Glad to see that." He didn't pursue her further, but slipped out of bed in one smooth move. His shirt hung over his shoulders, crumpled from sleeping in it. It was no longer a clean gray, but stained with her blood. Its open collar revealed the expanse of his chest, dusted with dark hair.

She hated how curious she was to follow the dusky trail of it further down. Shaking her head, she pushed away the blanket to stand—but stopped when the room started spinning again.

She looked back at Gavin. The sleepless night had drained his skin of its natural warmth, and a blue tinge darkened the bottom rim of his eyes. "If you're determined to get up, do it slowly. You lost a lot of blood and were pretty sick most of the night."

Violet took a deep breath and pressed her lips together tightly when warmth spread in her chest. "Thank you. For helping me."

He raised his brows, looking at her like she was about to grow an extra head. "A thank you? Perhaps you won't kill me after all."

She narrowed her eyes. "Don't push it."

Gavin grinned, shaking his head as he stepped toward the table covered in his healing potions. He inspected the labels on each vial with a growing frown. Mind still foggy with sleep, Violet limped her way over to where her clothes lay in a pile of brown and black, spotted with accents of dark burgundy. They were stiff with dried blood when she picked them up.

Violet scrunched her nose, any thoughts of an immediate escape dashed. She'd have to wait until she could wash these. She needed to blend in with the men in her old assembly, not become one of them. Actually, on closer inspection, she'd have to replace the pants entirely. That was right—Gavin had cut them open. Had said her life was on the line... "I don't understand why I reacted this way to a flesh wound. It's not the first time I've been hurt like this..."

"The cut went deep. You're lucky that we weren't too far from the inn. The lack of proper winter attire didn't exactly improve matters."

That sounded like she was only here still thanks to him and his healing magic, not that she was going to thank him again. She wouldn't point out that she would have been fine if he hadn't shown up at the tavern and chased her outside. Not after he'd been up all night, tending to her.

She prodded at the gauze and winced, shifting her weight to her good side as she limped toward the washroom. The noise of life out in the streets filtered through the closed window, and she could see snow from the storm last night piled high on the ledge.

By the time she returned, clean and wrapped in a flimsy towel that barely covered her ass, Gavin was sitting on the floor with a bowl of steaming stew in his hands.

How long had it taken her to wash up? He didn't have enough time to fetch them food. She guessed for someone born to money, Gavin could have paid the inn to bring them lunch to their room.

His smoldering gaze traced along every inch of her body that wasn't covered by the linen cloth she was wrapped in or her dripping wet hair. There was something intense in his eyes that hadn't been there the night before, and that alone had her stumbling on her first step into the room.

Violet wasn't one to favor modesty, and she was confident in the curves of her body and her athletic figure. Even so, she pulled the edge of the towel down, making sure it covered her as she shuffled over to the bed.

"Your food is on the table." He looked down, one of his hands brushing his hair out of his forehead. "The maid brought it up a few minutes ago. It should still be warm."

Her chest warmed as she peered at the tray of food

next to her. Even after all her sly remarks, Gavin got her food. She wished he'd stopped being so nice. It was difficult to keep on thinking of him as an enemy this way.

She sat on the bed, taking care not to aggravate her leg and reached for her food. Her stomach rumbled at the pleasant scent that rose to her nose. The bowl was warm and loaded with squash, potatoes, and dark poultry meat. "Why are you here?"

He looked at her, his spoonful of broth suspended in the air. "You know why."

"To take me back." It wasn't a question, and anger bled out of every word, like they were dripping with poison. "Why? Wouldn't it have been easier just to let me go? I doubt you came all the way here because of your burning, undying love for me."

Gavin released a resigned breath, then resumed eating, his brow furrowing as he kept his focus on something other than her. "Vera accused me of being an accomplice to your escape."

"The Crow?" Violet leaned forward, her thoughts sharpening at his words. "I didn't throw my blade at you...but they don't know that. I still hurt you. In what world does that mean we were working together?"

Gavin shrugged and dipped his bread in the stew, the tightness in his expression not softening when he met her gaze. "Does it have to make sense for the Society of Crows to get whatever retribution they seek?"

Violet knew full well that the answer was no. She'd

aggravated the Society beyond reason by attacking one of their members during a ceremony and by escaping right under their noses. She knew they would come for her, and it was likely that her punishment would be a life of imprisonment at the hand of the Society, at the very least. At worst, the King would demand her head.

But Violet didn't regret her escape. She would take the wrath of a kingdom over handing her future—her family over to the God of Shadows any day. She brought her hand around her neck and swallowed hard against the knot that had formed there. Guilt stirred anew in her gut, and she opened her lips to apologize. But Gavin spoke before she could say anything.

"It's not all your fault. I should have known better." His breath whistled between his teeth and he shook his head. "I defended your reason to escape because after they demanded to witness our... union, I was too mad to care about what might happen to me if I spoke my mind." His voice shook with anger. Was it directed at her or the Crows? Violet couldn't tell. Maybe both.

The archaic laws of witnessing a marriage inter-course had been abandoned decades ago, and no one cared whether the couple had sex during their wedding night. All they cared about was for a magical child to be born. The expectation of a pregnancy was high, and every person who went into a matched marriage knew this. So when Morgan had demanded to watch them that night, it was as if she was drawing pleasure from tormenting them further.

"I was thinking of escaping well before that." She

cleared her throat. Why was she being so candid with him? Maybe it was the suffocating remorse which settled in her chest when she caught sight of the scar on his chin and thought of the pain it must have caused.

After all, Gavin was as much a victim in this whole thing as she was.

He didn't seem surprised by her admission. He set his empty dish aside, reminding her that she hadn't eaten a bite. "I imagine that's the case, Violet, but they have no way of proving your intentions, only of condemning you for your actions after they demanded to witness us coming together. I don't understand why she did that. They already had what they wanted." He rested his elbows on bent knees, propping up his chin on his knuckles and hanging his head so that the curtain of his wavy hair fell over his face, hiding his features. She could only guess at his emotions.

Every time this man mentioned them lying with one another, her insides trembled with the way his inflection changed. As if he'd thought about it constantly. She pressed her legs together, cramming the bread in her mouth, unable to enjoy its buttery flavor on her tongue. She needed to sort through these confusing feelings and move on, or else she would fall prey to her cravings for him.

"You think they care whether they can prove that I planned to escape or not? There's no one in that city that will overrule the Society of Crows, even if I changed my mind and told them I was going to stay and obey their orders."

"We have a judge that sees to the protection of the kingdom's citizens and a fair king." At her snort of laughter, he furrowed his brows, crossing his arms over his chest.

"Your innocence would be endearing if it wasn't so likely to get you killed."

Gavin ignored her snarky comment. "Julius vouched for my innocence, but the Society demanded that I bring you back within a month. He appealed for it to be two months. With his good standing with the Crown, I don't doubt he will succeed."

She huffed, and put her soup on the table next to the bed, suddenly no longer hungry. "So, what are they going to do to you if you don't bring me in?"

"I'll be held accountable for two sets of crimes. Deserting the land, and refusal to comply with the match."

"That's absurd, but I don't doubt they'd still prosecute us for both crimes, even if you brought me in. To make an example of us. To show what happens if someone defies them."

"Julius wouldn't let that happen."

"You think your precious commander cares about us? He's the biggest snake of them all."

"You don't know what you're talking about." He raised his voice, his cheeks reddening as he got up from the floor, suddenly filling the space with his height.

"Were you in that meeting where he vouched for you, or did he just tell you that he did?"

Gavin pressed his lips together and shook his head. He stormed away from her toward the table where his healing satchel lay. "You like to think you know everything about everyone, so why should I bother answering any more of your questions?"

"Maybe I know more about your commander than you do, seeing how you seem to hold him in such high regard. Enough to throw yourself in the way of a knife intended for him."

He headed for the door, reaching for his heavy wool coat which hung from the wall. "I've known him since I joined the army, far longer than you. He is a good man."

Violet forced out another laugh. If only she could enjoy the way he frowned in response, but his naivety broke something deep within her, and the sympathy she felt for Gavin only angered her further. She had no right to care, and caring only gave him a weapon he could use to hurt her later. "Your rich boy attitude is showing, Gavin Luna. It's clear that wealth has coddled you your entire life and protected your family. If someone like Julius treats you with enough respect that you actually like him, then I guess it's no wonder you trust him with your life."

"What does my family—or their wealth—have to do with anything?"

"Where do I even begin?" She raised her index finger for emphasis. "One, only someone grown into a wealthy family gets to join the King's army when they are over sixteen. Two, they assigned you to the Valdor Assembly, which is known to be protected by rich men. Always sent last when it's time to fight against another kingdom or creatures that attack us." She lifted her third finger. "Three, you are naïve like a child. If you think that there is any way that they'll spare us once you and I get into the hands of the Crows, then you've got another thing coming."

His expression twisted, and his strained laughter barely hid his obvious anger. "If we go back, Julius will see that we are safe. He will send us to our next assignment immediately, away from the Crows to the Gold Kingdom. We'll be away from the city for a couple of years. The Crows will lose interest in making an example out of us."

"I'm not heading back to my certain death just because you trust blindly."

For a long moment, they stared at each other in silence, their hard breathing the only sound that filled the room.

"It must be lonely being you." Gavin said eventually, and his words pierced her heart. "I understand why you don't want to come. I meant it when I told you last night that I won't take you against your will."

"Then what do you want from me?" She tilted her head back and groaned. "If you know I won't give you what you came here for, why are you helping me?"

"I'm not one to let a person suffer—even if they got me in trouble."

The worst part was that she believed him. Gavin seemed like a man of integrity.

"Say what you mean. I didn't just get you in trouble. I ruined your life."

"Yes." He looked away from her, his lips curling into a grimace. "I figured you had a plan to escape when you came here. I want to escape whatever fate the kingdom has waiting for me as well. The Crows or an assembly will be sent here soon. I don't doubt that they are keeping an eye on my moves and will catch up to us."

"And you selfish bastard led them straight to me!" Her voice echoed through the room. She swung her legs over the side of the bed.

"You don't get to call me that. I'm in this mess because of you!" His voice strained. "I wouldn't have let them watch as I made you mine that night. Even though I knew the repercussions, I would have said no."

"But you didn't."

"The whole thing escalated rather quickly, Violet. But, my family had our back. Now I might never see them again. You didn't give me the chance to be on our side."

Violet's cheeks heated, and it wasn't anger anymore. It was an ugly feeling. She knew all about losing something. Life wasn't fair. But that was it, wasn't it? In the middle of her panic to protect her future, she hadn't considered about how it might affect Gavin.

Out of the two of them, she was the selfish bastard. "I thought they'd put the blame on me."

"Well, you thought wrong. Now I won't ever see my parents age, or my sister marry and bear children. Not without putting them at risk. Not unless you come back with me."

All this talk of his family brought back memories of her own. Unlike his relations, who were known merchants of great wealth and power in Plume City, Violet's family had been poor fishermen. They'd lived in a small house that bordered the Leona sea. Secluded, in constant fear of not having enough to feed everyone. She could still recall the last time she'd sat at that very table.

Her blood rushed hot through her veins as something returned to her that she'd lost long ago: clarity of how her actions affected others. The sinking feeling made her squirm. Since when did she actually care for this man? It was his family or her life. She'd had no other choice at the time...

Yet, she now understood his reason for chasing her down. His desire to get her to return with him didn't seem so ridiculous. If she agreed to go back and take part in the mad plan Julius had proposed, Gavin would see his loved ones again.

Gavin opened the door, revealing the dark corridor of the inn beyond, and the chill of a draft wafted across the threshold. "I know you won't listen to me, but I'm going to tell you either way. You aren't ready to travel across the mountains with your leg injury, and I need to regain my strength before I can heal you further. The cold sickness from yesterday has weakened your magic. Rest for today, and I will come back this evening to help you."

She raised her chin with a trembling lip. "And how will I know you won't betray me if I stay?"

He tapped his fingers against the door, and she felt naked beneath his unyielding gaze. "You don't. It's called a leap of faith."

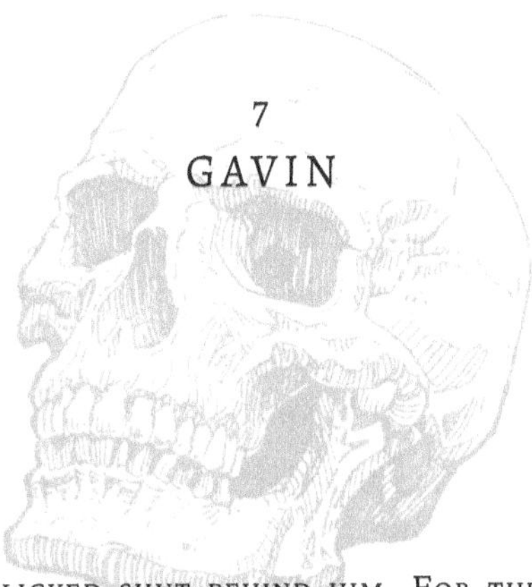

7

GAVIN

THE DOOR CLICKED SHUT BEHIND HIM. FOR THE FIRST TIME since he'd found Violet, the air he breathed wasn't charged with the scent of her skin. Cloves and a hint of vanilla. It was the worst kind of torture to know his presence wasn't welcomed even though they had been magically bound to each other. He rolled his shoulders, and the ache that stiffened his muscles eased as he turned his neck from side to side.

He didn't want to leave her here when, on his return, she could be gone forever. He might never see her again, nor get the chance to confess why he'd really chosen to side with her, although she'd thrown a knife at his commander.

"A leap of faith," he whispered to himself with a reassuring nod.

His concern for Violet leaving him behind was genuine and solely about her safety. He wasn't ready to admit—out loud at least—that it went far beyond his family's debt to Violet. Not that they'd discussed said debt. The past wasn't something Gavin had ever spoken to her about. In fact, Gavin doubted she even realized she had saved his little sister from drowning all those years ago.

He'd been so drunk on blackberry wine that he hadn't noticed that Elina had gone swimming while a storm approached. Had been too busy fucking that girl from his assembly. Never again would he be so irresponsible. It should have been him diving into the depths of the lake that afternoon, not Violet.

Gavin closed his eyes, the image of Elina's lithe body swaying limp in Violet's arms still vivid in his mind. It was a memory that could have concluded in his worst nightmare if it hadn't been for her. As his father had told him afterwards, his foolish boy actions that day had almost cost them Elina's life. It was time he became a man.

He'd taken the words to heart. That version of him had died many moon cycles ago, the irresponsible side of him long gone and buried.

The wind whistled through the windows and their crevices, howling down the hallway and seeping into the fabric of his clothes. He could always go back to the Iron Kingdom and claim he'd never found her. Be done with this madness.

He shouldn't stay, especially when she'd made it so abundantly clear that she didn't want him. He could— should—let her go. It would be sensible for him to be rid of her. After all, she was a negative, hateful... beautiful strong woman who drew him in like a moth to a flame.

If he left now, he would never have to admit that, against his better judgment, his ridiculous waiting game had turned into a painful attraction. That seeing her name in the letter that announced his match had turned him inside out and into a mess of nerves. It was a part of himself he was eager to bury forever.

Falling for someone like Violet didn't feel wrong, however. Not when she'd jumped into the black waters of the Hulten lake and pulled out his thirteen-year-old sister without a second thought. He traced the scar on his chin and shook his head with a groan before walking away from the room.

Gavin had healed her now. She'd told him she wouldn't come back with him to the Iron City, even after he'd pleaded his case. What other reason did he have to stay?

Although she was much improved, she needed time to recover from her wound and the mild hypothermia. He didn't want her dying out in the dangerous Obsidian mountains while still injured.

The window at the far end of the hallway slammed against its frame, shaking the glass and the snow that stuck to it. Beyond it, flurries dropped from the gray sky, covering the small town in additional layers of white.

His sister once told him he was a man who craved danger and a masochist at heart, and him wanting to stay with Violet proved that. He was clearly going mad. Being so on edge was unlike him.

What did the Society expect would happen when they cornered someone like Violet and tried to bend her to their will? He'd witnessed her fighting plenty of times in the assemblies, and she moved like a shadow, barely visible with the quickness of her steps. Ever since he'd joined the King's army, warriors had surrounded him, but out of all of them it was her who stood out.

She rarely relied on her magic to accomplish her goals but counted on her impressive skills with weaponry and a healthy dose of mischief. What if someone came while he was gone and took her? He trusted that Julius had been truthful when he'd told Gavin he would try and stop the Crows from chasing after them. He wasn't sure if they would get the two months his Commander promised.

Julius hadn't known about his full intentions to not force Violet back into the Iron City against her will. On his way here, Gavin had almost convinced himself that if he explained his reasoning to her, she might come back voluntarily. Alas, Violet and him agreed on something. He was a naïve fool.

Nevertheless, Gavin had already accepted his destiny long ago, before finding her in that tavern. He would leave his family behind if it meant allowing Violet to escape a fate she clearly hated. Even if it meant becoming a deserter himself.

The innkeeper he'd met the night before was

standing behind the counter downstairs. Her eyes, much like his, looked darkened by a sleepless night. She didn't notice him approaching immediately, stirring a silver spoon through the teacup resting before her. Hand-painted flowers and leaves decorated its glowing white surface. A woodsy vanilla scent tickled his nostrils as he came closer, bringing a smile to his face. Rooibos, his favorite. "Good morning."

The woman jumped, raising her wide blue eyes to meet his, and up close he couldn't miss her drawn, tired face. Did he look the same? "Gods, you scared me!" She reached for a tissue to dab some spilled tea from the surface of the table. "What can I do for you, Mr. Luna?"

"Just call me Gavin." He tapped his fingers on the counter, and flashed her a smile. "I never got the opportunity to ask for your name last night."

She rewarded him with the tentative tilt of her lips. "I'm Laura."

He'd initially thought her swollen red face might be due to lack of rest, but now that she used the same tea stained tissue to dab her glassy eyes dry, he knew something else was off. "Are you well?"

"Oh, I'm...yes." She brought the shaking cup to her lips and took a sip.

Something was off. Should he dig deeper? He doubted he'd be much help to her with the amount of trouble that continued to pile up on his plate. He needed to focus on getting a larger room for him and Violet to stay in tonight, or else he might end up throwing caution to the wind the next time she rubbed that fine ass of hers into him. Not only would it be disheartening if she pushed him away, but it also meant less rest if she didn't, and he needed all the energy he could get.

Maybe this once he'd just have to keep his concern to himself. "That's a nice Rooibos you have brewing there."

"You can tell what it is? I guess it does have a particular scent..." She looked down at her steaming cup, but then sniffed a shaky breath. "What can I help you with Mr.—Gavin? How is your wife doing this morning?"

"She is better today, thank you, which is why I'm here. I would love to rent a larger room for the day. I need some rest, but our bed is too small with the both of us crammed in there. And I don't want to disturb her while she is still recovering."

Laura's face fell, and she shook her head. "I'm afraid not. We had a few patrons arrive late last night. Must be the storm that forced them away from their travels since we rarely get so many this time of the year."

He eyed the chairs by the chimney warily. They stood bare by the fire and looked far more appealing than sleeping on the floor in his room.

"... a healer," Laura said. Gavin looked up and met her eager blue eyes, shining anew like the night before. He blinked with heavy lids and stifled a yawn before attempting to digest her words.

"Pardon?"

"You said yesterday you were a magical healer?"

He froze, alarm bells ringing inside his head. He glanced around the room, but it was a quiet morning, and they were alone. Only the sound of the crackling logs kept them company. "I said I was a healer... but I don't recall specifying that I was a magical one."

Laura's eyes lit up as she reached for his hand. Her small fingers were damp and deceptively strong, her grasp firm enough that he wouldn't be able to pull his hand away easily. She took a deep breath, and Gavin had the sense that his attempt to stay out of this woman's business was about to become a thing of the past.

"I don't mean to bother you, but I must ask for your help. I received news this morning that a beast has bitten my niece. She is very ill and not responding to our town healer's medicine. Maybe you can help us with your... magic?" She whispered the last word, her cheeks burning red.

There was no way he could use magic today without resting as well. Nor did he want to leave the inn—and Violet—alone for too long. Laura's lips trembled again, while unshed tears accumulated in the corners of her eyes at his silence. "She's just a little girl, Mr. Gavin. My sister fears we might lose her soon."

Elina's face flashed across his mind's eye. Damn the blessed gods.

Laura didn't know it, but she'd spoken the words that would make him turn his life upside down if it might help. Supporting children and the young recruits the army gathered had become a lifelong mission for him ever since he'd presented with the gift of healing. Especially since the day of the accident in the lake. Her words rang alarm bells inside his head and filled him with foreboding. "What kind of beast?"

She squeezed his hand so tight he had to press his lips together in order not to complain. "A werewolf."

This time, Gavin tore his hand away. Uneasiness stirred in his gut. He remembered the statues out front, the wolf in mid-transformation, the man holding the symbol of peace between species. He narrowed his gaze at her. "A shifter?"

She hesitated for a minute before nodding. "It's the second child he has attacked this month. Three the month before. The bite is not the problem. It is the curse that lingers that's killing them."

"What curse?"

"The one that comes with a werewolf's bite, of course. The one that infects humans with their rabid sickness. Grown people sometimes can't survive it, much less our children."

Oh no. These people were terribly misinformed. They still believed in the myth of a shifter's bite causing infection, and that it would turn humans into wolves during a full moon. Still, a werewolf was not the creature that crossed Gavin's mind.

The Archana Sídhes were both beasts and men. They hunted humans, driven by the hunger of their curse, and they looked an awful lot like a shifter to an untrained eye. No brew made by a non-magical human could vanquish the curse left behind by their bite. He wasn't even sure he would be able to do anything, even if he was rested. "I'm completely depleted after last night, Laura. When I asked for the extra room, I was not lying. I can't heal your niece if I don't get some rest."

"How long do you need?"

"Four hours, perhaps, ideally more…"

One moment, Laura was standing in front of him, and in the next she'd disappeared behind the counter. The loud crash of pottery breaking on the wooden floor followed. "Bugger. What a mess, I broke the bowl." She grunted and stood up, beet red and gasping for air. A brass skeleton key swung in front of her like a pendulum. "I own a little place across the road that's just for me. You may use it to rest, Mr. Gavin."

"Oh no, there is no need."

"I insist. Please—I—I hate to have to ask this of you. I know we are but strangers—you might be our last chance."

That was true. Magical healers weren't common in the world, and much less so ones who traveled around these remote parts of the kingdom. Gavin hesitated. "Are you sure?"

Laura didn't allow him to second guess the offer any further. Instead, she tossed the key in his general direction. With his slowed reflexes, it hit the planes of his chest, and he nearly dropped it as he tried to catch it in his clumsy fingers.

"Sorry." She didn't feel sorry at all if the small, hopeful smile was anything to go by. "I'm very sure. My rooms are in the green building. There are steps to the second floor, the door is painted yellow with flowers. It's not much, and it's all I can offer. But you may use it to rest, and you can take your wife with you. I will be eternally grateful if you can help Myna."

"All right. I will leave my wife to rest here and use it just this afternoon. Come and get me in four hours, and we shall go to your niece's home." He raised the collar of his coat to guard against the chill outside. He turned to leave, but paused. "You mentioned more travelers arrived last night?"

Laura nodded and looked down at what he assumed was the guest book. "Seven of them took my last four rooms."

"Were they soldiers or magic-wielders?"

Understanding shone behind her lashes, and she seemed to ponder the question. "They weren't built or dressed like you, all fancy and strong." Her already red cheeks darkened further, but she continued on, undeterred. "They were more like what I'm used to seeing crossing these parts. Merchants, traders—farmers, perhaps. I don't think you have anything to worry about."

He nodded and swung his satchel over his shoulder. Feeling the weight of it always calmed his anxious thoughts. "I will see you in four hours."

"Thank you, Mr. Gavin."

"It's just Gavin," he said. "Let's hope there's something I can do to help."

8

GAVIN

The wooden floors creaked under his feet as he made his way toward the window in Laura's kitchen. It was equal parts charming and cluttered, with a mixture of knick-knacks that suggested she was a collector of painted plates and knitted blankets. He smiled softly, shaking his head, craving the normalcy of her life, away from the politics of being a magic-wielder. He pulled aside the sheer curtain and peered at the streets below. Two men in heavy coats were shoveling horse droppings toward the sidewalks. The snow had turned into a brown slush, pushed aside by the passing carriages. This window gave him a perfect view of the inn and its worn planks of wood. They were covered in a light layer of moss, roughened by the harsh seasons of the mountains.

He wondered if Violet was sleeping right now—or perhaps she was already on her way out of Scoria.

A knock on the door made him jump before a tentative voice sounded from outside. "Mr. Gavin, are you awake?"

He let the fabric drop from his fingers, picked up his boots, which lay next to the modest couch, and walked toward the door to let her in.

Laura strolled into the kitchen, checking that everything was in its original place with a fleeting glance. "Did you get some sleep?"

"I did." He folded the extra blanket he'd used to shield himself against the chill of the day and placed it on the table. "Thank you for offering your home."

His aching shoulders loosened when she didn't mention Violet leaving the inn while he slept. He reached for the pillows which lined the couch that stood against the far wall, needing to busy himself and to fill the uncomfortable silence that descended on them. His nose itched with the plume of dust that billowed in the air as he attempted but failed to puff them up like the maids in his family home.

"Oh, you don't have to do that!" She rushed toward him, plucking the offending item off his hand and tossing it into the corner with a sigh. "I've spent little time here ever since I bought the inn. I'm ashamed of the state of the place."

They both stared at the small dining table and the glass vase with dried flowers which decorated its surface. The petals had long since fallen onto the table-cloth, withered away to brown shades.

Laura's eyes and nose weren't red anymore, but

they remained puffy, and Gavin could tell she was itching to remind him of the help he promised.

"Do you want something to eat? Perhaps some tea as well?" She walked hastily toward the yellow kitchen cupboard and took out a loaf of bread wrapped inside linen and a basket of aged cheese and dried meat. "I'm afraid the bread is stale... I baked it a couple of days ago but ended up not eating it. I have little else to offer here..."

"It's fine, this will do." He sat at the table and crossed his ankle over his knee, letting his weight relax on the creaking chair.

"Will it help you with energy? I mean... will it make it so your healing magic works better?"

"It helps." Hopefully his smile would soothe her nerves. He tore off a corner of the bread she had offered. The hard rim had grown tough, but it still had a pleasant fermented taste. Sour and nutty, just the way he liked it. His smile grew, and she visibly relaxed.

"Does it drain you to use magic all the time?"

"If I do it carelessly, yes."

She picked up a piece of cheese from the plate and took a small bite. She was sitting so straight that he wondered if she'd injured her back at some point. Or maybe it was her normal stance—or she was uncomfortable at having a man inside her quarters without a chaperone present.

"Are you running away from the King? Is that why you asked about the people who arrived at the inn last night?"

The air in his lungs whistled out in one long breath. He took his time to chew slowly, careful not to appear too bothered by her questions, but his fingertips prickled with his awakened power. It was like the magic was answering the call of his own panic. Gavin met her studious gaze with wide eyes, but he found no judgment there, just pure curiosity.

"I'm not. Not yet, at least." He paused, looking out to the street.

"But you will?"

"It's better if you don't know the details. It will be safer for you."

She nodded and chewed her cheese more quickly, looking like she relaxed a little. "I hope your Mrs. heals soon, before the next blizzard hits. It gets pretty bad here during the winter, and while last night's storm was uncharacteristically early, it makes me wonder if winter will come earlier this year."

They ate in silence until the bread was finished and only half of the dried meat remained on the plate. Then they left the warmth of her home and headed for the outskirts of town.

For a small city with few visitors, Scoria was a busy place. From carriages pulled by giant horses and riders wearing traveling coats to farmers pulling crates with goods off their wagons and into stores, every corner of it was bursting with life.

The ambiance dulled the further away from downtown they got, where the alleyways narrowed to four feet wide. The whispers of an attack had clearly made it this far, and people slammed their shutters closed when they crossed in front of their houses. Gavin followed Laura as she turned into a street cobbled with blue and black stones. The homes here had small court-yards with clotheslines strung across them that were full of tattered outdoor furnishings. There were no merchants to be seen, nor carriages or farmers to be heard. Just an eerie silence.

Gavin couldn't shake the feeling that he was running out of time. Not only to help this child, but for Violet and himself as well. Julius had stressed that Gavin only had little time to return and bring her back home, no matter what—or he wouldn't be able to stop the Society from enacting their punishment. It had taken him almost a month to track her down, and he'd only found her because he'd ignored his commander's recommendation to go west instead.

What if Violet was right, and he was too trusting of Julius and his intentions? Even though his commander had taught him to be a warrior, and saved him on more than one occasion. Maybe he'd always intended to reach Violet on his own, while he sent Gavin on a wild goose chase to the other side of the country.

The bitter taste in the back of his throat and the prickling at the nape of his neck alerted him to the mixture of dread and eagerness he felt to return back to Violet, and make sure all was well. Meanwhile, Laura paused in front of a home that blended into the rest of the street with its gray stone and washed-out wood. Moss cushions and ferns grew from the cracks in the wall. Even in the edges of this small town, these houses resembled the woods. A perfect place for an Archana Sídhe to attack.

The front door was marked with dripping white paint in the shape of a triangle, a line crossed through the middle of it.

Laura's rust-colored wool cloak stood out against all the gray shades surrounding them. She took a deep breath and gave him a shaky smile that didn't reach her sad eyes. "We're here."

"What's the symbol for?" He pointed at the white mark as they made their way past the iron gate.

"It signifies the fracture of the peace treaty with the shifters. It gets painted on the door of every victim of their attacks."

Gavin hummed and kept his doubts to himself. He wasn't here for politics. In fact, he'd had enough of that. His only job was to save the life of a child.

He ducked through the front door of the small house, under icicles that dripped frozen water onto the skin of his neck. A small hand wrapped around his biceps, stopping him before he'd fully made it in.

"Mr. Gavin, are you leaving Scoria tonight?" Laura's voice was a whisper, rushed past tight lips. "Because of the people that checked into the inn last night?"

He turned fully toward her. "I don't know. I have to talk to Violet and see how she's doing first. But we can't stay for long."

"Tomorrow, then?"

A trace of suspicion caressed the back of his mind. "Why are you asking?"

Laura took a deep breath, focusing on the white paint that still shimmered wet on the door. "Would today be enough to heal Myna?"

Ah. The questions made sense now. Of course, she would be worried one day of healing wouldn't be enough, and if he was honest with himself—it was not. "I don't know yet, not without seeing her first."

"If you could stay in my place—along with your wife, of course—do you think you might reconsider staying a couple more days?"

"I can't promise that, Laura."

Even though outside it had been freezing, the atmosphere inside the house felt worse. The home was built for shorter people than him, and all its angles and corners were crooked, like a block puzzle put together by a child. He wondered if these humans were magical without knowing it, as it seemed like only their sheer willpower was keeping the building standing.

He paused a couple steps in when the heavy scent of rot and death welcomed him like an old foe. His gut twisted—not because he was unused to the smell, but because he knew that whoever was upstairs moaning in pain had little time left. He'd been expecting the voice of a child, but the reality of hearing it was far worse than he could have imagined.

A woman walked down the steps with the slow gait of someone who was defeated and ready for the nightmare to be over. She paused midway, clutching the banister with a white-knuckled grip. Her eyes were red-rimmed, and tears streamed down her round cheeks. "Who is this?"

Laura sighed while she shrugged off her coat and dropped a basket with supplies on the table. "This is Mr. Gavin. He is a healer, and he can help Myna. He has... magic."

The woman on the stairs paled and took a step back up. "We don't want magic in this house."

"Belle..."

"No, Laura. Magic and magical creatures are all the same. They curse us and take from us, the weaker kind."

"I understand you're scared," Gavin said, "but if your daughter was bitten, she needs my help. I might save her life."

A child's screech of pain bounced off the walls of the small place as if in answer.

Belle was racing up the stairs in an instance, not sparing them another glance. Meanwhile, Gavin's magic buzzed around his hands in a light shade of gray that made the air crackle around them. The urgency that burst through him vanquished all other thoughts or polite conversation. "I'm going upstairs to help your niece."

No law in the world of Caztian, magical or not, could prevent a healer from helping a child. Plus, all magical healers knew and held onto the same principles. Heal first and ask for forgiveness later. Sometimes those who were sick or suffering weren't in the right frame of mind to make the correct choices. He'd rather save a child and face the scorn of a mother blinded by fear of what he was than forever regret not saving someone's life.

The feel of the room upstairs was just as odd as the rest of the house, but he no longer cared about its defiance of physics. He chased the trails of a soft aura that flickered in and out of the child lying in the bed. The soft yellow light of a gas lantern in the corner broke apart the long shadows of the furnishings.

It was hard to mask his concern with a friendly smile, especially with the girl's rattling cough. "Hey, what's your name?" He kneeled at her side.

She looked up at him with wide blue eyes, and her frail body wracked with shivers that rocked the bed. "M-Myna." Her expression, though pained, was alert.

"I'm Gavin. Your aunt has brought me here to help you. May I look at your wound?"

Myna flashed a nervous look at her mother who stood by the foot of her bed. Belle did a poor job at masking her panic or frown, but she nodded either way.

"You'll only look, right? Not hurt me like the other healer?"

"Myna…" her mother warned.

"I'll try my best," Gavin said. "I promise you that by the end, you will feel better. I've been told I have the healing touch. Maybe you can tell me if they were lying to me all along."

He schooled his features, trying not to bring any

more fear and anguish to this family, especially as he peeled the bindings away from the child's torso. It oozed pus from deep, bloody puncture wounds. Four large canines, wide enough to be the size of his thumbs. The imprint of a wide, powerful jaw had marked her, and the curse tainted her veins black.

"A beast, indeed," Gavin rasped, and his magic came to his calling, warming his fingertips as he pressed them against Myna's feverish skin.

"Those damn shifters. Myna is the second child this month to get bitten." His mother dabbed a tissue over her cheeks and blew her nose loudly.

"Where's the other one?" Gavin asked. Their darkening expressions were answer enough. Dead.

He imagined triangles painted on another door, one he hadn't been able to reach in time. His magic soothed Myna's pain while he cleaned the wound with gauze. "This is the bite of a beast, but not that of a werewolf." He didn't raise his eyes from the child, not even after their startled gasps. "Nor that of any other shifter." He probed at the blackened skin around the puncture wounds. Liquid continued to drain from it, signaling an acute infection that had been allowed to fester for too long.

He removed the useless remnants of the human healer's attempt to solve this: a paste made from mud and withered leaves.

Cursing under his breath, he pressed harder on Myna's stomach, and his hand heated further. Yellow liquid turned clear and bloody as the spell pulled out the infection bit by bit. Too slowly for his liking. He could only blame his lackluster performance on his utter exhaustion.

"If it's not a werewolf, then what?" Laura sounded skeptical. "The locals say they saw a werewolf around the woods during the full moon, waiting to attack. To turn us into one of them."

"Larger than any they had seen before," Belle added.

"A werewolf's bite doesn't curse," Gavin said. "Those are myths created by non-magic-wielders because nobody teaches you any better. Shifters are born, not made." At their blank stares, he continued, "This was an Archana Sídhe."

"An Archana what?" Laura frowned.

"A Sídhe is a type of fae that curses with a bite. They aren't common, but they are wicked and very dangerous."

"Are you certain?" Laura pressed a tissue to her nose, to block out the rotting smell which emanated from Myna's tattered flesh.

"Very."

"A fae?" Belle's skin reddened with annoyance. "That's ridiculous. It was a giant wolf shaped like a man."

"Sídhes are shapeshifters, and during the full moon their bites are poisonous. Their victims, if they're non-magical humans, will become cursed Archanas, whose sole task it is to infect more innocents and grow the Sídhe an army."

Belle and Laura glanced at each other.

Gavin cleared his throat. Perhaps better to come at it from another direction. "Werewolves by comparison aren't cursed and called to bite humans. They are a race of people with unique magic, like me. Some are good, and some aren't. Like with any society. But they don't curse or hunt humans during the full moon. Archana Sídhes don't usually hunt for humans either—unless they're battling a war amidst their ranks. On those occasions, there have been recorded cases throughout history when they have."

"Why would the fae do that?" Belle asked,

"To create an army of cursed 'disposable' humans to have under their control. It could tip the scales in a battle." Gavin shrugged and pulled his satchel to his side, withdrawing a couple of vials.

One was a disinfectant and the other a potion to fight infection. He paused when he reached for the wrappings in his bag. The roll was nearly depleted, and Violet would need new bindings around her leg when he returned to their—his—room. "I will need large, clean cotton rags, hot water, a candle, and coffee."

"Coffee beans?" Laura's confused tone was barely audible over the hiss of pain coming from Myna's chapped lips.

Gavin glanced up, opening the disinfectant vial and emptying it over his hands. He rubbed his fingers together before it all evaporated into the air. "I prefer it brewed. Black with no sugar."

"Oh, of course. I will get you some." She rushed

down the stairs, and her sister kneeled beside him. Her face, which had been marred by suspicion until now, had lightened with hope.

"This is the calmest she's been since she was bitten." Belle swallowed and reached for her child's hand. "Can you fix her?"

Could he? The infection went deep, but Myna's body was answering to his magic with the eagerness of someone willing to fight for survival. He smiled wryly. He couldn't promise anything until he'd sorted this out. Claiming that he could heal the infection would be a lie, and it went against the healer's call. "I will try my best, ma'am."

She pressed her lips into a fine line. "Will you stay here the rest of the day? You can rest downstairs. It's not much, but it's comfortable—"

"I'm afraid I can't. My wife was also injured and suffered from hypothermia last night. She's currently staying at the inn. I have to check on her."

The child howled in pain when Gavin pressed harder to get the last of the pus out. Her clammy hand wrenched out of her mother's grasp and clasped Gavin's arm instead. "I-it hurts!"

Gavin's eyes flashed to her mother, and he scrambled to get the last vial of purple liquid from his satchel. He pulled out the cork with his teeth and handed it to Myna. "Here, child, this will make it better."

"What's—?" her mother began, but Myna had already downed the liquid without a second's hesitation, eager to stop the suffering. Her body relaxed into the mattress almost immediately, her breathing slowing until the potion pulled her into a peaceful slumber.

"What was that?" Belle snarled. "Don't give her anything without me saying it's fine for you to do so." She leaned forward, observing the slow movements of Myna's chest as if she were expecting them to stop at any moment. But her child only breathed calmer now that the pain was gone.

Perhaps Gavin should feel guilty about handing the potion to the child without letting her mother decide whether he could do so. But he didn't. "It was my last sleeping potion, and I don't have time to explain every potion or its ingredients to you because you won't understand them. I need to heal her now, or I won't be able to save her at all. For that, I need to clean the wound without stopping every few seconds." He went back to doing just that, sinking his fingers into the open flesh and allowing his magic to sew and heal the tissue.

A potion like this would put a grown person to sleep almost instantly. Gavin wrapped the child's torso with clean cotton rags and let the air escape his lips as he eased onto the floor, registering vaguely that Laura placed a steaming mug of coffee next to him.

He studied the peaceful face of a girl who could be no older than ten, so close to the age his little sister had been when Violet had saved her from drowning. He'd do everything to try and save her, too.

9

VIOLET

VIOLET WAS NOT A WOMAN TO SIT IDLE. BEFORE SHE'D LEFT the Crown's army, they'd only had one personal day a week. She had always spent those days in the library, learning as much as she could about the world outside of the Iron Kingdom. About the laws, new and old. And about ancient spells that might help her evade Dargan's reach.

She'd quickly understood that you could never truly hide from a god...

The longer she sat in bed, waiting for Gavin to return, the more the walls seemed to cave in on her. She grabbed her blouse, which lay folded on the bedside table. It was time she stopped lingering. Packing her things would be a good start. Plus, she needed to find her weapon, so she had it on hand just in case.

She finished tying up the laces of her shirt, covering herself in something more than her undergarments.

A leap of faith, Gavin had said, but then he had disappeared.

Steps outside the door stopped her mid-thought, and her heart sped up as she reached for her knife on the table. As the door handle turned, and the candle beside her blew out in a sudden gust of wind, drenching the room in darkness. She ignored the sharp pain that claimed every nerve ending in her thigh as she leapt off the bed and across the room just before the door swung open.

A man moved past the threshold with careful steps, and Violet jumped out from her hiding spot with a scream. She pushed against him with her smaller frame and pressed her blade against his neck. It didn't matter that he was much bigger than her. The skills of a trained warrior had made her the weapon, fast and deadly.

"Are you going to do it, wife?" His voice sent a shiver down her spine, just as her knife dropped away from his throat. His Adam's apple bobbed when he swallowed. Her legs weakened when her eyes met his.

Gavin's scent embraced her as the blade fell to the ground. His tense posture eased, and they both stared at one another, too close, the warmth of his body burning through the fabric of her shirt.

"I thought you were someone else." Violet stepped away from him. With the surge of adrenaline dispersing, the ache in her leg was hard to mask as she limped back to the bed.

His light gray coat looked darkened by water. He adjusted the brown satchel that hung across his chest.

"I didn't think you'd be here," he murmured under his breath. He withdrew a small parcel from his satchel and threw it at her. "These are for you."

"Was I supposed to leave?" Violet unwrapped the cloth, revealing butter-soft leather. New pants that surely cost a fortune. She wasn't sure she could pay him back for these and the healing. "Why get me these if you thought I'd gone?"

He hesitated before taking a short inhale, then bent to pick up her abandoned knife from the ground. "I hoped you'd stayed... but half expected you to be gone."

"I considered it, several times," she admitted. It had been a surprise how his parting words had burrowed into her icy heart. The bitter loneliness that was her constant companion had become too much to bear. Every time she replayed them, she couldn't shake the finality of what her attitude might bring her.

Being alone, waiting for Dargan to take her. In the past, she'd thought that would be preferable. That it would be worse to fall for someone and get lost in feelings which could lead to a false sense of security. To crave for a family that would be taken away.

She was strong enough to survive this situation. She didn't care about what they'd try to do to her, but if the Shadow God or the Crown took her future child away, like the Society of Crows did when they ripped her from her parents' arms.

That would break her, and Gavin was a man she

could easily make that mistake with. Damn, but she was almost there.

Still, she hadn't left today. Even when the sun had set and led the way to the night. Violet had stayed.

But why? What if Gavin had been with Julius all day long, planning to subdue her in the most embarrassing way possible? He could have lied to her all along, like all men did. They could have been waiting for her to get comfortable. A revenge for what she'd done to them.

She'd never made it out of bed, despite all her fears.

Admittedly, he'd brought her new pants. That didn't seem like the kind of thing he'd do if he wanted to trap her. Maybe being standoffish was unnecessary. It was smarter to stay one more night. She would accept the advantage of his healing powers, and then she would leave in the morning.

"Are you expecting someone?" Gavin's voice made her jump. She'd been staring at the door so intently, waiting for Julius or another member of his assembly to storm in here and arrest her, that time had ceased.

"Are you?" She steeled her spine, ignoring the dull throbbing in her wound, or the uneasiness in her gut. "Why were you gone all day? Speak now if you're going to betray me. If someone is coming, I'd rather not be blindsided again."

He ruffled his hair with his hand. Droplets of water ran down his forehead at the same time that rain tapped against the window. His wet locks stuck to his skin, still dripping over the sharp edge of his cheekbones and down his muscular neck. "I was out healing Laura's niece."

"Laura?"

"The innkeeper. You met her yesterday."

The curvy woman with the tight corset and fake smiles? Violet supposed Laura's large breasts and pretty blue eyes could blind any male. It wasn't as if he and she were a couple.

Laughter surged from her throat, high pitched and ugly. "Typical. She wanted you to do something for her. Healers like you are even rarer than sorcerers."

"A Sídhe bit Myna the night of the storm. The girl was dying." His words sobered her up. "She is only a child."

A child? The beasts usually went for adults. Their drive was to obtain more infected humans to feed their army. Attacks on younger people were rare. "The fae are in this city hunting youths?"

"Another child passed a couple of days ago. Myna is around ten. Not sure about the boy. The citizens believe shifters are behind it."

"It's strange that the fae are striking the young. They should know children won't survive the curse."

"It could be a rogue, cursed one... or maybe there's something else going on here. Something we—I—don't have the time to get involved with."

On that they agreed, at least. "Is the girl going to make it?" Violet asked.

"I'll need to see her again tomorrow, to be certain she's well before I leave this place." He rolled his sleeves up, the way he had done the night before. The gesture still sent flutters through her stomach. "How are you feeling?"

Like an insecure idiot plagued by mistrust. Maybe she could let go of it until midnight. Forget about the emissaries or that Gavin was supposed to be her enemy, here to take her back to the Iron City to stand trial for her actions and be killed for deserting the kingdom. Tonight, he could be an ally of sorts, a man who was helping an innocent child—and her, too. "I'm fine."

"Let me see your leg. I need to make sure you didn't tear the stitches." He beckoned her to scoot to the edge, and kneeled in front of her without waiting for an answer. She'd always liked a man who took charge and didn't fear her scorn, so she sat still, awaiting his touch far too eagerly.

Ugh, since when had she become this pathetic?

Gavin unwrapped the bindings from her thigh, his brows knitted tight as he looked at her wound, tracing the edges of the sutures. "It's better. Are you suffering any lingering effects from hypothermia?"

"I'm feeling like myself, minus the bad leg." And with the addition of the damn flutters in her stomach. They just wouldn't leave her alone.

Gavin hummed, and his hand warmed with a healing touch, numbing the lingering pain of her open wound. If she was putting her suspicion away for one night, it opened up all kinds of questions. Would he end up leaving the kingdom like her? Had she truly stolen his chance to see his family? She tucked a strand of her hair behind her ears, but it sprang back out, moving over her eyes.

"Did I hurt you?" He lifted his gaze. "You're not breathing."

"No. I-I'm sorry, Gavin."

"You're sorry?" He didn't hide the skepticism in his tone, and it burned in the pit of her stomach, running through her like wildfire.

"Please, don't make me repeat it."

"What are you sorry for? Throwing a dagger at me or attacking me yesterday when I found you in the alleyway?" He returned his focus back to his task, his jaw clenching. A moment later, the warmth of his breath caressed the bare skin of her leg, raising goosebumps wherever it touched. "Maybe you're apologizing for being so agreeable to me all the time."

"I'd like to see how pleasant you would be if the people you thought were your friends abandoned you. Sold you to the Crown and humiliated you on their way out." She picked at her nails, trying to keep herself from fretting too much over his words.

He didn't know what it was like to have no one. To constantly look over your shoulder, waiting for an emissary to jump out of nowhere to take you or your future family to the gods.

"Not trusting anyone and pushing everyone away is a good way to make yourself an easy target for someone like the Crows." His stern expression softened, and she almost disliked that more. She could deal with snide comments about her personality. But she was unprepared for his niceness. "You hide behind this mask that's meant to protect you from getting hurt, but it also leaves you alone. You need those who will fight alongside you... For you."

Silence descended on them, so heavy with the truth that she felt it in her bones. Her eyes prickled with a warning of tears, and she glanced away from him. "Is it true that you won't be able to see your family again? That you'll have to leave the kingdom?"

Gavin pulled a roll of gauze from his bag. Thunder rumbled in the distance. "Yes."

"Then... I'm also sorry I'll be the reason for that." Violet let herself sink into the bed. She missed her own parents and her sister. She'd been so young when the Crown had taken her away from them. She was three and twenty herself now, so Thalea must be twenty. Violet spent countless waking moments wondering what she was up to. Whether her vibrant imagination was painting a different picture of her sister than reality.

Had she been in love? Had someone courted her? Perhaps she was even married already?

The Crown had seized her at eleven years of age, and the voice of her mother was all but an echo. Gavin had stayed with his family until he was eighteen, longer than anyone else she'd met in the army.

It didn't mean she wanted him to suffer the same.

Emboldened by her need to make it better, she reached for his face with trembling fingers. She traced the edge of the pink scar on his chin, smooth beneath the prickle of his beard. "I wish you hadn't jumped in front of the knife that night."

Gavin's breath stuttered, and his dark eyes searched her face. His turn to choose whether to give her another chance, or continue on with their constant bickering. "I know."

They stared at each other, the air crackling with a different kind of tension. Her gut twisted, and her skin grew sensitive to even the touch of the linen fabric of her shirt.

Then she let her hand fall away from his face, and the moment broke.

Gavin cleared his throat and sprang to his feet. "What happened to us wasn't good—I don't condemn you. I blame the Crows."

Interesting that he was leaving the Crown out of it. Gavin had called the King "fair" at one point, hadn't he? Presumably if you were born with a silver spoon in your mouth, the monarchy would appear less evil. But that was not a debate she wanted to get into right now, not when the weight of their conflict was lifting and she could breathe.

He continued to dress her wound, and Violet couldn't stop fixating on the places where his fingers touched her leg. Would he brush against her inner thigh, test the edges of how far she was willing to let him go? Maybe she wouldn't stop him at all. She struggled to focus on anything other than the tingling between her legs. A truce sounded better right now.

The two of them working together while they both crossed the mountains, found the shifters, and stole their way out of the kingdom.

She didn't desire to be alone... not really. Her odds of survival would be much higher if she had someone to trust if a Crow caught up to her.

Was she ready to take a leap of faith with Gavin? To trust that he wouldn't betray her like everyone else she'd cared about?

"Do you have siblings?" she asked, choosing the path of vulnerability. Hopefully it wouldn't come back to haunt her. She already breathed more easily, as if a bag of stones had been lifted off her.

He peered at her, and his features softened as if he understood what was happening. His cheeks turned a light pink shade. "I have a younger sister, Elina. She is thirteen."

The corners of Violet's lips tilted up. She watched him stand and walk toward the table. He drew out wrapped bread and some cheese from his satchel and brought it over to her. "It's fresh from the bakery. What about you?"

"What about me?"

"How old is the sister that's waiting for you at the edge of the mountains?"

Violet paused mid-chew, her heart hammering in her ribcage. "You know?"

"That your family's village is nearby, and that's the reason you headed this way? Yes."

She sighed, shaking her head at her stupidity. "I

thought they'd sealed the records unless a member of my household requested them?"

"We are married, Violet. Remember? In the eyes of the Crown, we have been one ever since we both received the letters."

Right. "So what, you went out searching for my history when I left?"

His damp shirt stuck to his back, revealing the shift of muscles beneath it as he strolled across the room. It was hard not to get caught up in his fluid movements. Or the way his messy hair accented his handsome features. Or his easygoing personality. Or...

"I looked into you the moment I learned you were going to become my wife." His tone was unapologetic, and Violet found she couldn't be upset about it. She would have done the same, had the Society of Crows not restrained her in her bridal chamber while she awaited the ceremony.

"Did you tell anyone about my family's village?" she whispered, and fear crawled up her back. The palms of her hands grew sticky with sweat.

"I didn't tell anyone where I was going. Julius commanded me to head west. The coastline is closer to the Iron City, and they assumed you were leaving the continent as soon as possible."

He was pacing the room like a caged cat, but she believed his words. Gavin dragged a chair underneath the doorknob, blocking it, and let his hand fall against the wood. He cast a spell under his breath, and a ward clicked into place right before her eyes, shining orange like a glowing shield of air which surrounded them.

She frowned. "Are we expecting company?"

"Laura mentioned that a few travelers arrived late last night." He hesitated. "She's also offered her place for us to stay. It might be a good idea if the Society of Crows is here, they're less likely to search a random, non-magical citizen's home."

"Why are you trusting her so blindly? What if she sells us out?"

That churning in her stomach was all mistrust and not jealousy. Right? They felt remarkably similar, some days.

"What would she gain by that? She needs me to help Myna, and I believe she is grateful."

The room hummed with the steady background noise of the wards. "If you trust her, then why the spell?"

"Because I need to heal you. You have to rest and eat. We should go before sunrise." He cleared his throat. "That is, if you agree that it will be safer there."

It took her a moment to weigh her options. "Does this mean you're leaving with me after tomorrow? To head across the mountains?"

Gavin looked her straight in the eye. "If you want me to. Then yes."

Three weeks ago

HER WEDDING WAS UPON HER. THE GOLDEN SUN SPILLED *through the large windows of the temple. She walked beneath pleasant greenery and flowers, petals drifting around her, spurred on by the wind that carried the scent of winter. The beautiful, untarnished blooms were at odds with the season, which could only mean magic aided them.*

Unlike the crown that rested upon her head. Drops of mud dripped from it onto Violet's face, rolling down her cheeks to end up on her ruined white dress. Vera had forced her to pick up the flower crown that betraying cock had given her as a parting gift.

Violet drew in a deep breath and let it ground her in the present, even as Vera's tightening grip sent a shock of pain up her arm. Did the Crow suspect there was a knife with her name on it strapped to Violet's thigh? Doubtful, but that made it all the more rewarding.

Logically, she understood this was a power play—and that if she wanted it to stop, she should act meek and apologetic. But she didn't want to act like she was sorry for plotting to flee the kingdom. She was only sorry she'd confided in her friends about her plan.

She'd tried to escape the night Vera had delivered the letter which bound her to Gavin. Admittedly, that hadn't been her finest moment.

It was an insult to the gods to wear something this filthy the day of her union to another magic-wielder. Especially one from such a prestigious, snobby family.

Yet, the Crow had placed it on her head, clearly intending to make her uncomfortable. In an act of rebellion, Violet simply let the drops of mud dry on her face. Pff—as if she would feel shame to be seen dirty by the likes of Dargan, the God of Shadows, or his sister Alera. This was who she was. If Vera wanted to torment her, she needed to up her game.

"Look at what a mess you are." Vera's voice was loud enough to travel down the chamber. Violet refused to give her the satisfaction of seeing how much it affected her. "Try hard to not do anything stupid. There won't be any more warnings."

"So I get one warning, and that's it?" The Crow's imposing aura crowded her own, spicy and stronger than anything she had ever felt.

"One's already one too many, in my opinion. You are trouble, girl. If it were up to me, I wouldn't waste anyone's day by escorting you."

Violet turned away from the woman, not wanting to

exchange another word with her. At this rate, she'd provoke her into doing something she would regret. Her fingers itched with the need to grab the hilt of her weapon and teach this bitch how much trouble she could be.

Quiet melodies played in the background. String instruments—perhaps a fiddle—were interrupted by the chimes of bells.

No—on second thought, that was the ticking of a clock. A massive pendulum hung at the end of the chamber, framed by stone arches. A marriage of old and new. Built from iron and brass, a soft musical sound echoed around them every time it swung.

Violet took in the massive structure and the markings of letters in an unfamiliar language. It was three o'clock, yet no one but Vera and her were here. The ceremony was supposed to start at three on the dot.

Where was her groom? The place was deserted except for the magistrate, an ancient man dressed in sharp golden tunics with a red sash tied around his waist.

As if her thoughts had called them, steps echoed behind them. Two men and one woman entered the temple. Violet turned and the moment her gaze met Gavin's, everyone else fell away. It was just him and her in this room, awaiting their destiny.

She devoured the sight of him a little too eagerly: the elegant velvet tunic that hugged his broad shoulders that tapered down to a narrow waist, emphasizing his trim body. Gold details hung from his chest: medals and commendations from battle.

They hadn't allowed Violet to wear hers, not after they

had stripped her of them when they'd discovered that she'd intended to escape. She tilted her head when Gavin stopped in front of her. His intense expression morphed into a grimace as he studied her in all her filthy glory. He was the light to her darkness, clean and polished against the dirt-stained picture she made. His brown thick hair was combed back, letting all the sharp angles of his handsome features shine under the flickers of candlelight.

His brows scrunched up in clear discontent. And yet, Violet appreciated that he kept looking at her face and not down at the mess of her gown.

She swallowed hard against the discomfort that swirled inside her gut, the insecurities of never being good enough. Of being all that Vera claimed her to be: filth, dirt. Worthless to the kingdom and to this man, who was the golden boy of his assembly.

"Cora," he said in a breathy tone that jolted her heart.

"We are getting married, Gavin. You can call me Violet."

"All right, Violet." Her name on his lips made her stomach flutter. They might have stood for longer, just looking at each other, if not for someone clearing their throat in the background.

Violet met Julius Coventry's piercing stare. His pale hair looked wet, smoothed to his skull. Wild strands curled over his ears. His white skin was peppered with pink freckles. A snide smile curved on his thin lips as he took in the plunging neckline of her dress, which left little to the imagination.

His tongue peeked out, and he sucked his bottom lip between his large front teeth. Had she not been staring,

Violet would have missed it. Her stomach sank, and her blood ran cold.

This was the man her snake of a commander had abandoned her to—the infamous Julius from the Valdor Assembly.

"It's about time someone introduced us, eh, Cora?" He extended his white-gloved hand. The ticking of the clock was deafening in her ears. "What happened to you? I hope you didn't run into any trouble on the way here."

False kindness to appease her soon-to-be husband. However, Violet wanted nowhere near those hands. They'd strangled multiple women in the past. Everyone knew it and yet nobody spoke about it.

"I can't say it's a pleasure," she said.

The second Society of Crows member who had to be present in her wedding stepped into her line of vision. Violet hadn't met her in person before. Judging by Vera's description of the woman, she could already guess she'd be as despicable as her chaperone. Morgan's hair was the same shade as Julius': a pale blonde. She'd stained her lips blood red, contrasting with her black uniform and bringing out the greenish tint of her skin. If Violet looked at them long enough, Julius and her appeared to be related—and around the same age.

"Watch your tone with your commander," Morgan snarled, letting her pronounced canines peek past her lips.

"Oh, calm down cousin. Violet is in shock about this whole affair." Julius' belly laughter was so loud it hurt her ears, but it wouldn't food her. His nostrils flared with a barely contained rage which promised suffering.

"It's Cora to you, Commander. You aren't my friend, so let's not pretend here." She turned away from the two of them, toward her intended.

Had it not been for the magistrate's presence or for Gavin's, she suspected Julius would have dragged her away by her hair. To get punished, no doubt. Nasty rumors circled about him in the other assemblies. They claimed he used canes and whips. That he broke people, and that their begging excited him. But he wouldn't break her, she would like to see him try.

Gavin's alarmed expression didn't waver, and she almost pitied him. A shame that this was his first real impression of her. Undoubtedly, no one had told him she rarely held back her thoughts and often led with her truth, whether it was unpleasant to hear or not. In this life, where a god owned you... Well. What was there to lose?

Violet doubted her fiancé truly knew what a monster his commander was. His growing displeasure made it clear that he was not on her side. And why did she even care? Other than the fact that Gavin was, admittedly, gorgeous to look at... Her stomach fluttered with re-awakened nerves as they pushed her to stand beside him in front of the altar, fear and attraction mingling until she could no longer tell them apart. It didn't matter. Violet needed to get out of here.

"It's time now." The magistrate's voice broke the silence that had descended on the group. Vera and Morgan stayed behind, and Gavin gestured for her to lead the way as they approached the statue before them. Alera, the goddess of life.

Violet turned to face Gavin, and they reached for each other's hands as the magistrate commanded. He rattled off *the laws of the kingdom and marriage, it didn't expand much more than the few scribbles of the binding letter she'd received. They were now one, unless they failed to make a child. Then it was followed by a binding spell, used to connect family together.*

Magic flowed around them like the waves of an ocean, golden circles enveloping both of them. In the background, Julius stopped scuffing his feet against the floor, and the Crow's hushed comments died down to nothing.

All Violet could see was the man in front of her. All she could feel was his tender grip, her heart sped up, and her stomach tumbled with excitement that was dampened by her nerves.

In another life, she would have been happy that the gods had looked down on her and granted her a kind, handsome husband. His gentleness didn't match the reputation of his assembly and their ruthlessness. Although perhaps he was just as evil and unscrupulous as them, only better at hiding it.

The spell settled around them, and the strings of gold vanished into their skin. And yet Violet felt no different. Everything was the same.

The magistrate stood tall, his frail frame swallowed by his tunic. He opened an ivory box with trembling hands. It was polished to shine like his bald head. Inside lay a silver dagger adorned with sapphires and emeralds. He stepped around the podium and came toward them, holding the blade. Up close, he looked even more ancient, although he was taller than Gavin by at least half a foot.

"Today, you are bound as husband and wife. Under the

laws of our kingdom and gods, you are one." His voice echoed through the large room, and he held out his hand.

Violet hesitated, but it wasn't worth her trouble to defy this command. She hissed when the sharp edge of the blade cut across her skin. Blood pooled in her palm. The magistrate picked up a golden cup from behind him and held it beneath her bleeding fist, squeezing it to coax the thin red stream out.

"That's enough," she snarled, pulling away from his grasp. Immediately, heels clicked over the marble steps, and another blade pressed against her neck. A reminder that this was not something she could escape. Or so they thought.

The magistrate's quirk of a smile sent another shiver down her spine. A trace of fangs peeked out from behind his withered lips, sending Violet's heart into overdrive. "Go on," he encouraged. "Getting agitated gets more blood out— much better that way."

It shouldn't have surprised her that the magistrate was an undead. Such roles were usually reserved for those kinds that lived long lives, although Violet had never seen one in the Iron Kingdom. When they had brought forth enough blood that her hand felt numb and cold, he repeated the procedure with Gavin. The healer, however, didn't complain. Clearly, his sense of self-preservation was more developed than hers.

Nausea churned in her stomach when the old creature drew the goblet to his lips and took a sip. He shuffled back behind his podium, with a skip on his step.

"Why the blood?" Violet asked, and the blade nipped at her skin, making her wince.

"*Quiet now, Gray.*" *Vera growled. If the insult was meant to hurt Violet's pride, it failed. She was proud to be a gray sorceress. Her power was not as strong as Vera's, but she knew how to wield a weapon better than most. And this would be the last time this bitch pressed a blade to her neck.*

"*Stop,*" *Gavin commanded, squaring his shoulders. The spice of his magic billowed around him. He was readying himself—but for what?*

Was he talking to her or to Vera?

There was no way he could engage two Crows and his bastard commander at once. "*Let her go. We've done what you asked of us. We are married. Isn't that enough?*"

Vera's shrill voice burned in Violet's ears. "*Oh! This is endearing. He thinks he can fight me.*"

"*Vera, Vera,*" *Julius interjected.* "*Let's not make a tremendous fuss about this. The child has a big mouth, and she's my man's wife now. Remember, Gavin's parents are benefactors of Plume City, and he is in excellent standing with the King.*"

Vera withdrew the blade from Violet's neck and slid it back into the sheath on her belt. Her crazed tone eased. "*Of course. If the royals like him, then I guess I can't have any fun.*"

Violet's hand twitched with the need to grab her own blade and use it to carve Vera a new face.

"*Speaking of what we demand of you.*" *Morgan spoke from the back, stepping toward Gavin and Violet.* "*We should head to the chambers for the union. Who would you prefer to be present during the act? Vera, myself, or the commander?*"

The room spun around Violet. Or maybe her legs were growing weak. Gavin's surprise was just as audible, a choked gasp that turned into a coughing fit. His cheeks bloomed bright red, and his wide brown eyes darted from face to face. "W-what?"

Had this not been about her wedding night—or a scenario that was becoming more real by the minute—she would have responded to his embarrassment in a provocative manner. Even under the unusual circumstances, heat rushed through her, knocking her off kilter. She pressed her legs together, trying to suffocate the tingling sensation that awoke in her core at the thought of sharing a bed with him. What was wrong with her? How could her own body betray her in a situation like this?

She fought the urge not to fidget under the room's watchful eyes. Could they see how her breathing became ragged? Could he?

Violet was supposed to hate all of this. But it was hard to lie to herself. To acknowledge that even though she'd intended to escape tonight, her attraction to him had been very real from the very first time she saw him a couple of years ago. Now, he was her husband.

"You both heard me. One of us has to witness the act to ensure the marriage is in fact consummated and the bond is strong and in place. It's the law, and it's necessary to prevent falsehoods in the unions." Morgan's red lips tilted into a coy smile that made Violet feel sick.

The words were a dose of icy water to Violet's heated thoughts. Morgan's blue eyes trailed down Gavin's chest, pausing at the edge of his pants as she drank him in like he was nothing more than an object for her entertainment. Violet tightened her fist around the pommel of her hidden blade and chewed on her cheeks, hard enough that she tasted copper.

"Neither of you are coming to our chambers," she said. "I have studied the laws extensively, and while they demand a Society member witnesses the ceremony, they don't require one for the wedding night." As Violet spoke, Gavin reached out a hand to hers, grounding her amidst her rising anger.

"Well, well. It seems we were wrong." Morgan walked around them in a slow circle. Her smile revealed yellowing teeth against red lips. "The peasant can read."

She stopped next to Violet, meeting her eyes, unblinking. Her smile transformed into a snarl, and in the next instant, her small hand grasped Violet's hair, pulling her back until their cheeks were pressed tightly together.

Morgan's breath reeked of tobacco with a hint of mint, as if she was trying to hide something putrid lingering in her throat. Violet winced, struggling as the Crow dragged her across the floor and away from her groom.

Dimly, she registered Gavin's panicked voice in the background, and through a veil of tears, she could see Julius holding him by the podium. He tried to wrestle out of his commander's grip but wasn't able to break free. Meanwhile, Morgan had already dragged her back toward the exit.

She lifted Violet by the hair and neck and brought her lips against the shell of Violet's ear. "I will watch him fuck you tonight and have you recite all the laws you think you know." Her voice was so low that only Violet could hear her. "And if you don't entertain me enough, I'll let my cousin have a go as well. I know he wants to, especially after you ran your mouth earlier."

This woman—this monster—was a sociopath hiding behind the veil of the Society of Crows. She abused her stronger magical skills to torment those she considered beneath her. But her confidence in Violet's weakness would be her undoing. She never saw the knife coming.

Violet tilted the blade, slashing through the fabric of her dress and pulling it out in a flash. She plunged it deep into Morgan's rib cage once, twice, meeting resistance between the bones. The squelching noise of blood and muscle tearing was all she could hear beneath her captor's screams.

Morgan clawed at Violet's shoulders, fists trembling, and dropped to the ground. Violet's hands were drenched in sticky red. She had just enough time to slice open the bindings around her wrists. The magic-canceling ropes she'd been wearing since Vera captured her fell on top of the Crow's lifeless form.

Chaos erupted. Screams pierced the air. But Violet didn't hover over the fallen Crow. Adrenaline flooded her as she fixed her gaze on Julius. Another monster that needed to be gone from this world. She hurled her knife by its very tip with all her strength, sending it flying across the room, just the way she'd been practicing since she was thirteen.

The blade whistled through the air, cutting through floating flower petals. Julius' eyes widened, but Gavin pushed his commander to the side, putting himself in the knife's path. The sharp edge nicked his jaw before it continued its journey and hit the podium, where the magistrate was hiding.

Nausea raced through Violet, and she emptied the contents of her stomach over the polished floor. But she couldn't stay a moment longer to see if he was all right. Vera was snarling loudly, and her magic, a much darker shade than Morgan's, bloomed over the room, drowning out Gavin's cries of pain and the magistrate's screams for punishment.

There would be no retribution—not today. Not for Violet. She ran toward the pillar which held boiling oil and a flame that illuminated the hall. She raised her palm and her magic burst forth, toppling the stone column so it fell against the drapes by the windows. They caught fire like dry kindling, and before Vera could even get close to her, the entire place went up in flames.

11
VIOLET

S HE STIFLED A YAWN WITH THE BACK OF HER HAND. WITH THE nightmares that visited her daily, she was struggling to gain enough energy to function.

The sun set on another day, dipping behind the treetops and the horizon of the mountains beyond. Violet let the embroidered curtain fall from her fingers and looked back at Gavin, who had been brewing the same potion the entire afternoon.

They'd overstayed their welcome in Scoria. If it were up to her, they would be long gone by now. Yet, a part of her accepted that her leg still ached, and that exhaustion clung to her body with the lingering effects of cold sickness.

When they'd moved into Laura's home, they'd settled into a comfortable routine of being semi-polite with one another. All this while, she'd been healing— both physically and from the wounds buried deep inside the marrow of who she was.

The looming threat of someone coming for her hadn't exactly improved her state of mind. The memories of her wedding haunted her, and sleep had been scarce. Besides, the Society was likely drawing closer now, seeking retribution for her crimes.

She took a long, deep breath to calm herself. Gavin was right, though. Even if the Crows were in Scoria, no one would suspect that they were staying here, in this dilapidated building where only locals lived. At least not without interrogating their host first. Unlike him, Violet didn't trust the innkeeper so blindly. A few gold coins tossed in Laura's direction would likely buy their whereabouts. That's what people did. They betrayed you.

She closed her eyes as the thought pulled her back to their wedding day. How her own commander had left her in the hands of the Crows: Vera, who'd walked her to the altar and forced her to wear a mud-covered crown, mocking her all the while. And Morgan, who'd promised to watch her and Gavin during their wedding night to make sure they consummated the union. Who'd promised her worse things, whispering them into the shell of Violet's ear when nobody else could hear.

She shivered with the memories. How the blood had splattered against her skin as she'd sunk the knife into Morgan's body. How she'd let the anger that plagued her seep out in the throes of her revenge.

"Anything new out there?" Gavin's voice pulled her back into the present.

"No one we should worry about, if that's what you're asking." Silence settled between them, leaving her to drown in her memories once more, in the hurt she'd caused. "Is she alive?"

The creaking of the chair told her he was shifting his weight. "Who?"

"Morgan."

"No, she's dead."

Violet tried to swallow around the knot in her throat, to chase away the chill in her blood. It seemed it was here to stay. "I... I've never done anything like that before," she admitted, shame distorting her voice. "Morgan was going to let him hurt me..."

She met Gavin's questioning gaze. Would he believe her if she told him what she knew about Julius? Gavin held that bastard in such high esteem. She wondered if he was purposely ignoring the facts. Did he really not understand that his commander was a monster known to kill women amongst the assemblies?

Morgan was aware of Julius' true nature, without a doubt. Or she wouldn't have threatened Violet with— how had she put it? Ah, yes. Letting him have a go. The outcome of which had been a very violent outburst on Violet's part—and Morgan's death. Still, it didn't ease the guilt churning within her guts to know that she could do such a thing. While she had been to battle many times, she hadn't truly hurt someone–let alone killed– unless commanded to do so. Even if this time had only been in self-defense.

"Let him?" Gavin asked. "Who are you talking about? The magistrate?"

"No. It's nothing." She turned away from him, taking a deep breath. "If you could not save her, then why on earth would you believe the Society of Crows won't kill me if I return home with you?"

Gavin was silent for a while, blinking slowly at the apparatus he used to make potions. Small glass tubes cake with residue, and brass knots that kept it all together. His jaw was clenched tightly. "Julius said he would protect you. Since you're now a member of the Valdors, and he is a high-ranking commander, he could pardon you. He told me he believed his cousin was out of line."

Ha! While it was true that Violet had only been trying to save herself, she doubted that snake of a man would have stuck his neck out for her. Especially after she'd tried, and failed, to kill him.

The law would have been on Violet's side, had the Society of Crows not been such a corrupt, evil organization. They held the kind of power that was meant to protect, but they enjoyed using it to torment the people instead. Morgan had been out of line when she'd insisted on witnessing their wedding night.

Violet hadn't broken any rule when she'd defied her archaic demands. She'd known what the actual scriptures required of them, and it wasn't watching while a new couple consummated their bond.

"And you believed him?"

"I do—did. I understand if you don't. Which is why

I'm here, alone." He turned to her, and his deep frown eased.

He was questioning his commander's actions, after all. Perhaps it was better if he arrived at the conclusion on his own. If it were up to her, she would let Gavin hate her for all that he'd lost and maintain the illusion that his commander was a good man. She'd already taken so much from him. She didn't want to continue the trend.

"Was your family near the temple on the day of our wedding? As I fled, I could have sworn I saw a man with a striking resemblance to you... except older."

Gavin nodded, but his eyes remained on his workstation. If it hadn't been for his hand freezing midmotion and the stiff set of his shoulders, she would have thought they were talking about what was for dinner and not reminiscing about that horrible day.

"They'd traveled to the city to meet you."

She held on to the table as the ground seemed to tilt beneath her. "They did?" Surely that pathetic sound wasn't her voice.

"My sister didn't come. They don't permit children to take the portals."

"I thought non-magic-wielders couldn't cross either. Shows how little I know about true wealth."

The scriptures didn't go into too much detail about the gods and the strange phenomenon that were portals. But everyone who survived seeing the Shadow God knew that Dargan always collected a prize from those who crossed through his in-between worlds. He was known as "The Collector" for a reason.

Gavin chuckled, and a pleasant smile with dimples remained on his face. Her heart fluttered at the sight of it. "Whatever you think my family's wealth is, cut it in half."

"I doubt most of us common folk get to meet the King in person."

"I suppose you're right."

Was Gavin's sister anything like Violet's had been when they were young? Thalea was a woman now, and probably nothing like she remembered. Regardless, Violet had always liked children. They were bright and innocent and all that was good in the world. They needed to be protected.

If she survived, she vowed to try and help those innocents that got dragged from their homes before they even made it into their adolescence. Like she had been.

"I would have wanted to meet your sister, even at that moment." She recalled the state she'd been in, her wild eyes and the blood that stained her white dress. "Actually, I take that back. She wouldn't have liked me. No one does."

"Elina adores you."

Violet stilled, his words knocking the wind out of her. "She knows me?"

His cheeks bloomed red, and the spoon he held clattered to the dish below. "They all know about you."

Oh.

Of course. What was she thinking? They had been engaged for a week, that was enough for his parents to learn of their son's match, although correspondence in the kingdom seldom traveled that fast. She evidently didn't have a clue of how much his wealth could buy.

Gavin continued tinkering with his salves, while Violet busied herself with the only book the innkeeper kept in this place, a fantastical story about other worlds. A very light read for her, but the only way she could occupy her mind while she was stuck here.

Violet was bursting with pent up energy. She closed the book, and dust plumed out of its brown pages. "We shouldn't just sit around like this for days while we are being hunted down," she said, though the Society of Crows wasn't pursuing him yet. "Let's train. Whoever scores first wins, and the loser buys our next meal."

That caught his attention. He put his ingredients down and turned towards her. "Now? In this small place, while you're injured?"

She shrugged one shoulder and stood up slowly. "We need to work out our energy and keep our skills in place. I shouldn't need to remind you of that."

He cocked his head to one side and lifted one brow. "And I shouldn't have to remind you that you almost died a few days ago."

"I'm fine to train," she said, and walked towards the living area while rolling her shoulders. "We can spar lightly. No kicking and no magic—that is, if you aren't afraid of me."

Gavin stood in one fluid motion, strutting forward in a wide stance. "I'm most definitely afraid, wife."

"I don't like it when you call me that." The living room was too small for this, but she was too stubborn to back out now.

"But you're my wife."

His words sent a rush of adrenaline that burned through her, and she attacked without waiting for him to go back to his potion brewing. Gavin was a trained soldier like herself, and a very capable one at that. He got out of the way easily.

She attacked and he ducked from her fist, again and again, leaving her craving for the normalcy of her speed. Her stiff leg slowed her down, but she refused to let that stop her.

"Are you going to hit me back or are you going to continue on with this dance?" She forced out in between gritted teeth before leaping, and barely held a hiss of pain behind her lips as her wound flared to life.

Gavin blocked her, but this time didn't move fast enough and she collided against his body with all her strength. They stumbled back a few feet, her legs tangled with his. Her sutures pulled and pain blazed with such intensity she lost her balance.

They fell too fast into a tangle of limbs and hard planes. She shouldn't enjoy his nearness, and the way his hands settled around her waist.

"Are you hurt?" he asked.

"I'm fine." She scrambled away from him and immediately missed the delicious warmth of his body.

"You were taking it easy on me. If you do that, how am I going to be ready to fight someone like the Crows?"

"You're injured and I'm your healer. It's not the right time to train."

"Whatever, you still owe me lunch," she said and got up to her feet, shuffling back to the table where she'd left the book.

He didn't argue, and maybe she'd been secretly trying to earn some of the free food she'd been getting lately. He walked back to his station and drop to the creaking chair without a word.

He'd spent most of the morning chopping herbs and grinding rocks, extracting their essence through a complicated apparatus with brass elbows and silver knobs. Its glass tubes were caked with particles of old magical potions. How did all these parts fit in his satchel?

Gavin hadn't left today to tend to the innkeeper's niece, most likely waiting for the cover of the night. He hadn't told her much about the little girl over the past few days.

His complete devotion to help the child made him a great healer—and a man too close to destroying the flimsy walls she'd built around her battered heart.

He put on a pair of round spectacles. Their thin black frame reflected the flames of his workstation.

"I didn't expect you to wear glasses," Violet muttered. She let her chin rest on her palms and studied him as he placed a mint leaf between his teeth, unaware that he was being watched. Or maybe he was just very good at ignoring her.

She stroked the recently cleaned tablecloth. The dried-out flowers had been the first thing she'd tossed. Violet had never been able to afford or been allowed to own her own home. It annoyed her that someone could choose to keep theirs this way.

Gavin flashed a look at her, straightening out of his hunched-over pose when he realized she was staring at him. "I only need them for potion brewing, it protects my eyes."

"I see." The corners of her lips twitched. She schooled her features before the smile could break loose and reveal that she was enjoying chatting with him. "They make you look smart."

He scoffed. "How do I look normally, then?"

Like a handsome trouble she wasn't supposed to want, but did regardless. "Without a doubt, like a giant pain in my ass."

Gavin laughed, shaking his head. A white powdery substance spotted his dark, wavy hair, remnants of a minor explosion a few hours ago. He had cleaned most of it off his face, but she found it so endearing that it was still clinging to the strands that she didn't have it in her to point it out.

For a moment, they stared at each other. It wasn't uncomfortable anymore. Instead, it awoke a pleasant sensation that extended from the pit of her stomach to her fluttering heart. "So, how is Myna doing?" she asked eventually.

"Better." He returned to his brew, dropping some oil into his small bowl and stirring it over the fire. "I've pulled out most of the poison, and she should be ready to walk in a few weeks."

"What are you brewing, then?"

"A muscle relaxant. It's for you."

"For me?" Her cheeks warmed.

"It'll help your leg when we are on the road, in case you experience spasms as it heals. And it might help with the nightmares."

Damn him, she hadn't realized he heard her at night. "I don't need a potion to relax my muscles. Quite the contrary. I need time to exercise so I can banish my pent-up energy. Either another training session or..."

She paused before saying the words that almost spilled out of her reckless mouth. A good fuck would work too, but she didn't want to give him the idea that she was open to it.

Judging by his growing smirk, he knew damn well what she was going to say. "Or what, wife?"

Her insides churned with a need that almost took down her last remaining defense against those dimples. This in between them would only make everything more complicated.

"Nothing you could handle."

He scratched his brow but didn't deviate his eyes from hers. "I always give it my best. I might surprise you."

She didn't doubt he would, and she was already in

too much trouble to continue on this line of conversation. "We should leave this city tomorrow."

Gavin sighed and nodded. He turned all the knobs on his apparatus and began breaking it apart into tiny pieces, stowing them all away inside his leather satchel. "I'm afraid you're right. I haven't been able to sleep properly for the past few days for fear of the Crows arriving. We can go after we've taken the last potion to Myna."

He stood and stretched like a cat. The movement pulled his tunic up, giving her a front seat view of his well-defined stomach muscles and how they dipped into his pelvis in the shape of a V. Violet's mouth dried at the sight. She needed to put some space between them before she threw caution to the wind and jumped him.

Intimacy wouldn't just mean plain sex between Gavin and her. Even if she avoided getting pregnant with a potion, she couldn't afford to make a mistake and develop stronger feelings for him than those that had already begun to build inside of her. It would only cement the magic spell that had linked them together ever since they'd wed.

Violet wanted him—badly—but she might want more than just physical connection. She had to resist temptation.

12
VIOLET

THEY STROLLED DOWN THE STREETS JUST BEFORE DAWN TO bring the girl the last batch of medicine. The veil of the night was a perfect cover for a Sídhe, and those bastards were a more dangerous foe to encounter than a Society member.

Energy buzzed through her: she wanted to meet this little girl, even though her home was on the other side of town.

Gavin cut through a narrow gate. Weeds grew on either side of an uneven pathway, brown and partially hidden by snow. Violet lifted her coat's collar, shielding herself from the cool breeze that picked up as they neared the house.

He'd told her about the symbol Scoria's citizens had adopted that signified the break of peace between humans and shifters. The triangle was still painted on the wooden door, an ominous white mark.

"I thought you'd explained to them that shifters aren't to blame here?" she whispered.

Gavin knocked twice and rubbed his hands together before blowing hot air into them. "I did. Not sure they believed me."

To judge by the emblem, they hadn't.

Candlelight flickered through the fogged windows, and steps clicked behind the door. Its hinges creaked as it cracked open, revealing a man a head shorter than Gavin and at least twice his age. He wore a thick, brown-striped robe and a scowl that matched Violet's for intensity. "Mr. Luna." His polite and raspy tone was stark against the quiet night. "We weren't expecting you so early."

Violet stepped inside the house. The iron wood stove sizzled, a pot of tea hissing on top of it.

"Who's there?" a woman called from upstairs. She moved down the steps moments later, holding a candelabra. The child's mother, perhaps?

"Mr. Gavin is leaving town today, and he wants to check on Myna," the man answered. He dipped into a dark corner and re-emerged with two mugs filled with tea leaves to pick up the pot from the stove.

"I see. She will be sad that you're going." The mother wet her lips as she shifted nervously. Violet couldn't settle either, and a sense of unease crawled up her back, demanding that she leave. These people appeared every bit as uneasy about her presence in their home.

The woman's blue gaze fell on her. "And who is this, Harry?" she asked her husband in Obsidian.

"Do I look like I know, Belle? She showed up with the healer."

Violet wondered if they usually spoke in their native language when Gavin was around. He didn't seem to know what they were saying, nor care much about it as he pulled things out of his spacious bag.

She could answer them and reveal that she could understand everything. And yet, the part of her that was used to spying for the Crown told her she should stay quiet. Keep her cards close to her chest and listen to all of their potentially incriminating conversations.

"Who is this young lady, Mr. Gavin?" the woman asked.

"Oh, this is my wife, Violet."

"We have heard much about you." Belle closed her robe with one hand, pushing her long golden braid back from where it lay over her chest. "Are you able to leave right now, in this dreadful weather? We heard you've been ill as well."

"Try not to stare our hosts down, dearest," Gavin whispered into Violet's ear. "Not everyone's out to get you." His nearness sent goosebumps over her neck. Her heart stuttered, and blood rushed to her cheeks.

Ha! Tell that to her former commander, who'd left her in the hands of Julius knowing what he was like. Or to the vipers who'd sold her to the Crows, who'd been her best friends. She peeled her lips over her teeth in what she hoped was a smile, but to judge by their pale faces, it came out as more of a snarl. Oh well, she'd tried. "I'm fine now."

Gavin scoffed, but he was smiling as he walked past her toward Belle. "Is it too early to see Myna?"

"She's still asleep, and we're trying not to wake her. It's difficult for her to rest with the pain."

"I understand. I don't want to bother her either, and I don't expect her to be worse than she was yesterday. Use the potions I'm leaving here." Gavin glanced up at the second floor, and his brows met in the middle with a sadness that was hard to miss. "We should leave you to rest. Please tell her I wish her well and take her to your regular healer by the end of the week."

"Will she be fine during the full moon?" Harry asked, shuffling closer to them. "Are we going to have to chain her so she doesn't hurt anyone?"

Silence descended upon them, and Violet was sure her face mirrored Gavin's wide-eyed and open-mouthed expression.

"Absolutely not," he said. "Myna isn't cursed anymore. If she were, she wouldn't be alive. Youths don't survive the bite of a Sídhe."

"But we've seen werewolf children," Belle argued, one arm pressed defensively across her stomach.

"Shifters are born that way." Given his tender nature, it wasn't often that Gavin's tone turned harsh, but it did now. "As far as I'm aware, you or your husband aren't shifters, correct?"

"Of course not!"

"Well then, that answers your question. Myna is not a werewolf. Nor will she ever become one."

"Gavin?" A small voice came from upstairs. Then the creaking of the wooden planks above their heads alerted them to a child on the move. Chastising Myna loudly, Belle raced up the steps to stop her.

Both men followed, but Violet hesitated before she trailed after them. She didn't have the gift Gavin possessed of being so at ease with strangers. And she wasn't ready to start learning it right now.

Still, her throat clogged when she saw the girl's frail frame lying against the headboard of her bed. Myna looked weak and sick. When she spotted Gavin, she let out the loudest, most vibrant squeal Violet had ever heard.

Her father laughed from the corner, and even the mother snickered as their child settled back in bed.

"Now that's the welcome I like to see from my favorite patient." Gavin flashed a look at Violet, right before he kneeled next to Myna. "No offense to you, wife. You don't receive me quite the same."

Pff. It wasn't like she wanted to be his favorite. She didn't. And the quiet voice in the back of her mind calling her a liar could fuck off.

"None taken," she mumbled, pulling her collar away from her throat. But the pressure she felt didn't ease.

His eyes sparkled with mischief, and her heart rate doubled. This feeling was new and scary. A different light shone on the man she was growing to care for far too fast to be happy about it.

This was what she wanted. Him and a family of their own. The clarity of her desire hit her like running into a stone wall at full speed. Violet could have had it all—if only her future hadn't been cursed by magic and the emissaries that hunted her.

Her chest constricted painfully, and she backed away before storming outside. Down the damn narrow stairs that blurred with the salty tears that were dripping on her lips, and out the door painted by a symbol of broken peace..

She sat in the cold for what could have been a couple of minutes or an hour. The distant sounds of the city sprang into life as the sun rose from behind the horizon.

"Are you all right?" She didn't move at the sound of Gavin's steps or at the low timbre of his voice cutting through the quiet. He lifted her chin with two calloused fingers so he could inspect her face.

"It reeked in there, and I needed fresh air," she lied, pulling away from his touch and ignoring all the places that were left tingling in its wake.

Gavin's lips parted, then shut again. "You can talk to me about it when you are ready," he said eventually.

Which would never happen. She glared at him and rose, ready to put some distance between herself and this place—and him.

It was easier to keep her emotions at bay when she had hated him. Admittedly, that had been challenging on the best day, and now everything was changing. Gavin was helping children even though it could mean capture. He'd healed her although he'd lost his family because of her selfishness.

Her feelings were growing too close to something she'd sworn she wouldn't give in to again.

He intrigued her. But love—that was a forbidden word for her. Her heart couldn't handle another blow or more heartbreak. Not after Cullen.

13

VIOLET

By the time they made it back to the center of town and to Laura's building, the morning sun cast shadows over the streets. Tumultuous gray clouds were approaching from the west side of the mountains. They had a couple of hours at most before the bad weather reached Scoria and might prevent them from leaving.

She might be new to being a fugitive, but she'd always been a pawn in someone else's game. A weapon forged from an early age, allowed only to be bitter about what they'd stolen from her. And now the reality of her sacrifice, the unfairness of it all... It was just too much.

The shape of the inn resolved itself, its dark wooden beams, green window sills and shutters rising tall from the morning haze. A wide set of steps led from the road to the main door with large stout columns and the two statues of the shifter and the human on either side.

Violet hadn't absorbed all the details the night

Gavin had brought her in, nor had she paid attention during the following days in the innkeeper's home. She allowed herself to appreciate the beauty of it all now, knowing they were so close to leaving. While this place was unique, she'd never return to this part of the world if she could help it.

They were still a fair distance away when a man with pale skin, golden hair, and a bushy beard walked down the steps. He wore a gray coat the same color as Gavin's. She didn't need to look at his features to recognize him.

"Julius." She heard Gavin's sharp intake of air just as the word left her lips.

Without a worry in the world, the commander adjusted his black gloves as he inspected his surroundings.

The feeling of ants that crawled up her back matched the sudden fear that clutched Violet's chest, paralyzing her. Julius hadn't spotted them yet, turning toward the four men that were standing near him in the street instead. Much like the commander and Gavin, they wore silvery outfits with the kingdom's insignia sewn over their hearts.

Their faces were a blur from this far away, brown belts, and fur scarves were a dead giveaway of who they belonged to. It appeared that the Valdor Assembly had found her, after all.

"Fuck!" Gavin's wide hand wrapped around her arm and whisked her into the nearest alleyway.

Violet's boots dipped into inches of mud, and she

let her numb body collapse against the wall behind her. "He came here with part of your assembly. Does that mean the time he gave you to take me back to the Iron City has run out?" She met Gavin's wild gaze. His skin looked pale and shone with a fresh layer of sweat.

"That's not my assembly," he said.

"What do you mean? They're all wearing your uniform."

"I know, but those aren't my brothers. I've never seen them before."

She straightened, and the reality of their situation sank in. All the pieces of the puzzle clicked together. Who these people were didn't matter, as they'd most likely been hired to help Julius with the dirty task of tracking her down and killing her. By wearing the army's uniform, they could avoid any questions from Scoria's citizens. Gavin clenched his jaw, and she knew he must have reached the same conclusion as her.

If Julius had come with his own hired muscle, it could only mean the King hadn't signed and approved this mission. And the only way this hunt would end was in bloodshed.

The pulse of her heartbeat echoed loudly inside her ears, drowning out other sounds around her. She didn't fear death so much, but she dreaded the way they would do it. Had she been sentenced to a warrior's execution, she would go fast and with little pain. But left to his own devices, Julius was going to rape and torment her.

"He's going to hurt me..." Her breaths came out in

shallow pants as she paced toward the dead end of the alleyway and back again. They were trapped. Stuck here, next to wooden boxes littered with animal feces.

The heavy weight of two hands landed on her shoulders, warmth seeping through her coat. She'd escaped for nothing.

"Hey," Gavin said. "Calm down. Violet."

She barely registered his voice. How could she settle down knowing the pain that awaited her? Adrenaline pumped through her body, bringing traces of nausea to her gut.

Gavin turned her by the shoulders, and her breaths eased when she met his gaze. "When you were talking about Morgan, was Julius the one you feared would hurt you?"

Her expression must have been answer enough because he dropped his hands like she'd burned him. "Fuck!" He looked back towards the inn with wild eyes, and his quick, shallow breathing gave away his panic. "They are heading this way."

He studied the buildings that loomed over them on all three sides. There were no windows on the bottom level, except for a narrow balcony to the right. It looked more of a hazard than not, to judge by the rotten wood that hung from what had once been the floor.

"Come on, climb up on my shoulders."

"What?"

"You'll be hidden up there until they take me away because you're small."

She frowned. "You think this man is your friend,

Gavin, but he isn't here looking to uphold this lie he told you. I killed his cousin and deserted the kingdom while being a part of his assembly. He's out for my blood."

"I know." He fumbled with his satchel, pulling it from his shoulders and dropping it over hers. Too stunned to move, she watched as he tightened the belt around her. "Do you recognize the difference between a healing potion and one that's meant to induce sleep? Never mind. If you're hurt, in my bag there's one potion that's tinted green. It's a strong healing brew. It can keep you alive until you find help."

"Why would that matter? I'm not hiding up there while you fight them."

Julius and his men must be drawing closer. She swore she could hear their voices, mingling with the din of the streets.

Gavin let out a deep breath, regaining some of his composure. "I would never forgive myself if he hurt you."

"If we work together, we have a better chance of escaping."

"Two against five? You're still injured, and I haven't really slept in days." He pushed her toward the building and underneath that death trap of a balcony.

"No," she protested again. "It's better if we stay together."

"You're going on that terrace."

Violet turned to him, but her angry retort died in her throat when she found his imploring gaze. He raised his hand to her cheek and trailed his fingers across it. "Let me do this for you."

Gavin had given enough already, and she didn't want him choosing her life over his. She shook her head just as his lips slanted over hers, stealing her words. He pulled away just as quickly, and she chased the kiss, wanting to hold on to the fantasy for longer.

"I wish I'd done that sooner," he whispered and rested his forehead against hers.

"You should have," Violet agreed. She stood still, dazed by his taste. And when Gavin hoisted her over his shoulders as if she were a paper doll, she didn't fight him off like she should have done.

The voices of the men were moving closer, definitely audible now. She knew there was little time to waste and fight him on this. Violet would not leave him alone to die for her, but she could let him buy them time. She'd hide until the group grew comfortable and took him away to where they were staying. Then she would strike.

She doubted Julius would be so careless as to kill a member of his own assembly, someone who wore the same uniform as him and had been in town for a while. It might be their best chance of survival if they didn't catch Violet alongside him.

Gavin was right. They were both tired, which would weaken their magic.

Violet settled her feet on Gavin's shoulders. Her body shook with her loss of balance, but she managed to drag herself onto the balcony. The wood, covered in a pillow of moss, groaned under her hands. She jumped over the gaps on the floor and landed on the side of the building.

With ragged breaths, she flattened herself against the doorframe, thankful it was painted black, allowing her clothes and skin to blend in. She knew how to disappear.

Gavin strolled toward the street, rolling his shoulders and stretching his arms over his head. Then he pressed his body against the wall behind a box, buying himself more time to cast one final glance at her.

Thunder rolled in the background, and the air crackled with static. The storm couldn't have made it here already, could it? Perhaps it was an emissary's warning. If she decided to fight these men, it might trigger one of the undying to come to her aid.

They would bring her Dargan's message and save her from this mess. Right?

No. While the idea was tempting, she didn't know who the next emissary would be. It might be a Luelle, old and jaded. Or a Cullen, manipulative and sly. Fuck him and them. Plus, having them come didn't guarantee Gavin's survival. They weren't interested in protecting his life. Just hers.

Better to go it alone... as always.

Violet stilled her movements and focused on the steps and voices just around the corner. The men must still be unaware that they were here.

Maybe they wouldn't find Gavin—or her.

Maybe...

"My boy, is that you?" Julius' voice traveled down the long alley, his friendly tone hiding a stiffness that hadn't been there on the day of her wedding. She peered over the edge of the balcony. The five of them blocked the road as rain pattered against the ground. Gavin didn't move or attack.

"Commander." His greeting came out stifled.

Julius stepped forward, tilting his head as he inspected the area, forcing Violet back into the cover of her hiding spot. Although she could no longer see them, her mind supplied vivid images of what was happening below. It was enough to hear: The stomping of boots over wet dirt and stone. The clanging of metal and rustling of heavy fabric that shifted with the calculated moves of trained fighters.

"I didn't expect to meet you all the way here, in the Obsidian town of Scoria. Didn't I tell you to find your wife?"

"You did."

Julius' tone hardened. "I recall commanding you to head west."

"I had my reasons to believe that wasn't where she was headed."

"Ah. Well, where is she then?"

"Not here, as you can see."

"And why are you hiding in this alley packed with shite?"

The squelch of hard sole boots over wet matter as Julius—or someone else—strolled close to the balcony. A bark of male laughter followed soon after from further away, as though Julius' hired muscle found all of this hilarious. Violet held her breath, not daring to move in case she might give herself away.

"It seems I've been around shite long enough, and my senses are dull to the foul smell of it."

"Whatever do you mean?" Julius laughed.

"I find it strange that you are here, when you assured me that you'd wait for my return to the Iron City." Gavin sounded entirely too calm for someone surrounded by enemies.

The silence that followed constricted her chest with a burning ache.

"I trained you well." The smell of spice and the sizzle of power signaled that more than a few of the men below were sorcerers. She could distinguish Gavin's magic from the rest with ease. It was familiar, earthy and warm. The other auras felt strange. "Where is Cora, my boy? I won't ask you again."

"She isn't here. I should have listened to you and gone west instead of wasting my time in Obsidian."

"On that, we agree."

Violet's hands prickled, damp with sweat as rain rolled down her cheeks, tasting salty on her lips. Her breaths sped up, and for a moment, the only noise around them was the distant yapping of a dog.

Then chaos broke loose.

The building behind her rocked with a spell gone awry, and static traveled with the raindrops that fell heavier upon them. Her hair stood up on end as a scream of agony reverberated against the wall.

Was that Gavin? She scowled and peeked over the edge of the balcony again—to see him withdraw his bloodstained blade and pull away from the two men that crowded him. This was her fault. Violet was the reason he was being cornered in this grimy alleyway, with a laceration on his brow and betrayed by someone he'd trusted.

Her gaze traveled to Julius just as he removed a silver bar from his coat's pocket. It extended into a long staff that snapped together, catching the gray light of the rainy sky. He jumped toward Gavin, and the tip of the weapon hissed through the air, barely missing his face.

Gavin hopped back. Despite his agility, he wasn't fast enough to duck Julius' next attack, not when a spell hit his side at the same moment. The metal caught him in the gut, and he fell to the ground with a silent cry.

Violet clawed at her own legs, using her own pain to subdue the scream that wanted to tear from her lips. She watched in horror as Gavin tried to get up, his arms sinking deep into a puddle of mud just as a blast of energy lassoed around his neck and tightened from the back.

His hands rose to the thick cords of the magic-canceling rope, and he thrashed about as another spell hit him full force. It came from a bounty hunter with a short stature and terracotta skin. The third man who wasn't torturing Gavin at the moment was kneeling beside his companion who lay dead in the alley.

Julius strolled around the place, kicking over

another crate full of animal droppings. It spilled all over the ground in a large, smelly pile.

He must think she was hiding inside them. Tears pricked at Violet's eyes and rolled down her face as she pressed against the façade of the building, Gavin's words echoing through her mind.

I would never forgive myself if he hurt you.

Let me do this for you.

I wish I'd done that sooner.

"Where in God's name is she, Gavin?" Julius snarled. The loud pounding of fists hitting flesh made her flinch. The grunt of pain that came after tore at her heart.

Her anger bubbled over, harsh, demanding, and all-consuming. Tears streamed down the mess of her face. She took a calming breath before peering at what was happening below and immediately regretted her choice.

"I. Don't. Know," Gavin answered, and Julius' staff met his skull with a crack. Gavin's eyes rolled into the back of his head. She pressed both hands to her open mouth, muting the scream that almost broke free.

The short bounty hunter caught Gavin before he toppled onto the filth on the ground. His body slumped with a dead weight, and the wavy curtain of his hair hid his face from her. "Should I slit his throat now?"

"No." Julius walked around and kicked over the next crate, cursing when he only found it filled with more of the same. "I don't need witnesses that can link me to Gavin's death. I wasn't expecting the boy to disobey me and come here."

Violet might have believed he was remorseful if he hadn't been the one to crack Gavin's skull with his steel weapon. She tightened her grip around the pommel of her own knife.

"Then what? I doubt hitting him on the head will make him forget this," the other, red-haired bounty hunter grunted. "Besides, he killed Tierre."

"Then celebrate. You get to split Tierre's reward amongst yourselves," Julius commanded, just like she'd thought he would. Behind the mask of a nice man there was only a monster. "Gavin is coming to the commissary with us. He knows something, and I need that to find my prize. You take Tierre's body outside the city and burn him where he can't be found. Dispose of the uniform somewhere else."

Julius walked to the last crate and raised his hand. A ray of gray light spiraled from it, colliding with the container. Feces and wood rained over the alleyway.

"The bitch isn't in Scoria." The short man spat on the ground. Julius peered around the alley with a deepening sneer. His icy eyes slipped over the balcony—and missed her.

Blind bastard.

"Oswald, I thought you were smarter than that." Julius resumed his usual jovial tone that masked his jab at the other man. "This boy is hiding her whereabouts, but not for long. You'll find that I'm quite persuasive with people. They give me the information I want."

She watched them as they dragged Gavin out of the alley, his boots pulling the mud into the street in two trails. His head tilted to the side with the motion, and she spotted his slack jaw and the blood that trickled down his temple.

He would have demanded that she leave town if he were awake. Violet had never considered herself someone with a death wish, nor a hero hiding behind a scowl. Following these cocks would mean a low chance of success.

And yet, her mind and heart demanded that she do something. Maybe she was an idiot after all.

14
VIOLET

SHE STOOD ON THE BALCONY UNTIL SHE WAS ABSOLUTELY certain they wouldn't return to the alley, although every part of her itched to move. The sun rays filtered through stormy clouds. Her fingers were numb from the icy rain. Her stomach rumbled with the lack of food.

Violet couldn't leave through the same road those bastards had taken. Apart from the mess of crates on the ground below, she was sure Julius suspected she was nearby and working with Gavin. He'd probably posted one of his goons to watch out for her on the street.

The wood creaked under her feet as she probed the tall doors to her left. The knob didn't budge, clearly locked from the inside, but the panel gave way a bit when she rested her weight against it.

She peered at the sky, and her vision blurred with the heavy rain. The waiting game always paid off. The bolt of a lightning ray was followed by a crack of thunder that made the doors and flimsy windows shake, and Violet's magic bent the doorknob under her tightening fist. She slammed her whole frame into the only feasible escape path with all that she had. Again and again, until the door fell open and dropped her into an empty, dark room.

She choked with the dust that bloomed around her and sat up, lifting her hands. Her magic illuminated the surrounding area. She rose and tiptoed past the peeling wallpaper and the stacked pieces of old furnishings covered in blankets that had once been white but were now spotted with mildew. At least she was alone and safe in here.

Until she opened the door to the adjacent suite—and the screams of a naked woman greeted her. A man leaped away from the bed and backed into the corner of the room, cowering behind a wingback chair. His wide-open mouth took over most of his face, and his half-erect cock swung around like a pendulum. If only she could unsee it. "Whatever my wife paid you for information, I'll double it! You tell her I was never here." He tried to pick up his pants in an attempt at modesty. "All you women have a price, don't you?"

Her fleeting gaze lingered on the woman in bed. Should she ask for directions now? Best not. She took off across the room instead, running toward the main hallway.

From the inconspicuous looks of the building, Violet would have never guessed a brothel conducted its business here. How could these people ignore the heavy scent of animal feces drifting in from outside? She crossed the deserted hallway toward the staircase, and found the foyer on the ground floor busy with men sidling up to scantily clad women in half-hidden booths. Most of the patrons and prostitutes ignored Violet, even with her magical aura buzzing around her. She jumped down two steps toward the exit. Thankfully, it led out the back.

What a sad place. Still, she didn't have time to think about these people, not when Julius might be torturing Gavin. Julius had revealed the information about their plans and whereabouts so easily—too easily in her opinion. In the middle of the day and out in the open. She wasn't naïve enough not to suspect a trap. Perhaps he'd known she was there in the alleyway all along, although he hadn't been able to find her.

Scoria was one of the rainiest cities in the Obsidian mountains. However, she hadn't seen the weather this bad since her arrival... which meant the streets were deserted, so anything unusual would stand out. At least the absence of onlookers would give her enough time to defend herself if some bastard awaited her in a shadowy corner.

She was cold, fatigued, and hungry, and the storm raged as she made her way to the inn through the back roads. It took a while because she lacked exact knowledge of the buildings in town. While she didn't trust Laura herself... Gavin had.

A leap of faith.

Violet found her alone, sat behind the counter as

usual. A breath left her as the tension in her shoulders eased. This one time, she wouldn't have to battle to get information. She could take a few minutes to collect herself before she had to go and fight for Gavin's freedom.

The innkeeper yawned.

"Psst."

Laura uncoiled and turned in her stool before her blue gaze met Violet's. Her plump red lips fell open. Then she ran toward Violet like a soul called to purgatory. Her slender hand grabbed at Violet's wet coat, and she pulled her into the cramped pantry.

"You can't be here," Laura said, out of breath. Violet had to give her points for bravery. Not many saw her scowl and dared to touch—let alone grab her—without permission.

"A commander of the King's army arrived earlier today, looking for a black woman with purple eyes."

They stared at each other knowing well what that meant. Violet shifted her weight away from her sore, throbbing leg. "Did you tell them I was here?" Her words lacked any heat, and Violet didn't believe Laura harbored an ounce of hostility toward her. Not that she had a good record when it came to trusting people.

"What? No, of course not. I owe Mr. Gavin my niece's life. I'd never want any harm to come to him."

"If that's true, you can help me find him. The men that were here earlier today took Gavin somewhere to be interrogated." Violet cleared her throat. She had to avoid the horrid details of what would happen to him to protect Laura, in case all of this went awry. "They said they were taking him to the commissary. Is there such a place here?"

Laura seemed to mull it over before nodding. "Yes. But, it has been abandoned for quite some time. It burned down half a year ago after an altercation with the shifters."

Definitely a trap then.

"What building would the King's men take their prisoners to? Is there anywhere you can think of?"

"Yes," Laura whispered. "The gaol is rumored to be underneath the governor's home. The high-ranking commanders stay there whenever they visit Scoria. It's the large building on the outskirts of town. You can't miss it."

Ah. Now that made sense.

Violet placed her chilled hand on Laura's shoulder, and even though the innkeeper flinched under her touch, she remained in her spot. "He was right about you."

Laura blinked rapidly. "Mrs. Luna?"

Violet's heart skipped at hearing the surname. Luna. Because she was supposed to be his. Had she taken his name when they wed? The Magistrate could have changed it automatically, although she hadn't requested it. Not that it mattered. The marriage was a farce, after all, even if her heart ached with the thought of it.

"Yes?"

"I've heard that the gaol has another, less

frequented entrance underneath the temple. By the crypts." Laura's brows rounded as her gaze darted around the small room. "People in town say the place is cursed, which keeps most away. Use that one instead, as I imagine it's not guarded."

Violet nodded, not saying thank you out loud. Words weren't her strongest quality, and she was grateful to Laura for her help. However, knowing herself, her own mistrust would accidentally slip out in a snarky remark. Best to say nothing at all.

With a tilt of her head, she was out of there.

THE GOVERNOR'S HOUSE WAS A LARGE BUILDING FOR SUCH A small city. Standing three stories high, with gesso-stained plaster and walnut-colored windows, it rose proudly against the night sky. A stone chimney with iron pipes jotted from its clay roof, billowing smoke into the air.

Violet watched from her spot between two bushes as a guard walked the perimeter of the home. He looked miserable, wearing a tall fur hat, drenched and dripping rain water onto his face. She herself felt a bit less like a drowned rat after she'd spent the rest of the afternoon in Laura's rooms, warming up and waiting for nightfall. It had seemed safest to hold off until then before any rescue attempt. She could only hope Gavin hadn't suffered for it.

There weren't many guards in place. She'd counted

five, three by the entrance, taking cover from the weather, while the others took turns walking the gardens. No magic hugged their bodies, and being this exposed to the unforgiving elements would only make them more sluggish and tired.

An easier target for a trained soldier like herself. Still, they outnumbered her, and five against one were odds she'd rather avoid. Especially since they were likely not the last line of defense she would meet.

Maybe the entrance by the crypts would have been a better choice, but who could guarantee it was even there? She'd debated heading there instead as she waited, but she couldn't just put Gavin's life in the hands of a human who listened to the town's gossip, however well-intentioned. Plus, even if it was real, Laura had mentioned that it could be cursed.

Violet didn't have time for what could be or what ifs. She needed certainties. Flattening her lips, she shushed away the nagging voice in her head. The path she was going to take toward the building was now burned in her mind, as she'd been obsessing over every stone she could see from her hiding spot. She took a sharp breath to calm her frazzled nerves and set off.

Running through the grounds, she became only one more shadow of the night. Her magic sheltered her from view.

Violet jumped over the five-foot iron fence, ignoring all the ways her muscles objected. The metal squeaked as she pushed her body over the vertical bars and avoided the sharp, rusty spikes at the top. The movement strained her hip, and acute pain shot through her wound, a firm reminder that she was still healing.

She sneaked through the garden like a thief, past bronze statues of male figures wearing elegant tunics. The evergreen shrubs that grew against the outer wall of the building proved to be a safe hiding spot. The guard who was completing his second round of the house blew warm air into his hands, rubbing them together before grumbling something under his breath.

Violet almost felt sorry for this poor soul, and what she had to do. She lay in wait as he marched closer to her hiding place. When he wasn't looking, she shot a ray of energy into the bush opposite her.

The guard stopped, his head snapping toward the moving leaves. Turning his back to her, he approached the bush with tentative steps and nudged the area with one boot. At the same moment, Violet leaped after him, aided by magic. Two fast steps, and she was upon him.

The scream died on his lips, and he fell to the ground beside her in a tangle of limbs and sharp bones. She pressed her hand over his mouth and rested her blade against his throat. "Move a muscle and I'll cut you. Nod if you understand."

Her Obsidian was rusty, but the guard swallowed and nodded.

"The King's commander brought a prisoner here this afternoon. Where is he?"

"I-I can't. He'll kill me if he finds out I told you."

"It seems to me you don't realize your current

predicament, then." With steady hands, she nicked the skin of his throat with the edge of her blade.

Of course she didn't intend to harm this man past this demonstration of power, even if he didn't cooperate in a timely manner. But he didn't need to know that. Especially since the looming sensation that she was running out of time weighed down on her.

"The gaol is a series of tunnels underneath this entire property. Not all of us have access, and I don't have the keys. I swear." His voice shook as he blinked the raindrops from his pale lashes.

"Where is the entrance?"

The man pressed his lips together, and Violet lowered her blade to his neck once again with a growl. "About ten feet south from here, behind the ivy. Please, I have a family—"

She smacked his scalp with the pommel of her dagger, hard enough that he sank into the ground unconscious almost immediately. Her breath clogged her throat as the sound of Gavin's skull being smashed by Julius' metal staff echoed in her mind. So similar to what she'd just done.

Feeling queasy, she dragged the guard's body behind the bushes where she'd been hiding before. Then she dug through Gavin's bag, which was still hanging across her chest, and pulled out a thin rope. She didn't have to use much to tie his arms behind his back and his legs to the bush. She used Gavin's gauze to gag him so he couldn't shout for help when he regained consciousness.

Her actions shamed her. She'd been commanded to do similar things in the name of His Majesty the King. This was different. This had been her choice, and while it had bothered her all the times she'd done it before, now she questioned it. Could she have gone about this differently?

Maybe if she'd taken the crypt's entrance, she wouldn't have had to knock this man out...

The gate was easy to spot when you knew what to look for, although it blended into the wall, painted in similar shades of cream and white. A curtain of ever-green ivy shielded it from view.

Picking locks was something she'd trained in while she was a pawn in the King's army. She had excelled at it. She pulled two metal pins from her hair, and the section they'd held back curled into her face, obscuring her vision as she proceeded with practiced ease.

Sweat beaded at her temple as she jiggled the bars inside the keyhole. The click came soon after, and the gate eased open, allowing the muggy air of under-ground tunnels to whiff out.

It was impossible to see a thing once the door had swung shut behind her. She stepped down polished stone steps, taking one at a time until she found the softer ground below.

It took her eyes a while to adjust to the pitch-black darkness. It took her even longer to get her bearing as she set out through the tunnels. She hadn't expected them to be so mazelike. She didn't want to use her magic and drain her energy further. Nor was she sure what awaited her once she got out of this labyrinth.

How long had she been here? She continued on the path with the strongest breeze running through it, hoping it would lead her inside the governor's house. The surrounding scent of mud cleared the further up this way she went, and the air warmed up, which was a good sign she was getting closer.

"Well, look who came to play," Julius' voice rang over her, smug and suave. The hairs on the back of her neck stood on edge. She pulled her knife with a trembling breath and turned around—but met no one.

How did he know she was here? Where was he?

Her surroundings spun around her as she turned again and again, trying to find the bastard anywhere in the carved rock that cut her off her on all sides. Wait. Which way was the back and which the front? Where had she come from?

"Cora." He chuckled, his tone that of a good-hearted greeting, and yet it felt nothing like it in her current situation. "There you are."

He appeared from the shadows, a mirage come to life. His power had hidden him from view all along with a shielding spell. Easy for someone like him to master, whereas it was impossibly hard for gray sorcerers like herself. She'd ran her energy reserves dry when attempting to cast one while crossing the yard.

Her heart stopped, and a nip of pain extended from her skull down to her neck. The numbness traveled to her limbs, a sudden cold that burned underneath her skin.

She registered the thump of her knife as it fell into the mud below. Her surroundings flowed like ocean waves. She fell, and everything appeared to go in slow motion, until the arms of the snake wrapped around her body. With little care, Julius draped her over his bony shoulder.

Panic rushed through her as the numbness continued to hold her limbs prisoner, and her sluggish mind struggled to come up with ways to escape. Although she tried to grab the fabric of Julius' coat, everything refused to move—why couldn't she even do something so simple? There was no scent of magic in the air. No ropes tying her down. Nothing hurt.

"Save your efforts to fight it. It's a well-crafted brew known to paralyze every limb. It even makes some people forget what happened to them while under the influence. You don't have to worry about that, Cora. You will be eternally sleeping by then."

The dim tunnel moved around her, and she registered the screech of rusty hinges as a door opened and shut behind them. They entered a large hallway with stone flooring and gold-framed pictures hung on the walls, fuzzy around the edges of her vision.

Julius strolled through it like he owned the place. He whistled a cheerful, macabre tune, ignoring the guards that sneered as they passed them by—at her, or at Julius? She'd never know.

A familiar voice called to them. A sound that pulled

at her heartstrings and made the adrenaline already pumping through her body double. She opened her eyes and tried to focus on the words.

"Is she all right? Should I call the healer, sir?"

"No." Julius' deep timbre rolled under her stomach, and his hands came up her thigh, squeezing. Although the sensation was dulled, her stomach revolted at his touch. Nausea twisted her gut.

"Should I bring her dinner, then?"

"There won't be a need for that either. You see, Cora is not a guest. I don't want word to spread about her being in my chambers. Is that understood?"

Silence.

"Is that understood?" Julius repeated with a snarl, abandoning his false politeness.

"Quite, sir."

"Good. I would hate for you to encounter issues while I'm here." Julius shifted his weight, turning away from the man, dismissing him. "Make sure no one disturbs me."

As he moved, Violet could finally see the man. His tired expression matched that of his daughter, Myna. Harry's eyes widened when their gazes met. His jaw, covered in a dusting of blond beard, jutted forwards as it clenched tight, his knuckles whitening where he clutched the wooden handle of a mop.

Laura must have heard about the separate entrance from her brother-in-law if he worked here. Not from a town's gossip. Which meant that Violet's stubborn refusal to follow any advice she was given had cost her not only her own life, but what was far worse... she'd failed Gavin as well.

She couldn't even tell if tears wetted her cheeks. This was a nightmare, and she'd failed Gavin and herself.

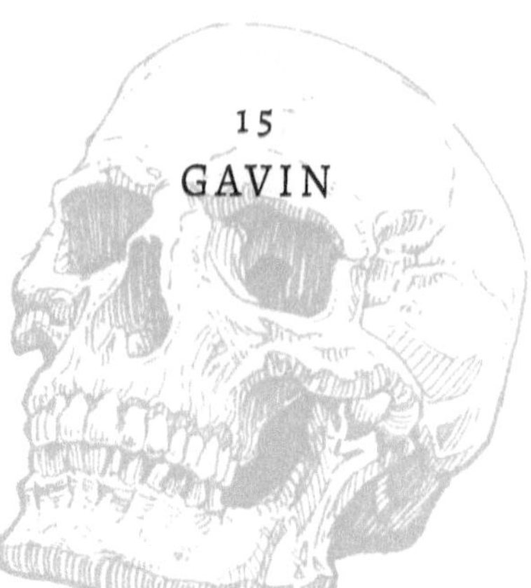

15
GAVIN

GAVIN WOKE TO A HIGH-PITCHED SOUND RINGING INSIDE HIS ears. Besides the intense headache, the whole room wobbled underneath his body as dizziness wrecked him. He groaned, inching his hands over the hard, cold ground, only to stop when he met resistance around his wrists.

The ropes were tight enough that they bruised his skin, and while he could move his arms, he was clearly bound to the wall behind him. These weren't just the regular, twisted hemp cords, but the ones the army used—imbued with a spell to repress magic.

At least the room was dark. Tucked in the far corner, a light flickered, away from his sensitive eyes. His breathing sped up as he probed the back of his head with a tentative touch. The pain pulsed to his jaw, like shards of glass embedding themselves in the bone. He sucked a breath through gritted teeth and his fingers touched the sticky texture of blood that matted his hair to his skull.

His symptoms could only mean he had a concussion. But to know how bad it truly was, he needed a rational mind and his magic. His chest hollowed out with a sorrow unlike any he had felt before. The memories of what had happened were within reach, but foggy.

He must be in an underground prison somewhere in Scoria, though there was a possibility they'd brought him to another town in the Obsidian mountains. On their way back to the Iron City—

As soon as that thought entered his mind, he pushed it aside.

They weren't taking him back to the city. He was going to get killed here.

The six-foot-wide cell was encased by rusty black bars, and a bucket stood in the corner, still caked with waste from the previous occupant.

Gavin studied the dark gray walls, looking for a sharp edge he could use to cut through the ropes. He spotted white scratches running along the stone, some vertical, some crisscrossing in a pattern. Frowning, he leaned closer and discovered remnants of darkened blood smeared over the white streaks. Claw marks, left behind by the poor soul that had been here before.

The rotten scent that clogged the air could only mean one thing. That person had died in here and then been decomposing for a while.

Gavin jolted up onto wobbly feet, and for a split second his vision blackened as the room spun around him. When everything steadied once more, he opened his eyes and met the unnatural golden gaze of the neighboring prisoner. He had a beard so thick it covered most of his features and wore black clothes that blended into the background.

Gavin jumped back with a shout. He slipped over a suspiciously wet patch on the ground and landed on his side with a grunt.

"Are you all right in there?" The deep voice bounced around the room.

Gavin rolled onto his back and swallowed the heavy nausea that surged through his body. He tried to ignore the intensity of his headache, but panic kept rising to the forefront of his mind, making it increasingly hard to do so.

"Just great." He struggled with the bindings around his wrists, and his magic leached away further, becoming a distant drum beneath his skin.

He stared at the cave-like ceiling above him. The perk of presenting with the healer's gift was that his body was incredibly efficient at healing itself. It was increasingly difficult to deal with his now dormant power, especially when he needed it most.

The images of what had happened earlier came to him in flashes. Much though it hurt, he couldn't deny it any longer—Julius' true nature was out in the open. His betrayal spoke for itself. Gavin's friend and mentor for the past six years had turned out to be a monster. How could he have got it so wrong?

But amidst all that, the memory of Violet's lips eased the bitterness that snaked through his gut. Where was she now? Had she made it out all right?

He wondered what lie Julius would spin to his parents when he returned and announced Gavin was dead. Maybe he would blame Violet for it all.

"You've been unconscious for a couple of hours," the man with the golden eyes said, filling the silence. "Looks like you had a nasty blow to the head. Are you well?"

"Well is a stretch. But it won't be the thing that kills me."

No wonder Violet acted the way she did. After this betrayal, Gavin wasn't sure he'd ever be the same. He sat once again, draping his arms over his knees. "How long have you been here? I hope not long enough to have seen the person who was in my cell decompose."

"Oh, I saw him, all right. They removed the body right before they tossed you in."

"Great. My day keeps getting better and better." So the wet spot was unfortunately what he'd thought it might be. He scrunched his nose and pulled himself as far away from it as the ropes would allow.

"Same. The commander dragged me in here with his pawns a night ago and—" He paused, and the distinct sound of metal scraping over stone bounced off the walls. Shackles? Maybe this prisoner wasn't a magic-wielder? "—actually, I guess I don't know if it was that long ago. I've been in and out of consciousness for a while."

"What does the commander want from you?"

"He didn't tell me when he poisoned my drink." The growl that rolled from him was definitely not human. A shifter.

At the beginning of the day, Gavin wouldn't have dreamt of finding Julius in Scoria. Now here he was—with Julius poisoning shifters. Every moment seemed to reveal another hidden layer of the man he'd thought he knew so well.

Gavin sat back, staring wide-eyed at the large shape of the man. His unnatural irises made sense now. "Are you from the shifter colony nearby?"

The man's laughter was bleak. "I'm not from this land. I didn't even know there was a colony close by."

"Hmm. The townsfolk believe a werewolf has been attacking the citizens. They're claiming the peace treaty has been fractured."

"Treaties are unbreakable and bound by the magic of the gods. Have the shifters done anything to breach the terms?"

"I just arrived in Scoria a few days ago myself. But there have been a few attacks... A child got killed."

"Scoria... in Obsidian?" The man seemed to ponder the name, but Gavin couldn't read his expressions from this far away. Not when whatever wasn't covered by a beard was dirty. "If a shifter killed a child, our laws would deal with the issue. Have they got any proof?"

"No, because it wasn't a werewolf who did it, even though they want to blame one for it."

"What do you mean?"

"That the town saw a wolf-like creature attacking these children, and the simple answer was that a shifter did it. I helped a family whose daughter had been attacked. She was cursed and dying."

The deep rumble of his neighbor's voice sounded almost amused. "A werewolf's bite doesn't curse."

Gavin let out a heavy sigh. "I know."

"So, a Sídhe is hunting in this town, and the commander brought me to what—put the blame on me? Why capture a shifter from all the way in the Iron City for that?"

"Your guess is as good as mine. But if people are growing angry and are demanding that they capture the werewolf doing this, but that shifter doesn't exist… Well. The governor might grow anxious. I doubt this small town has the manpower to declare a war against the shifter's village…"

"Ah yes. A rogue outsider is the perfect scapegoat." The other man grunted, and Gavin heard the distinct thump of what could be his head hitting the wall. Once. Twice. Thrice.

Was this man a lone wolf, then? Gavin didn't know or understand much about the shifter world and their lifestyles. Usually, they kept to themselves. But what the man said made sense. Being alone made him the perfect target for a scumbag like his commander.

"If they kill me without allowing me to speak, the governor of this place can deny his people's demands to seek retribution by a more official route." His gravelly laughter boomed around the place. "I guess it could be a temporary solution to avoid a war, as the Sídhe will continue on and more will die."

"Yes." Gavin rested his head on his knees, and Myna's drawn face flashed through his mind. This was a stopgap that would only appease people for a few weeks. Until the fae hunted again.

Seemed like both him and his companion would die soon. They were fucked... but at least Violet was safe.

It was hard to tell the time inside this place. But if it was past sunset, Violet might be near the shifter village by now. Or camping in the forest.

"Why are you here?" the shifter asked.

"The bastard that took you is—was—my commander. Let's just say we disagree on what we think is right and what's wrong."

"But you weren't with him and his assembly that day at the bar..."

"That's because he wasn't there under the command of our King. The men that are with him are paid mercenaries, and I believe they wear our uniforms so people don't question what they're doing." Gavin cleared his throat, but the emotion clawed at his chest.

"Like drug a shifter in a bar on the outskirts of town?"

"Yes, exactly."

Gavin couldn't ignore how much Julius' betrayal hurt. If he looked back at all the interactions between his commander and other people in the past, everything became tainted. All the times he'd sent Gavin away when things grew tense. All the women that had joined the Valdors and then mysteriously deserted only months later. He wondered if they were still alive, and had actually ran away?

He was a fool. If he'd been more aware, he could have helped so many people. His blind faith in Julius' better nature had been nothing short of naïve.

But Gavin wasn't going to cover for him any longer.

"He came to kill my wife here in Scoria," he elaborated. "I opposed him, and here I am."

"Did she escape?"

"Yes." He sighed and held onto the memory of the taste of her lips. Her words, warm in their goodbye, had planted a seed of hope that perhaps his feelings weren't one-sided after all. That she'd wanted him to kiss her just as much as he had.

"I wish there was some alcohol around here. It seems you and I are dying together." The man's accent became stronger. He'd said he wasn't from this land. Was he even from this kingdom?

"Yes, I guess we are. I'm Gavin, former healer of the Valdor Assembly. Nice to meet you...?"

"Mios..." The man paused, and for a moment, Gavin thought he wouldn't say anything else. Not that he needed to. If this was a lone wolf, he probably preferred to keep things to himself. "... Lionborn."

The cold nipped at his skin as the ringing in his ears returned. Shock sliced through him.

"Lionborn? As in—the shifter royals from the Gold Kingdom?"

"Estranged royals."

His accent made so much sense now. "But you aren't a wolf at all."

"That's correct. Not that your commander stopped and asked what my animal side was."

Surely Julius wasn't oblivious to the fact that he'd start a war if this man was killed by a commander of the King's army. He couldn't be. Right?

Maybe this massive oversight wasn't a coincidence at all. Maybe it was what his commander had intended all along: a war between rival kingdoms. A coup to overthrow the King.

16

VIOLET

THE ROOM'S WALLS WERE AT LEAST TWELVE FEET HIGH, WITH dark-stained beams and windows with black, crisscross details. A warm, inviting place—now tainted because Julius was dragging her there to die.

The fire burst alive as he extended his hand toward the charred logs inside it and dropped her without a care onto a large, stiff leather sofa. She landed face down, pressed into the rounded cushion and unable to move away.

"Make yourself comfortable, dear, we have a long night ahead. I'll have fun teaching you the true meaning of pain." He laughed while patting her ass with fingers that lingered. Her skin grew cold and clammy under his touch, and her gut coiled as bile rose to the back of her throat. She tried to move, but it was impossible with every inch of her body still paralyzed.

Julius wandered away, leaving her alone in the sitting area. As the fire dried her damp coat and she closed her eyes, she registered the rustle of his clothes hitting the ground and the distant tapping of steps moving further away. Then a splash.

A bath. Julius was bathing, which gave her a window to escape, however small it might be. If her history with Dargan had taught her anything, it was that her life was important to the so-called gods of this world.

The God of Shadows demanded the second born in her bloodline, and if all else failed, he wanted her, which meant he wanted her alive. Even though she'd been caught by this cock of a man, and she was a lonely, miserable soul, she wasn't alone in this.

Julius had misjudged her desire to live, and with it, her power. He'd been smart when he'd taken her ability to physically fight him, as that was her strongest suit. But since he hadn't made sure she was unable to use her magic, he'd given her a chance. A minor mistake for him might mean the difference between freedom and escape for her.

Her fingertips twitched, and her skin glowed a pale gray that became brighter and bolder. Then Violet did what she'd avoided doing ever since she'd learned about Dargan's claim on her. She prayed to the god she hated most.

"Are you going to let this man kill me and lose your slim chance of getting what you say I owe you, Dargan?"

Nothing happened.

She breathed out and focused on her memories of

the emissaries, hoping that would somehow bring her closer to Dargan. The image of Cullen's handsome face flashed through her mind, and her heart twisted at the vision alongside the hate that bubbled up like an old foe she'd never forgotten. Then Luelle's hunched shape and the red aura that matched her tunic followed.

The older woman hadn't cared about Violet slitting her throat open… because she was eternally cursed and forever claimed by a god. Violet didn't have the same willingness to perish here, not when doing so would also mean Gavin would meet his own demise. All because of her.

She tried to close her fist, and nothing happened. Her frustration burned hotter. Would raising her body temperature burn away the poison that paralyzed her?

"Dargan, I don't care if I die tonight. That way, you'll never get what is owed to you. I won."

The air swirled around the room, a cold blast that contrasted with the heat her magic called into being. The sound of steps followed moments later, muffled by the rug. Her eyes snapped open, her heart suddenly pounding like a hammer.

Was Julius back? Was this the beginning of her end?

Violet tilted her head to the side. Only a fraction… but she was moving! Her excitement didn't last long when her eyes fell on a pair of polished black boots standing on the red carpet.

Fuck. He'd come.

"Lies." His soft voice, a mixture of bored and entertained, echoed in her mind. A freezing sensation crawled over her skin like an icy touch. Could he feel her panic? Her need to escape? Her stomach clenched, and she struggled with conflicting impulses, torn between the need to look away and her curiosity to see more of him.

"It's not a god's way to save their pets from the danger they've got themselves into."

"T-then go." The moment she spoke the words out loud, calling his bluff, the panic of being next to a god eased. She shifted her head a tiny bit further to look up at his tall silhouette. Backlit from the fire behind him, his features were as sharp as the blade of her forgotten knife. Even bathed in shadows, he was gorgeous beyond belief. It was his gaze that was the most breath-taking, shining with its own light: a golden hue that matched the glowing crown over his head.

"Cora, is that you?" Julius' tone carried an edge of surprise, buried beneath barely controlled anger.

"I suggest you move. You don't have time to waste," Dargan whispered inside her thoughts, and his solid form faded.

Was he kidding her—how could she go? Unless... Violet held her breath and moved her arm. No longer paralyzed, she rolled from the sofa and to the ground, landing over Dargan's polished boots.

The air burned her lungs. It tasted like frankincense with a suspicious undertone of smoke. Her arms shook beneath the weight of her body as she pushed herself to her knees. In the background, the sloshing of water was unmistakable as Julius exited his bath.

"Time to go."

She didn't have a second to glare, yet she stuck up her middle finger. Dargan's amusement was clear from the shifting of his brow and the tilt to his now semi-transparent lips. Then he faded fully, dissolving in a trail of mist as Violet forced herself up to her feet.

Her legs trembled like a newborn fawn, and she tumbled toward the fireplace, barely catching herself on the stone mantlepiece. The prickle of its texture sliced her skin as she trudged toward the door.

Her sorcery no longer aided her. Her weakened body lacked the substance to continue to call on her power. So instead she saved what little energy she had left and pushed forward with sheer force of will.

"Where do you think you're going?" Julius had abandoned all of his false politeness.

Her heart skipped a beat as she tried to move faster. There was no chance she'd make it out of here—he was already so close. Violet reached for the cold tip of the cast-iron fireplace utensils hanging from hooks on the wall. She wrapped her hand around the poker just in time, a split second before he yanked her against his wet, naked body.

He struck her hard, and she would have fallen to the ground if he'd not been holding her up. The noise of the slap rang through the room, and the pain pulsed into her cheek and gums. His hand wrapped around her throat and squeezed her windpipe, hard enough black spots danced across her vision.

Her jaw ached where he'd hit her. He dipped his

nose into the crook of her neck and inhaled her like she was a bouquet.

Violet hoped the scent of that alleyway still clung to her skin. That he got a good whiff of the crates of shit he'd so willingly kicked over. But instead of leaving her alone, he pushed into her, letting her feel his hard erection against her stomach.

"You do not know how long I've wanted to do this to you."

Tears pricked the corners of her eyes. He loosened his grip, and she sucked in a deep breath, her throat like fire. His lips traced the skin of her neck, and nausea rolled in the pit of her gut. She would never let this happen, not without a fight, not even if traces of his poison sucked the energy from her body.

"Fuck you." She spat the words and tightened her hand firmly around the handle of the cast-iron poker.

"I intend to do that to you. Hard."

It wasn't time to strike yet. He was too close and pinning her arms to her body with his own. Plus, her weapon was too long to cause enough damage if she attacked him now.

She needed to stab him with it.

"I'm delighted the boy refused to follow through with the Crow's demands the night of your wedding. He could have fucked you then, and I would have gladly watched, but it would have been hard for me to hold back. No such complications now you're a wanted criminal. I can have my fun." His tongue traced the edge of her jaw, while his hand traveled along her torso, clasping one of her breasts roughly.

Violet pressed her lips into a thin line. She wouldn't fall into the trap he'd set. She wouldn't give him the pleasure of hearing her beg for mercy.

"Not so mouthy now, eh, Violet? Where's your fiery spirit? It isn't fun without a fight."

"Let go of me, and we'll see if you're willing to fight fair." She regretted her words as soon as they left her lips. Not because they were untrue, no. But she didn't want to feed into this sick fantasy he'd clearly been harboring for a while.

Julius mouthed at her neck and bit her clavicle, and his hand continued its downward path.

"I will cut that hand off and throw it into the fire," Violet threatened.

A wave of laughter bubbled out of his throat, and his red-rimmed eyes pierced hers, just as he pushed a finger past the fabric of her pants, digging it into her skin.

Despite the pain, Violet didn't allow any noise to escape. Instead, she bucked against him—hard. He stumbled back a step, but not enough for her sluggish arm to swing the poker up to truly hurt him.

He slammed her into the wall with all his strength a moment later.

Even though her energy was dwindling rapidly, she pushed him again, calling on her last reserves. Her magic burst from her skin, burning the air with its spicy scent.

She brought the poker up with a newfound quickness, aided by her power. Julius' eyes widened. Probably realized that he'd failed to restrain her magic, that bastard.

Too late.

She speared him without waiting for another second to pass. His naked chest was completely unprotected, and the sharp end of the metal bar sank into his ribcage meeting little resistance.

He gasped and let go of her, stumbling backward. He grasped the poker and pulled it from his gut with a wet sound that brought forth tissue and blood. Moving fast as lightning, Violet picked up the dustpan and swung it hard against his head, knocking him out on the spot.

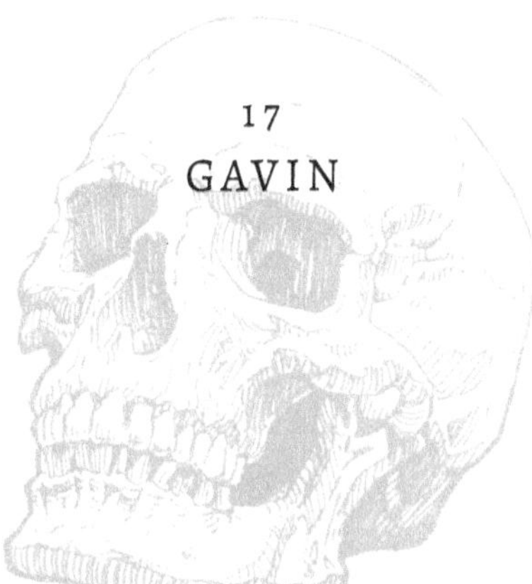

17
GAVIN

Steps echoed off the cave walls, growing louder as they drew closer. Beneath the stomp of wooden soles on stone, a scraping sound of something being dragged along the ground filled the space. Whoever was approaching was speeding up. The door screeched, and bright light from outside bled through the gaps.

Mios rose and almost hit his head on the ceiling. It took Gavin longer than his pride liked to pull himself to his feet, using the filthy wall for support.

A middle-aged man wearing brown pants, a white shirt, and suspenders entered the room. "Mr. Gavin."

"Harry." Gavin strode toward him and winced when his headache reminded him to move slowly. Myna's father was gasping for air like he'd run all the way here, his complexion shiny with sweat. His eyes widened as they traced Gavin's battered face.

"I feared it was you they had imprisoned here." He

looked around, making sure they were alone, and stepped closer to Gavin's cell.

Then he fished a ring with hundreds of skeleton keys from his pocket, each with a different shape and size. "I'm getting you out of there."

Gavin tried to move closer, but the ropes wouldn't let him. "Hold on."

"If I don't get you out, they will kill you," he said.

"Would they find out it was you who released me?" At this point Gavin wasn't sure how far Julius would extend his punishment to Harry's family if he were to find out the truth.

"I owe this to you."

Gavin grunted, reaching for the bars. "Listen, Julius likes to hunt down people who break the law. Did anyone see you come here?" It wasn't like he wanted to die, but he also couldn't take anything lightly that would ruin this family and their future.

Harry looked up with worry etched in his brow, his face sober. "No one saw me, and he has your wife."

"I beg your pardon?" Gavin stepped forward, not caring that the cords of rope rubbed his wrist raw. "What do you mean? Who has my wife?"

"The commander from the Iron Kingdom took your Mrs. into his room just now. He... he doesn't seem like a good man. And he asked me not to disturb him."

"Was she awake?" Gavin's skin turned clammy and hot. He pulled harder on his ropes, and the metal of the bolts which fixed them to the wall groaned with the tension.

"Yes, but she wasn't moving."

"It's the same poison he used on me. It keeps you paralyzed and awake," Mios said from next door.

"I'm going to kill him," Gavin said.

Harry yelped in surprise and jumped back, stumbling to the ground. "I'd forgotten the shifter was down here," he mumbled to himself as he got back up.

Mios' shackles were much longer than Gavin's, and he wrapped his hand around the bars next to Gavin's cell. His bright shifter eyes dilated into the darkness. "Then get out of here."

Harry had recovered his composure and was back at the cell. He didn't wait for Gavin to answer, jamming a key into the hole before cursing loudly and attempting another.

"I'm also releasing him." Gavin pointed at Mios's cell with his jaw.

Harry's lips trembled as his gaze flashed to the shifter. "You are? But he's a criminal."

Gavin didn't know Mios well enough to assure Harry he wasn't one—although he believed the shifter about being a Lionborn. "He's not here for what they claim he did."

"But—"

"What reason did Julius give you all for his imprisonment?"

"That—that he's the one attacking the city, responsible not only for Lee's death and Myna's bite, but that others in neighboring villages also suffered at his hands."

Mios scoffed loud enough that it bordered on a growl.

"We've already talked about who's actually attacking your city, Harry," Gavin said. "And it is not a shifter."

At least Harry had the decency to look abashed at his words as he tried another key. "Yes, I suppose you did tell me that. But it's hard to deny what you see with your own eyes."

"Only if you're an ignorant man with serious prejudices," Mios snarled. Anger instantly shone behind Harry's glasses. Undoubtedly, he felt emboldened by the iron wall that separated Mios from them.

Gavin sighed. Mios reminded him of Violet and her never-ending fire. The thought was enough to ground him in the present. He needed to get to Violet. Nothing else mattered. "Open the gate, and I won't let him hurt you. However, I can assure you that, even if the attacks had been committed by a werewolf, it was not Mios who did it—he is a lion shifter."

Harry's lips fell open, and he studied the other prisoner with renewed interest. "You are?"

"In the flesh."

A click echoed through the empty hallway. Harry had found the right key.

"I can't believe I'm doing this," he mumbled to himself as he unlocked the gate. He walked over to Gavin, gagging the moment the putrid scent of death hit him.

Holding his breath, he pulled out a small pocket

knife. Intricate designs that resembled tree bark decorated the polished bone handle. Even though the blade was dull and rusty, it cut through the fibers of the rope without any issue.

It was Gavin alone who stepped inside Mios' cell a moment later. Harry stayed behind by the door, keeping his distance from the shifter. "I have no key for those." He shrugged, pointing at Mios' cuffs. He looked embarrassed, perhaps at his fear at the other man.

Not that Gavin could blame him. Mios' hands were the size of shovels, and his muscles stretched out his clothes. To anyone else, these were just garments, but not to Gavin. He'd visited the palace often enough to know that someone had made these with the finest materials. They'd even embroidered a lion crest with delicate stitching on the side of his shoulder. Black against black, designed to disappear for anyone who wasn't looking for it.

His pants were frayed at the cuffs, and he no longer wore boots or socks. His feet were raw and bloody. Was this the treatment all of Julius' prisoners received? How many had been innocent?

"Don't bother with the cuffs. It's going to take too long, and the bastard has your wife. Bring the knife. I can get these off with that." Mios pointed at Harry's blade.

Myna's dad stayed where he stood, although he dropped the weapon to the ground and kicked it in their general direction.

Mios crouched, picked up the blade with two

massive fingers, and handed it to Gavin. "Push the point into the keyhole until you locate the spring."

Had anyone ever cuffed him before? Gavin lifted a brow while following his guidance. He found the spring shortly after and pushed the blade down harder until the edges scraped the metal sides and the bar on top loosened around the shifter's wrist. The next one snapped open much faster than the first, now that he'd learned the trick. As soon as the cuffs were off, Mios tore off the ones on his ankles himself.

Gavin stepped out of the cell and toward Harry, holding his gaze. "Thank you," he said.

"You don't owe me a thing," Harry said. "I'm the one who is eternally grateful." His lips shook in a wobbly half smile, but his weary eyes flashed back toward Mios. He cleared his throat. "What now?"

"Can you take me to where Julius took Violet?" At Harry's nod, Gavin rested a hand on his shoulder. "Then you will leave this place for the night."

Harry nodded again, his cheeks reddening as they moved into the empty hall. "The guard is asleep, he drinks too much White Mule liquor... so getting out of here should be easy. The commander's chamber is on the third floor. The last room in the west wing."

They stole out of the dungeon-like prison, sneaking past the sleeping guard and replacing the keys on the rusty hook on the wall beside him.

Gavin's magic was still healing his wound, and warmth spread outward from his chest. With the pain mostly gone, clarity of thought was no longer an issue.

They arrived on the third floor undisturbed. The hallways here were wide, and warmer than the cells below by at least twenty degrees. Even at nighttime, it was bright enough up here that it took some time for Gavin's eyes to adjust to the light of the gas lamps that hung on the walls. The emptiness around them was a blessing, but it wouldn't last. "How are we going to get out of here once I have Violet?"

"I will wait for you here," Harry said, indicating a linen cupboard near the stairs. "There is an exit that's ancient and only used by the custodians. It will take us to the temple of the gods, near the crypts."

"What about the men that were with the commander? Have you seen them?"

"I'm afraid not. I can't even tell you how many were with him. I saw a few of them leave. After they put you in the cell, I imagine." Harry pointed at a set of double doors. "Your wife is in there. I hope your Mrs. is safe."

18
VIOLET

SHE STOOD IN FRONT OF THE FIREPLACE, STILL HOLDING THE metal bar she'd speared the monster with. Blood dripped from its pointed tip, soaking into her mud-caked boots.

Julius was dragging his body toward the door. His breaths wheezed and rattled as he gasped for air and struggled with the effort of crawling away from her.

She should be ecstatic to see him so desperate. Exactly the way he'd wanted her to be. Slithering over the floor like the snake he was. In the back of her mind, she was aware that Gavin needed her help, and yet she was frozen where she stood. Her blood no longer pumped hot with anger. Instead, she shivered with a cold that made little sense, especially when she was standing right next to a fire.

The skin of her face prickled, the feeling of ants biting her everywhere Julius had touched. Everything in her life was already tainted... and now this. Her heart ached so fiercely that it bordered on physical pain. She was a disappointment. She should have stopped Julius sooner. Instead, she'd allowed him to live despite knowing he was doing this to people.

It had been easier to turn her face away and pretend it didn't happen. After all, everyone else ignored it, so who was she to raise a flag and call attention to it?

It hadn't affected her at the time, and with a god pursuing her, Julius Coventry had been the least of her worries. What a fool she'd been. Her gut twisted with a sudden need to empty itself.

Julius gasped for air, pulling her out of her stupor. He raised his torso up on shaking arms, almost at the door, but then collapsed on the floor.

Dargan's voice was a whispering memory in her mind. Time to go. Although he was no longer here, she obeyed his command almost blindly, following the bloody trail Julius had left behind. Maybe she should end him now, before she went to find Gavin. The most evil side of her reared its ugly head.

Hadn't he wanted her to suffer? Hadn't he told her how he'd hurt her—rape her? Fuck him. Completely ignoring him and the blood pooling on the ground, she stepped over him and headed for the door. If he hadn't been such a monster, he'd have the most skilled healer she'd ever seen at his disposal.

The door was locked from the inside, the key stuck inside the brass plate to prevent anyone from opening it from the other side. Gavin's face flashed through her mind, lighting a new fire within her to move her numb body and gather the remaining dregs of her energy.

She cracked the door open and peered outside. The hall looked dim and empty. Taking a deep breath, she tightened her grip around the bloody handle of the poker. She closed the door behind her and locked it, dropping the key in her pocket.

A slow death was what that bastard deserved, and she was happy to provide it.

Two large men stormed out of a set of double doors on the other side of the hall. Violet's heart leaped, and for a moment she stood frozen in her spot. She lifted her makeshift weapon—and dropped it again. There was no need to attack or escape. She would recognize him anywhere. The way he walked and the wide set of those shoulders. Silence draped over them as she studied his handsome face in the shadows. Her husband—Gavin—was here.

Violet's legs gave way, too numb to hold her weight any longer. She sank to the floor, and he ran to her. The messy waves of his hair barely covered a dried patch of blood that was smeared down the side of his face.

"Hey... are you all right?" He kneeled in front of her, one of his hands resting on her thigh, burning through the cloth of her pants. Why was he concerned for her wellbeing? Ridiculous—he was the one who'd got hurt, not her.

Yes, she wanted to say, but the word stuck in her throat.

A second man came into view, towering over them. She flinched away and tried to get to her feet.

"It's all right, he's with me." Gavin's grip around her leg tightened. His fingers trailed down her cheek, and it was only then that she realized her skin was damp with tears. She let go of the metal bar and grasped his hand like a lifeline. Everything else faded into the background.

Even though he could have escaped, Gavin had come to save her. He hadn't abandoned her or betrayed her like she would have expected him to—although perhaps that would have been easier. A sob left her lips, and she launched herself at him, crushing her lips to his. The kiss lasted less than a heartbeat, but was returned just as eagerly.

"I was supposed to be the one finding you." She pulled away, frowning. "But I'm happy you found me instead..."

"If you receive me like this every time, you'll have a hard time getting rid of me." Gavin glanced at the door behind her. The cords of his neck tensed as he swallowed thickly. What was he thinking?

"Where is Julius?" he asked.

Did Gavin want to go in there to make sure his old friend was, in fact, dead? Did he even want him to be, or was Gavin the sort of man who forgave quickly enough to keep even a monster alive?

Maybe he'd want to help Julius, instead?

Violet sniffed and wiped her wet nose with her arm, buying herself time to process her contrasting emotions. The glee that Gavin was alive and the dread that Julius might still survive threw her off kilter.

She trusted Gavin, but she also knew that he was all good… when she was not.

"He's no longer our problem." She patted the key in her pocket to make sure it was still there, relaxing when she felt it beneath the layer of her wool pants.

Julius had minutes to live—at most.

Gavin pressed his lips together, still glancing toward the door. Eventually, he nodded and returned his focus to her. "You haven't answered my other question," he probed gently.

"About what?"

"If you're all right."

"I'm fine." Violet tucked her hair behind her ears, and Gavin's gaze zeroed in on her neck. He reached for her and traced the spot where Julius had strangled her with the lightest of touches. She flinched away.

"Did he do that to you?" He pushed the words through gritted teeth.

Violet stood up and wrapped her arms around her chest, trying to hold back a heave with little success. Shame burned through her, but she pushed it down. It wasn't her fault that Julius had touched her.

It could have been much worse than a bruised neck, and she was far from a damsel in distress. She'd taken care of the problem herself. "He didn't hurt me more than I hurt him, I can assure you of that."

"Are you sure he's dead?" the man in the back growled. It was an unnatural and beastly sound. She glanced over Gavin's shoulder at him. He had sand-colored hair, and pale skin that was golden by the sun. His features were streaked with filth.

Why was he questioning her?

"I speared him with this when he was strangling me, right through his gut." Violet lifted the poker, still wet and smelling of blood. To judge by the flare of his nostrils, the shifter noticed that detail. "What is it that you doubt—that I could deal with him myself, or that I'm smart enough to tell when someone is dead?"

Not that she'd checked if Julius had stopped breathing altogether. But she was confident he'd die soon, so it didn't matter.

"That's not what I said." The man crossed his massive tree trunk arms over his chest. Violet stuck her chin up in the air and leveled him with her best scowl.

Gavin sighed. "Julius kidnapped Mios from the Iron City," he said. "He was poisoned and tortured. I'm sure he just wants to make sure Julius has got what he deserved."

"I don't know you, but I don't doubt that you made him suffer... which is enough for me." Mios' gaze settled on her face, honing in on the marks on her neck. If only she could cover them. "He also sold me to this town to be hung for the deaths they believe the wolf shifters have committed."

Right. That sounded like Julius.

"And they would have caused a war between kingdoms, if we'd have let them get away with it," Gavin said.

"What do you mean?" she asked.

"He means I'm a Lionborn, and there will be repercussions for imprisoning me," Mios growled.

Violet's cheeks warmed. She had heard that name before. Everyone in the world of Caztian had.

Although they no longer ruled the Gold Kingdom, the world still considered the Lionborn royalty. Even though their crown had been taken, they were still powerful, feared, and revered. She didn't want him as her enemy.

"I should have let you kill Julius on the night of our wedding," Gavin whispered as he stepped closer to reach for her hand.

"No, you needed to save him then. I like the way you show your character. You're better than me."

He stared at her, and his lips tilted down into a grimace. "That's not true."

"It is."

The hallway was too quiet. The only noise she could discern was the sound of their soles against the ground once they set off. Gavin and her stilled when Mios tilted his head and sniffed the air.

"Someone's coming." His face transformed in front of her eyes. The straight bridge of his nose widened as fur grew out of his skin. His white teeth elongated, and she had to fight the urge to turn around and run when his rounded pupils fixed on her.

Yet he was still half man, half lion. Not fully changed into an animal form—something she'd heard only royal shifters could do. Gavin cursed just as three guards walked around the corner.

The slash of their swords being drawn echoed through the hallway. But it was the growl of the beast that had the men freeze in fright as the cat leaped through the air with his long legs. He landed beside the guards, expertly dodging their blades, his claws slashing across one guard's chest in a crisscross pattern.

Blood blossomed to soak his shirt as he fell on the ground. Mios pushed the next guard against the wall, and the crack of bones reverberated around the space, making Violet wince. As the third guard lifted his blade to strike Mios, Gavin released a spell that knocked him down.

Just like that, silence descended again, leaving behind only Mios' hard breathing as he shifted back into his human form. He shrugged his tattered coat to the ground in pieces, wiping the blood from his fingers off on his pants with a scowl that rivaled her own.

"So... what now?" Violet asked. She sounded breathless even though she'd barely moved this entire time.

"Harry is waiting for us. He said there's another way out of here that will prevent us from having to deal with the guards."

Harry? So Myna's father had released Gavin from wherever he'd been held. He must have told him that Julius had taken her here as well. She swallowed against the thick knot that formed in her throat. "Is it the exit by the crypts?"

Gavin tilted his head. "How do you know?"

"Laura mentioned it before I came to help you. I should have listened to her."

Alas, her stubbornness had almost got her killed. Gavin's belief in the good in people had saved them. Even after someone he clearly cared for had hurt him, he maintained the same spirit.

He trusted this lion shifter—who he'd only just met—hours after being betrayed. His faith in people was shocking. It lit a need within her to protect him from the evil out there that would take advantage of his goodness.

And yet, he'd been right. Violet hated to admit it, but she'd been wrong about that entire family. Damn it. She'd have to learn from this.

She'd never trust easily, not when everyone she'd considered a friend had betrayed her. But she would try harder. For once, she'd gained an ally in Gavin. A true friend. And she wasn't afraid to admit she wanted more. Maybe they could grow closer while they traveled across the Obsidian mountains.

THE TEMPLES OF THE GODS WERE LARGER-THAN-LIFE buildings made of cream-colored marble and rounded columns. Violet had only been to the one in the Iron City, back when she'd still revered the deities.

She hated them now.

This one was no longer standing. Instead, it was merely the ruins of a grand monument, tucked away in an overgrown garden amidst a mess of petrified weeds and half covered in melting snow. To her, these chipped chunks of marble and stone represented the fall of the gods. Dargan's displeasure at their neglect must be great. Good.

They slipped past the fallen columns that held pieces of the crumbling ceiling afloat. Everything was now drenched in the fresh rain that fell over the city.

The crypts lay at the very back of the place of worship, hidden behind tall shrubs: an ominous building with massive front gates built from bent metal that formed intricate flowers. The rumor was that the crypt was cursed, and Violet was inclined to believe them. Neems—the haunted, angry souls of people murdered in horrible ways—hovered on certain magical grounds. The right components were present here to have them linger.

"She should have mentioned that I didn't really have to go through the crypts to get to the governor's house from here," she grumbled to herself. In fact, the hidden path ran parallel to the crypts, which made for a swift entry and exit from the building, ultimately avoiding the spirits.

"What are you talking about?" Gavin turned to her, his wavy hair sticking to his face. His breath was a plume of steam in the chill air.

"Laura—" She shook her head. "Never mind."

He looked at her like she was completely insane. Truth was, if she could blame someone else for her mistake, if only in part, then it would relieve the suffocating pressure on her chest. But it had been her utter lack of trust in people that had cost her so much. It could have been Gavin's life next, if it hadn't been for Harry. They could all be dead by now.

She chewed her lip, guilt and self-loathing clutching her tightly. Harry led them to a wall of laurel trees so thick and high that they completely shielded the outside from view. He pushed the leaves aside.

Behind them, a heavy wooden door slumbered, perfectly camouflaged by a cascade of stems and evergreen vegetation.

"Go to the inn." He wrenched the door open. "Let Laura give you enough supplies so you can safely make it across the Obsidian mountains. Then leave. They will start hunting for you soon." His eyes landed on her, and they softened. "I'm sorry this happened to you all."

He said all, but for some reason she got the impression that he mostly meant her. And his pity would normally have set her teeth on edge. Except this wasn't that... It wasn't pity, not really. Not at all. It was sympathy. He'd saved Gavin and her. She was grateful beyond belief that her face was already wet because she didn't care for strangers seeing her cry.

They were free, and Harry should be safe as well. Since so many guards had seen Julius bring Violet to his chambers, and she'd escaped unscathed, they'd undoubtedly believe she'd been the one to release the prisoners. Harry could sneak back under the cover of darkness and pretend he'd never seen anything.

They had at least until sunrise. Dawn was already beginning to break behind the stormy gray clouds and the peaks of the conifer trees dotted across the side of the mountain.

Hopefully she would never have to set foot in another garden of the gods again, or return to this place. Now they just needed to find the inn for a short refuge, to gather some food and warm clothes. And then they'd depart for the shifter village.

19
VIOLET

THE STREETS WERE DESERTED WHEN THEY LEFT THE INN AND made their way toward the stables at the edge of the city. Violet had stolen a mare back in the Iron City, and she hoped that the stable boy had kept her well fed and clean. She'd paid him most of her coin for it.

In hindsight, she should have held on to more of her gold earlier in the trip. Still, there was no way to make it across the mountains without a ride while being pursued, so keeping her mare well fed and happy had been important... even if it meant she went hungry.

The walls of the stables were aged red brick that stood out amongst all the other gray buildings. Light shone behind the window by the front gate, and the scent of manure and hay became stronger the closer they came. Gavin fixed the thick, knitted hood of his new clothes over his wild hair and rang the bell twice.

The door cracked open, and a youthful, freckled

face peered out from behind it. "We're closed. Come back later."

Gavin's hand shot out and held the door open as the young man attempted to shut it in their faces.

"We want our horses, boy, and we need them now. We're leaving Scoria before the storm hits." Gavin sounded friendly and stern at the same time. He exuded the kind of confidence that made Violet's stomach flutter and caused heat to rush through her body.

The boy's eyes rounded, bouncing from Gavin to Mios' giant form, finally landing on her. A healthy dose of panic flashed over his features before he swung the door open.

Dense blobs of snow fell from the sky. No one in their right mind should leave in these conditions. Not unless they were running away.

"Do you have your stall slips?" At their blank expressions he sighed, shaking his head. "I guess I don't need them, let me take you through."

Mios didn't have a horse. He'd assured them he would travel in his animal form, although Violet doubted whether he was equipped to do so. Lion shifters usually lived in deserts, not in snowy forests in the middle of the Obsidian mountains. Regardless, the shifter leaned against the outer wall, keeping watch while Gavin and her stepped inside.

From the outside, the place appeared to be multiple stories high. However, once inside, it was one large space split into stables. Thick wooden beams held up the vaulted ceilings, taller than most temples in small cities like this.

The stableboy pointed them at their horses' boxes, and Violet and Gavin went off in different directions to fetch them.

It didn't take her long to find her mare. The beast pressed her snout into Violet's hand, welcoming her. She was a beautiful palomino that Violet had ridden during many army missions. When she'd left the city, she'd instantly known which horse she'd be stealing.

Twenty-one strutted with the eagerness of a beast that hadn't been exercised for a while. She shook her head all the way toward the room where the saddles were stored.

Gavin joined her there with a beast with dappled gray fur that stood out against his fine, cognac-colored tack. The stallion was at least eighteen hands, a thoroughbred that dwarfed her own. "This is Hillar," he said. "He's been mine since I was eleven." He brushed the horse's beautiful, shiny mane before cinching up the saddle.

"You're from Plume City. Isn't that a long way from the Iron Kingdom?" she deadpanned. "Wouldn't it have been easier, not to mention cheaper, to buy another horse than to take him all the way with you?"

Gavin's cheeks darkened. "It would have—but it wouldn't have been Hillar."

"What makes him so special to you?" Her curiosity spiked. She'd never truly attached to a horse like that herself. This mare was the one she'd always been the closest to, but Violet hadn't even named her yet.

"My sister gave him to me when she was three."

"She bought you Hillar when she was three years old?" she teased with a growing smirk.

"Well, not like that. She picked him for me from the lineup. And that counts—right? She used to love gray horses... Still does." He grinned and scratched the horse's neck.

"You sound close," she said past the pain surging up the back of her throat. Once upon a time, Violet and her little sister Thalea had been the best of friends, too.

Mina was much younger than Gavin, but now Violet knew they loved each other. And he'd never see her again. She'd ruined this for him.

Would she change the past if she could? Stay in the Iron City, with everything the Crows and Julius had planned to do to her? Could she have settled even though she would have been required to have a baby? Not that Gavin would have forced her to—but the Society of Crows would have.

Violet couldn't have stayed for long. However, she didn't have to leave that night, either. Things might have been different if she'd considered that maybe the man she was marrying was honorable and good. That they could work together, instead of against each other.

"We are very close," Gavin agreed, and cleared his throat from the emotion that distorted his voice. His gaze remained glued on his horse as he finished fixing the saddle. He secured the sacks of food and other supplies Laura had provided for them, actively avoiding looking at her.

"I would change it," she whispered. "You were right. I was selfish on our wedding day, and if I could, I would've stayed and worked with you. I know I've said it before, but I'm truly sorry, Gavin. I was very young when I was taken from my family, but I still remember how much it hurt."

"I'm not angry at you anymore."

"You should be. I wouldn't blame you if you were."

Gavin stepped forward and reached for her chin. Her heart sped up as he traced the edge of her jaw. "I'm thankful to you. Sure, I can't see Mina right now, but she is alive today because of you."

"What do you mean?"

He let out a resigned breath and straightened. "Do you remember the accident at the Hulten lake three years ago?"

How could she forget? On that fateful day, the first emissary had appeared in her life, claiming that she owed Dargan her future son or daughter. Although of course, Cullen hadn't told her that at first.

"Yes?"

"I took my sister swimming that afternoon... and I got drunk with a friend. I didn't see how rough the lake had become because I was so out of it."

"The storm hit out of nowhere," she reassured in a weak tone. The ground suddenly seemed to be moving under her as her past and present collided, narrowing in on her. Her fingers tightened around his arms, and the images barreled down on her.

The pleasant scent of sweet water surrounded her. The fish she'd caught flapped about inside the bucket by her feet. She'd loved fishing her entire life—as the daughter of a fisherman, it ran in her blood. But that afternoon in the lake, the sky turned black suddenly, and the wind kicked up waves high enough to rock her boat.

She wasn't far from the shore, and the screams of two girls called her to the deep end.

The first girl she pulled out was young and lithe, with tawny skin and raven hair. Violet was an excellent swimmer, and with her magic aiding her she could drag the child into her boat, even though the waters were treacherous.

Then she chased after the fair-skinned girl with golden hair, diving into the murky waters. Deeper and deeper, until her lungs burned with the lack of air. But whatever Violet did, she could never get to her, could never reach her.

It was the first emissary who hauled Violet out of the water before she drowned herself in pursuit of the girl. She later found out there had never been a second girl at all. Cullen's special power was to create mirages —a gift that ran in his bloodline and was coveted by the God of Shadows.

He'd tricked her into believing he'd saved her that afternoon—when he was the one who'd almost killed her with his storm.

"I rescued your sister?" she asked, pushing down the bitter memories. After Cullen had taken her back to shore, Violet had met the little girl she'd saved and her brother. Gavin's features were a blur in her memory, like she'd been placed under a spell to forget him.

She remembered vaguely that a drunken fool had offered to help her feel better. Which now made sense, since Gavin was a healer. More missing puzzle pieces coming together.

Cullen had declined Gavin's offer of help, likely because he had his own devious plans to nurse Violet back to health and make her fall in love with him so she would carry his baby. Then he could have delivered the child to Dargan with a golden bow. The bastard.

"You did," Gavin said. "I was an irresponsible idiot. I was so out of it that I lost track of where she'd gone." He scratched the back of his neck while his cheeks turned an even deeper shade of red.

"You told me that she loved me when we were back at Laura's place. You meant that."

"Yes, and so do my parents. They were so happy that you were going to be my wife, and I..."

"You what?"

He swallowed and combed his hair away from his face, breathing faster as he looked back at her. "I have been half in love with you for the better part of three years."

Violet's pulse raced, and all the places his body touched hers tingled with a sudden awareness. His muscular arms flexed underneath her hands when he reached for her waist. She couldn't possibly tell him she'd also been thinking of him for more than a year now, obsessing over him from afar.

While she'd been very good at denying it before, he'd completely torn down all the walls she'd built around her heart to protect herself from further heartbreak. His words made her giddy in a way she'd never allowed herself to be in her life.

Violet couldn't promise him a forever, but she would enjoy being with him for however long Dargan and his emissaries let her. She rose up on tiptoes, and everything fell away the moment her lips touched his. All that was left was the softness of a kiss that caught fire.

His breath hitched when she pulled the hood of his coat off his head and dug her fingers into his hair. She'd been craving to do that for so long. His tongue traced the edge of her mouth, and she opened to him, eager for more. He tasted like home.

Violet pressed herself to him until there wasn't an inch of air between them. She wanted to suffocate the fluttering need that burst to life between her legs. He growled, and his hands trailed down her spine and hooked underneath her ass.

Then she registered a muzzle nipping at her hair. Right. Twenty-one had got tired of waiting. Her warm, steamy breath hit the nape of Violet's neck. She swatted at her mare, but the beast was as stubborn as herself.

Gavin laughed against her lips and pulled away.

There was something close to adoration shining in his eyes. She didn't deserve it. "We need to go," he said, although his resistance bled away when she drew him into another kiss.

She didn't want to come back to reality, not just yet. She wanted to stay forever inside his arms. Allow his kisses to wash away all lingering traces of Julius' touch, of all the hurt she'd endured in the past.

The sound of leather boots tapping over stone resonated in the background, and both of them broke apart.

Mios came through the doorframe a moment later, tilting his head so he didn't hit it on his way in. Now that he'd cleaned himself and trimmed his beard, he looked ruggedly handsome in his new clothes, standing with a powerful and elegant stance. His ebony scarf held as many melting snowflakes as the mane on his head. "Sorry to interrupt."

Was he? He appeared mildly uncomfortable. Mostly, he looked annoyed. Probably because he'd been outside in the snow while they were in here, getting extra cozy.

"Weren't you supposed to be keeping watch?" Violet asked with a smile.

Mios raised an eyebrow and met her grin with one feline of his own. "Weren't you two supposed to be getting the horses?"

"We got sidetracked." Gavin cleared his throat and shifted away from her.

"I saw. The town is stirring, my love birds, and I

saw at least three suspicious looking fellows nearby. They looked like guards."

"We should go." Gavin nodded and dropped one last kiss on her temple before the three of them made their way out of the stables. They waved their goodbyes to the stableboy, but he was chatting animatedly with the horses and paid no attention to them.

"Are you sure you don't want to ride a horse?" Violet asked. "Twenty-one is very sweet-tempered, and I can go with Gavin."

"You named your mare Twenty-one?" Gavin's offended tone wasn't lost on her. Well, what did he expect? Strictly speaking she wasn't even her horse.

Mios reached for her mare's tack after adjusting the hood over his head. "Horses rarely like shifters, but if you really don't mind it—I am still recovering from the poison. I need to preserve my energy until we know what awaits us out there."

He was right. She could still feel the poison lingering in her bloodstream as well. Out in the mountains, they might encounter a Sídhe, or who knew what else. Their time in Scoria had ended, and Violet was ready to head back to her hometown of Sagewood. Hopefully, she'd see her family again at long last.

Talking about Mina had only made her miss Thalea more. She hoped she could say one last goodbye before she left this kingdom for good.

20
VIOLET

THEY RODE WITHOUT STOPPING, OTHER THAN TO REST AT night. A sigh of relief left her lips when the rough dirt roads slowly gave way to cobbled stone. The first homes appeared shortly after, some with wooden shingles and others covered with thatched roofs. This was so different from the imposing buildings of the Iron City. Even when compared to Scoria, the shifter village of Tulahn appeared rudimentary.

Their horses' hooves clanked along, and the homes became more polished-looking, made from stone and hardwood. The snow which had been falling on them for the better part of the day had stopped, but the chill in the air still left Violet's fingers numb. They must be high up the mountain by now.

Carts pulled by oxen clattered over muddy streets, creating a steady background sound, and soon the small stands of a market came into view. Few people bustled between the stalls, either working or browsing the vibrant array of herbs on offer. Their rich aroma blended with the crisp scent of winter in the air, and Violet's stomach grumbled loud enough for everyone to hear.

"We'll get some food soon." Gavin's voice was gentle from behind her.

"I'm fine." They had stopped to eat just once after they left their camp in the morning. It had been enough to tide her over until they reached this village.

"There aren't many people out," she whispered. In a place where everyone's senses were heightened, she wasn't sure anything was a secret.

"I suppose few would enjoy being out in this wonderful weather, though I have to admit... I quite like it myself." Gavin shifted closer to her to keep their conversation private. His soft lips grazed the sensitive skin of her neck, right underneath her ear.

Violet could blame her damp clothes for the way her body shivered at that. Although she'd accepted that his nearness affected her and wanted nothing more than to pursue this building between them. "So you enjoy being cold and wet?"

"No, but I like having your round ass grinding against me as you try to get cozy."

"Hush, everyone here can listen!" As strangled laughter left her lips, her stomach fluttered with a pleasant sensation. Violet hadn't felt it in so long, she'd almost forgotten what it felt like. Gods, but anticipation was delicious. Her body instantly melted into his, and the hard planes of his muscular chest fit perfectly against her back. It would be so easy to become used to this. She felt dizzy with how much she wanted him.

"Let them. It will give them something to talk about."

She turned toward him and caught the sparkle of mischief in his eyes. "Aren't all rich men like you taught to be gentlemen? You had me fooled, Gavin Luna."

"I would be happy to show you all the ways I can be ungentlemanly, then."

Mios threw them a look from over his shoulder, lifting one shapely brow before he focused back on the road. "She's not wrong. Everyone can hear this nonsense."

A beat of silence, then Gavin's roll of laughter shook her with its intensity, and she followed suit. Even from his profile, she could see Mios' serious expression cracking as his lips morphed into a small smile.

This was it. A first in a long time, for her to be joking around with others. To feel free, even though she was a deserter and her days were numbered. She'd stopped herself from connecting with anyone ever since Cullen had betrayed her... maybe even longer than that—since she'd been taken from her family. Violet had one thing to thank Julius for, and that was that he'd shown her what she really wanted. She was done sabotaging herself out of it.

Whatever time she had left before Dargan came for

her, she was determined to enjoy it with Gavin. If he'd let her... And she hoped he would.

Mios dug the heels of his icy boots into Twenty-one's stomach and rode ahead, just as four men strolled out into the main street and toward them. They weren't as large as their companion, but they still towered over most regular people. The largest one walked ahead of the rest. His skin was darker than even her own, and his piercing features were half hidden behind a thick beard with salt and pepper strands.

Where Mios moved with elegant and precise steps, the wolves stormed in with the confidence of a pack. Violet hadn't had much contact with shifters before. They had their own world and rules and rarely welcomed magic-wielders into it.

"Lion, you are far from your prowling lands." The male's voice rang deep. To judge by his growly disposition, this must be the alpha leader of this colony. He clearly wasn't happy to see another shifter riding into his town. "Your kind haven't been in this part of the kingdom for more than a decade..."

"I assure you, I'm not looking for trouble."

"You brought magic-wielders with you." The alpha's lips peeled back, displaying teeth that contrasted against his lips. "They aren't welcome here."

His copper-colored eyes pinned her down like a deer under a predator's stare. She had to battle her instant need to flee. To remind herself that she wasn't the prey but their nightmare.

"Have they been here before?" Mios asked.

"No. But they are all the same, and when they arrive, those damn Crows are never far behind." He spat on the ground in their general direction and crossed his arms. "State your reasons for intruding on my land."

"Since when does a lion have to justify himself to a wolf? Our treaties allow me safe passage through your territory... and your kind receives the same courtesy when crossing mine."

Was Mios an alpha? Violet didn't know much about the lions and their hierarchy. Was he a prince—a king, even? A duke of sorts, or an estranged heir?

Perhaps it was time Gavin and her asked him some questions. He was one of the Lionborn, the closest thing to royalty the shifters had, and his presence alone inspired respect, even from her. But there was so much they didn't know about him.

To judge by Gavin's intake of breath, his hope to avoid any confrontation was running out. She almost felt sorry for him. It seemed that he'd always be surrounded by people with big mouths and stormy dispositions.

The werewolf snarled. "If you're here, then it's my issue."

Mios hummed and looked around the place leisurely. Violet followed his gaze, trying to see what he saw, and now she was no longer distracted by Gavin, the picture grew clearer. She saw the battered walls, dirtied by unforgiving winters. And she saw the remnants of a battle not long past, from the shutters that hung crookedly from their windows to entire sections of roofs that were missing as though a storm had hit. Or, more likely, as though a large animal had been jumping from shop to shop, tearing everything apart in its wake.

"It seems you've been doing a piss-poor job of protecting your village if a Sídhe is tormenting your town, hunting in the one next door, and riling up the humans against your people. Soon, you'll be calling for help from our laws to protect you from them."

The man's eyes widened. "How do you know about the Sídhe?"

"I was kidnapped by a commander of the King's army to deliver me to Scoria's governor. We realized their aim must have been to appease the town and serve them some retribution against our kind."

"But... you're a lion."

"Well, he didn't exactly stop to ask me what my beast was."

The man looked around. People had begun to gather under the awnings of their buildings, staring at them. He pointed at Gavin and herself. "And what about them?"

"They helped me escape," Mios said.

"Let's move this conversation inside. I need you to explain to me what you know."

Mios lifted his sharp chin and narrowed his gaze. His one-size-too-small coat barely contained his arms as they bulged inside their sleeves. "While I want to help you, wolf, don't think for one second that you can tell me what to do. You can invite us to stay, as guests. Then I will share with you what I saw. And when I return to my homeland, I will make sure that someone from our court comes to investigate the governor."

The other shifter glared back at Mios. To judge by the worn expressions of everyone around them, his pack must be tired of dealing with this problem as well. "And why would I care what your court may or may not do? Lions have dwindled in numbers. You have been displaced out of your crown, after you lost it to the blood-drinking creatures of the night."

Some of the bystanders cowered behind the wooden columns of the shops, as if they feared an attack. Twenty-one shook her head, clearly sensing the tense atmosphere, and danced on the spot, spraying wet snow everywhere.

"If you say so—it must be true." Mios smile was positively feline. "We will leave, then."

Violet opened her mouth to protest. While she had little to offer in gold, she could at least buy herself a satisfying meal. Her stomach grumbled again, and she was sure that this time everyone around them could hear it.

"Don't." The alpha wolf growled, then turned back to the crowd. "Erden, come here and take our new... guests to the cabin. Bring them meals and dry clothes." He paused, sending Mios a withering look. "Once your basic needs are met, you can amaze me with your all-encompassing knowledge of how I can save my people from war. I'll be in the house next to yours."

Contrary to her expectations, Mios stayed seated on top of her mare, unmoved by the condescending tone the werewolf used. The alpha wolf turned and left without another glance back. The three other males followed close behind him, but not without spitting on the ground in what was evidently a sign of them not being welcomed.

On second thought, Violet really wasn't sure she wanted to stay here, even for one night. It seemed safer to deal with the winter storm. She would prefer to be rested if she had to fight for her life and freedom, but they were better off alive than dead.

"I don't like this," she said. "We should just keep going. My family's home is not far and the Crows could be getting closer to us as we speak..."

"Rest is important, Violet," Gavin whispered. "We've had a rough couple of days, and we need to sleep properly if we want to stand a chance to cross the mountains and leave the kingdom."

"I know that. But we aren't welcome here, and after everything that's already happened, I don't want to worry about these people and everything else as well."

"We will be fine here for one night," Mios said. "These people have been going through something bad. You can see it on their faces, even the buildings are showing signs of it. It's normal for them to be wary of strangers. Besides, alphas aren't inclined to show weakness in front of another alpha."

A stout man stormed toward them, widening his arms and looking like a puffed peacock. His bushy auburn brows nearly covered his small eyes, a funny look as he was the least intimidating male she'd ever seen. "Come on, I don't have all day."

21
VIOLET

T**HE LOG CABIN STOOD ON THE OUTSKIRTS OF TOWN. I**T SAT ON a spacious lot and was surrounded by a giant patch of dirt that might have been garden beds at another time of the year. Tree branches, chopped down to roughly equal lengths, fenced off the perimeter of the place.

Erden fetched a set of keys from his pockets and opened the door. The three of them cautiously stepped in. The musky scent of moisture hung heavy around the place. Violet doubted anyone had stayed in here for a while.

"There should be some food and things to cook a meal in the kitchen. I'm sure you can make yourself useful and fix up something for the men, eh?" Erden's black gaze met Violet's. Turned out he was a cocky idiot with a death wish.

Gavin's sharp intake of breath should have been enough to hold her back. She didn't want trouble. But then again, she also wasn't the rational type. Violet stepped forward before he could stop her, resting her hand against the doorframe as she looked straight at the man. "I don't cook, Bill. I imagine you do, though—so I expect you to bring us our food, since you were commanded to. Make sure it's warm, and no spitting in it. My friend Mios would smell it."

Perhaps messing up his name on purpose was childish. But she was hungry and annoyed, and it was worth it when his face revealed his feelings.

"Bill?" Erden's expression shifted from angry to confused just as she shut the door in his face, firmly locking him outside.

"Tedious man," she grumbled, and waited where she stood until she heard the crunching of snow as he stomped away from the house. "Do you think he'll actually bring us food? I doubt you two have ever cooked a thing in your lives?"

Gavin and Mios exchanged a look before the lion strolled into the kitchen, scratching his brow. He opened some cupboards and hummed before reaching for a ceramic container which had fabric wrapped tightly around the lid with twine. "I can try to make something. Not sure how edible it will be, though, as I've only cooked for myself before."

"Really?"

"Don't look so surprised. I've been traveling on my own for half a year now. I had to learn at some point."

She craned her neck to see what he was doing, but after a while she got distracted by the newness of the quaint place. Aside from the smell, it appeared mostly clean. A rustic table with two chairs stood underneath a window that overlooked the garden. The small sitting room came complete with a chimney and one stiff-looking couch, wrapped in animal furs.

To her right, a narrow, dark corridor led to two doors in the back.

Violet headed toward the hearth, trying not to wince when pain shot through her wound with each step. It felt like shards of glass had embedded themselves below her skin. She cursed internally at her luck and hoped Gavin wouldn't start fretting over it.

Her current filthy state wouldn't help her ward off infection, either. She called for a fire spell and aimed her hand at the half-burned logs in the fireplace. Flames licked the wood, warming the place.

"Violet, I saw you limping. How is your leg?"

So much for him not noticing. "It's fine."

Gavin's forehead wrinkled, and he followed her closely as she walked past him and down the corridor toward the back of the cabin. She didn't have her familiar knives with her anymore, but Laura had given her a couple when they'd left the inn in the early morning.

There were two rooms on this side, both with narrow beds with handmade frames that matched the fence outside. The hay mattresses were stiff although they were covered in furs. The feather pillows dipped beneath her probing hands. While not ideal, this would do for one night.

She walked over to the small set of drawers by the

window, in search of extra linen. The scent of wood, dust, and moths tickled the back of her throat, and she wrinkled her nose, trying not to sneeze.

On the far side of the room, a large copper tub stood in one corner, hidden behind a wall made of horizontal tree trunks. Their uneven shapes left holes gaping between them. A poor attempt at privacy… but it was something.

When she rejoined the rest of the group in the sitting room, Gavin was just coming back in from the outside. He stomped the snow off his boots on the front door mat, holding a couple of buckets full of water. He placed them over the wood stove in the kitchen area. Mios already had something boiling. Stew, to judge by the aroma.

"There's two empty rooms at the back." She hobbled toward them.

Gavin dried his hands on his pants, studying her leg as if he expected to see blood or even a bone poking through her clothes at any moment now. "You can take the room. I can sleep out here."

Did she even want that? Oh, how things had changed. While her attraction to him had always been there, she'd held it off for so long. Now, she just wanted him close.

"I need to check on your leg," Gavin continued. "Don't think I didn't notice how you're walking."

She opened her mouth, ready to tell him she was fine again—but then again, being touched by him, even if it was only to heal her, didn't sound half bad.

"Thanks," she said. "After we eat and bathe, though. I feel like my clothes are going to walk away from me at any moment."

He laughed. "Same."

ERDEN CAME BACK WITH VENISON, ROOT VEGETABLES, AND A large carafe of ale. Violet found infinite joy in calling him by the wrong name again, especially since he made a point of not speaking to her when she opened the door.

The stew wasn't half bad either, and by the time the three of them huddled in front of the fire, her clothes were dry. Her stomach was eager to be filled with something other than cured meat and stale bread, and the fermented taste of beer made for a nice change.

With their tongues loosened by the alcohol, they'd shared more in the last hour than they had during the last two days of traveling together. They had left behind the horrors the three of them had lived through under Julius' hands, and if she closed her eyes, she could almost fool herself into believing that Mios was a long-lost friend instead of a stranger she'd only just met.

Was that how Gavin was able to connect with so many people so readily? How did he manage to get complete strangers like Harry and Laura to do what they did for him?

"So I take it you two are running from your crown?"

Violet's gut feeling was to tell him to mind his own business, she wasn't about to air out all of their secrets to a near stranger, even if she did like him. However, after all that happened with Harry and Laura, she wanted to try to be more open. "The Society of Crows is chasing me down for escaping my husband."

Mios's gaze traveled to Gavin, and his shapely eyebrows arched. "I thought you two were married?"

"We are…" Gavin said.

"It should be easy to go back and tell them you are together, no? No need to keep running."

If things were that easy, but she didn't want to get into the whole child thing here with the both of them.

"There is nothing easy when it comes to the Society of Crows. They are a bunch of corrupted pricks." She said instead, "and I did kill one of their members on the way out, Morgan was demanding to see us come together during our wedding night, which is illegal. When I challenged it, things got ugly. She threatened to let Julius–well. She's dead now."

Why did she need to explain all of this out loud? It didn't matter how she said it, and how much he hated the bitch, she still felt guilty about it.

"See you come together?"

Shame and anger churned inside her by just remembering that day. She hated she became flustered all over again, and it became even worse when Gavin's eyes burned into her, with an intensity that melted everything in their path.

"Consummate our marriage, have sex, fuck—"

"Ah, if someone had demanded to watch me take my beloved, they would be dead too." Mios agreed and leaned back in his creaking chair.

The cracking of the fire filled the silence that came over them, and his words did appease her. Maybe opening up wasn't so bad.

"So, what about you? What brought you to the Iron Kingdom?" she asked Mios, spooning some stew into her mouth. The wind howled through the gaps of the ill-fitted windows, bringing a breeze that burrowed into the deeper layers of her clothes.

Mios stared intently at the crackling fire. For a moment, she thought he might ignore her question, and her curiosity spiked higher with every second that drifted by without an answer. "I'm looking for a god stone," he said eventually.

"And what's that?" Gavin placed the empty bowl by his feet and leaned forward. "Is it a magical artifact?"

"It is. A powerful and rare one at that."

"It must be, to make a Lionborn leave the Gold Kingdom," Gavin said. "What does it do?"

Another moment slipped past as Mios seemed to deliberate how truthful to be. This time, the silence stretched long enough to grow uncomfortable. Violet kept spooning bite after bite into her mouth to avoid saying something. "It's said that a god stone hides your magical abilities. They are somewhat of a myth, but I know for a fact that they exist. I've seen one in the past."

Wait a second. Violet's heart was beating too fast

all of a sudden, and time seemed to contract and expand around her. Was the god stone the artifact Luelle had said she needed? Could it be the same as the Stone of Clemency?

If this rock could hide one's magic from the world... could it also hide it from a god? Violet's throat closed up as she inhaled sharply. Her body prickled with a rush of adrenaline, and she fought the sudden need to pace around the room and demand some answers.

Gavin's face, in contrast, still looked relaxed, although his gaze flashed to meet hers before returning to the shifter. "Surely that can't exist. If it did, then everyone would be trying to get their hands on it to avoid being drafted into the army."

Good point. Her mind had been so focused on the possibility of escaping Dargan that she hadn't even considered any other possible uses for such an object. The freedom that children would gain if they got to escape being pulled from their homes...

"It's extremely rare," Mios admitted. He let his body sink back into the sofa, crossing one ankle over his knee. "I only tell you this because you saved me, and that deserves my trust. But I'm sure you understand what people will do in order to get their hands on such an artifact."

The answer was obvious. She knew, deep down, what she would do to free herself. To have a shot at a normal life with Gavin.

People would kill for this stone... and perhaps, so would she.

"I only know of the ones held by the four kings and queens of Caztian. When the kingdoms were first formed, the royal families split a large stone and divided it amongst themselves."

"Your family was part of the first royals, no? Wouldn't you have one of those if the myths were true?"

"No, not us. The shifters never called for the ire of the deities. Our goddess never threatened us with extinction like your gods did to the rest of the people living in this world." He shrugged with a sigh. "So we never got our cut of the gems. If my family had one, I wouldn't be out here trying to find it."

The legend of how the new world had been formed was heavily debated either way. There were indeed those who believed that the leaders of the old world had given sacrifices to the gods, and in turn the wicked bastards hadn't destroyed everyone living here.

Pff. Violet didn't believe a word of it. But even with her skeptical view of everything, she knew myths and legends were based on reality. The god stone was the only lead she had right now to find what Luelle had suggested she needed. It could be a way out of this mess. And that alone deserved some consideration.

"So are you going back to the Iron City? And then, what—buy it from the King?" Gavin followed Mios as he got to his feet, his empty wooden bowl held in his hand.

"No, King Urien would never give me his. Although it would be much easier if I could simply purchase it."

"Why not? Believe me, I know him. He doesn't seem to care for material things."

Mios' harsh laughter bounced off the walls. He walked toward the kitchen and poured some more ale into his metal cup. "If I told you, you wouldn't believe a word of it."

"Try me." Violet's voice was a whisper that not even Gavin heard. But Mios' head turned to her, his eyes narrowing as he studied her closely. "Please."

"It's said the royals promised their second-born child to the gods. That it was their biggest sacrifice to save the planet. The deal was that if their heir displayed a magical trait, the gods would take them to serve as emissaries—the messengers between the deities and the royal families. My parents always said the Gods claimed the children of the royals when they turned twenty, as they are no longer babes to nurse."

"What happens if the heirs don't get the magic gene at all?"

"Then the gods move on to the next generation. So, the royals found an artifact that would make the gods believe all new royal heirs, after their firstborn, were simple humans without magic," Mios answered Gavin, before taking another drink.

Violet's breath rushed from her lungs all at once. She had been twenty when Cullen came for her, even though her magic presented itself when she was eleven. "What it's stopping the gods from taking the firstborn?"

In her case, Dargan lay claim on her if she didn't give birth to anyone.

"I don't know all the details. It's all passed down in galas through drunken lips. But I can speak from what I know, and they tied the royal blood to the land of every kingdom. The deal protects the royal firstborn from the gods."

Well fuck, she wasn't a royal. Tears pricked her eyes. "So it does hide you, even from the gods?"

"Yes." Mios' gaze pierced hers, and all else fell away. Could he see Dargan's mark on her now? Did he know?

The gods needed to collect second children of a family to fill a quota of emissaries. It made sense. They weren't going to be killed, but used as connections between the deities and the people of the world. Forever enslaved.

If she got her hands on one of those stones, she could hide from Dargan. And once she had a baby, she could use it to hide them instead.

"Are you trying to find it to protect your second child?" Gavin asked, his voice pulling her from her musings. But the spark of hope remained.

"It's not for me," Mios said. "A friend of mine has unknowingly repressed her magic for years. It's only a matter of time until the Crows find her. If it hides magical people from the gods, it must surely do the same with the scrying mirror the Society uses."

The mirror was rumored to find all magical children in the world. Myth claimed that it had been given to the Society of Crows by the wicked gods, to be used to maintain "balance". Whatever that meant. In the end, Violet had always suspected that the gods saw Caztian and its inhabitants as mere playthings to toy with.

Mios downed his drink before placing the cup on the surface of the kitchen counter. "I need to meet with the alpha now. You two should stay here, as shifters are protective of pack information. Try to get some rest. If I'm not back by midnight, then leave this place without me."

22
VIOLET

HER FINGERTIPS WERE WRINKLED PRUNES BY NOW, AND THE water had turned from boiling hot to lukewarm. Yet, it was hard to find the motivation to get out of it, even though the chill of the air increased when daylight disappeared from the sky, giving way to night.

A bath was a treat, especially given the state she'd been in, and she was determined to enjoy every bit of warm water by lingering in the copper tub for as long as possible.

A knock on the door had her peering over the rim of the tub before Gavin's voice filtered through, making her stomach flutter. "Violet, you didn't go to sleep on me, did you? I need to check your leg."

She pressed her lips tightly together to kill the idiotic smile that appeared without permission and took a shaky breath to gather her strength and calm her frazzled nerves. "I'm not asleep. Why don't you come in?"

She climbed out of the tub, spotting Gavin by the door. He was staring open-mouthed at her through the holes in the privacy screen. Her heart hammered when she met his dark gaze across the room.

"Would you hand me my shirt? It's on the bed." She watched him fret while he looked for the item in question. His cheeks were bright red when he tentatively approached her, and his eyes followed the droplets of water that trailed down her naked body.

He cleared his throat and turned his face away. "Are you sure I should be here? I can come back later."

"Do you want to leave?"

He flashed his gaze at her. "No."

"Then stay." The heat inside her veins flared, burning through her like wildfire as she shrugged on her shirt, not bothering to do up the laces at the top. She wasn't one to waste time, and if she was going to seduce him, spending energy lacing herself up tight was a wasted effort.

The fabric stuck to her skin, doing a poor job of hiding her curves. "Should I sit or stay here?" she questioned.

"Y-yes. I mean, whatever you want." Gavin swallowed and turned his body toward her as she stepped out of the tub enclosure. She had to commend him for attempting to keep his eyes glued to her face, even though she could feel his gaze burning her back as she strolled to the bed.

He'd brought a tray with ripped strips of linen—he'd no doubt borrowed them from one of the sets of drawers—and a bowl of steaming water. His hair was still wet, although tamed from a bath.

Gavin kneeled in front of her and placed the tray to his side before rubbing the back of his neck. "Did you re-injure it when you entered the governor's house, or while we traveled?"

"Governor's house." She didn't want to relive that moment, not now. Right now, her entire focus narrowed in on him and the way his fists opened and closed as he settled more comfortably on the floor.

He pressed his wide palm over her outer thigh and focused on her cut. He did a decent job at masking his features, and the only thing that gave away his nerves was the quickness of his breaths. A couple of stitches had torn at some point, and the edges of her wound looked redder than she'd remember.

He drew his finger over the injury, and waves of magic rolled through her body, numbing the pain. She gasped as he touched the inside of her thigh, steadying her leg while he healed her. As she exhaled, his hand moved higher, and the ache vanished, leaving behind only his touch, tracing fire over skin.

Her center tingled and ached with the rhythm of her quickened heartbeat. Gavin frowned. "Does it still hurt?"

Her face warmed. Of course he was only thinking of her injury, while she was here burning with the need to be touched by him. After all they'd been through, she craved him—the man she was falling in love with. It was a frightening word to attach to someone, especially in light of her past.

Her fingers prickled, all her senses fully awakened. She swallowed. "No—yes…"

"Yes or no?" The air of his breathy laughter hit her skin, and gooseflesh erupted on every inch of her leg that his hand skimmed.

Enough of this silliness. She took a deep breath to settle her nerves, and only the giddy sensation of needing him remained. He was her husband. She shouldn't feel ashamed of desiring his touch.

This was more than an attraction to a handsome man. Gavin had saved her life and helped her understand her own self-destructive behavior. He'd chosen to help her even though he might not see his family again.

Now it was her turn to choose him over everything. She'd give him the only thing she had left: her heart.

"I am hurting—but not there." Violet placed her hand over Gavin's, pulling it up the inside of her thigh, drawing it closer to where she wanted it.

Gavin's lips parted as understanding flashed behind his dark eyes. He tilted his head back, revealing the wonderful thick lines of his neck. His Adam's apple bobbed when he swallowed heavily. His fingertips continued to inch upward, even after Violet dropped her hand, allowing it to fall away from his. He traced small circles over her supple skin. "This way?"

"Higher," she breathed. He touched the edge where her leg met her pelvis, right where the signs of her arousal were becoming ever more evident beneath his touch.

"Violet..." He held his breath and shifted his weight on his knees. She opened her legs slightly, allowing him an unobstructed path to her aching core.

He dropped his gaze and pulled her closer to the edge of the bed with his other hand, then lowered his lips to her skin, following the lazy trail of goosebumps he had woken before. He teased her sex with his hand, right where she ached the most.

"Is it here that you're hurting?" His breath hit a wet patch on her leg, and desire roughened his tone. He pushed her legs wider with the weight of his shoulders —and slipped a finger inside her.

Pleasure exploded around his touch. It felt warm, with an edge of spice that burned and soothed the ache in equal parts. The power of his healing magic was completely different when it caressed her from the inside.

Violet gasped in surprise as desire surged through her, making her toes curl. She grabbed his shoulders as his lips collided with her aching center, and her moans died in her throat.

It was too much and not enough. He took her with eager strokes of his tongue, matching the pace his fingers had set inside her. She supported her weight on the mattress with one arm and wrapped the other hand through the strands of his wavy hair, pulling him closer.

Pleasure coiled tighter as he flattened his tongue

against her, and soon she came undone, falling over the precipice in a quivering mess.

Gavin stood slowly and studied every inch of her on display. Freshly exposed skin pebbled with the chill of the air as she shrugged off her shirt. Then she reached for him, clawing at his shoulders and capturing his lips with her own in a demanding kiss.

The bed screeched over the floor, banging against the wall. She pulled his tunic up his torso and tore it off, revealing an expanse of skin wrapped around tight ropes of muscle. Moles and freckles peppered every part of him that she touched. She was ready for him again.

Violet undid the ties of his pants and pushed them down the generous curve of his ass, letting her fingers play along the two dimples of his lower back and up his spine. He broke away from her lips and traced kisses down her jaw and neck.

He was iron wrapped in velvet when he pushed inside her. At first, he set a rhythm that matched what he had done to her beforehand, but then he slowed down. As if he was savoring her.

Violet rarely liked slow, tender sex. She preferred hard fucking over making love any day. But this was different. She'd never felt this way for anyone, and her need to take her time filled her as surely as Gavin did. She relaxed into it, and he pushed deeper until every inch of him was buried inside her, palming one of her breasts.

"Gods, you're tight. Does that feel better now?"

Gavin grunted against her neck. Then he lifted her up from the bed in one swift move and pushed her against the wall, thrusting inside her. The room shook as he continued his wonderful torture. "Or do you need more? Is this ungentlemanly enough for you?"

"Yes," Violet said in a breathy tone.

He seemed to be everywhere at once. His teeth nipping at her neck, his fingers digging mercilessly into the line of her ass, sending her over the edge. Her vision blackened as pleasure ripped through her in waves that took her breath away.

When his pace faltered, a trace of panic rose to the back of her mind. He was close. She couldn't let him come inside her. Not unless she wanted to risk losing her battle against Dargan, before she'd even had the chance to tell Gavin about it. She needed to give him a choice...

The moment she came down from the cloud of her orgasm, she pushed him hard enough that he stopped and stumbled away. Then she sank to her knees and took his cock in her mouth. His fingers dug into her scalp with a surprised groan as she moved up and down his length, matching the rhythm of his hips. He came in her mouth a split second later.

His taste was intoxicating. He watched, breathing heavily as she licked all of him. Then he bent down and picked her up from the ground and threw her on the bed, pulling a roll of laughter from her.

The light of the moon seeped through the window, grazing the ridges of his abs. He continued to stand and stare, watching her crawl under the blankets. "What are you doing over there?" She patted the bed beside her. "Bring your ass in here."

"Since you're asking so nicely..." A slow smile spread over his face as he climbed underneath the sheets alongside her.

She wrapped around him like a limpet, loving the way his breaths tickled her face and how his fingers caressed her shoulders.

"I would never have guessed you enjoyed cuddling," Gavin murmured.

"Not sure what gave you that impression. I'm the sweetest—most cuddly—person, you know." She burrowed her nose into his skin and grinned at the soft snort of laughter that came from him. It was endearing in the best possible way.

This time, she didn't stop the smile when his lips brushed over her head. "You taste sweet, but that's only for me to know."

Her cheeks burned. "And now Mios undoubtedly knows it too... I'm pretty sure he can hear through walls."

Gavin cursed. "I'm going to have to kill him. A pity, really, since I like the man."

She laughed and enjoyed the quiet sense of peace that suffused her. "Gavin?"

"Hmm?" The lazy movements of his hand over her skin grew weaker as sleep began to pull at him.

"I'm sorry about what happened to you with Julius.

I know what it feels like to be betrayed. I wish you'd never had to go through that."

He looked down at her, blinking, before he let out a tired sigh. "I wished I'd killed him before he ever got the chance to touch you, Violet. I should have suspected something was off. There were signs I ignored because I couldn't believe he was so awful... He sent me the other way, and it didn't even sound suspicious to me until a couple of days ago, after you spoke to me. I should have questioned him more."

"I know the feeling," she admitted.

"Are you afraid of becoming with child? Is that why—?"

"Yes."

"I can brew a potion to prevent it, when we settled somewhere safe," he said.

Would that be enough to deter Dargan? She doubted it, but smiled up at Gavin with a sleepy smile. Then her eyes grew heavy with a sudden exhaustion, closing on their own and taking her down into a dreamless sleep.

23
VIOLET

"Had a good time last night, eh?" Mios' lips twitched with mischief as they headed out of the cabin. The chill morning breeze blew the mane out of his face, revealing his handsome profile.

Violet could have blamed the cold for the way she blushed or the soreness between her legs on riding a horse all day yesterday. She wasn't a bashful woman, but this situation left her longing for more privacy. What had happened between Gavin and her meant so much more than just a romp in the sheets.

They had taken that next, very intimate step. Before, it had been easy to lie to herself, to tell herself that Gavin and her weren't truly married. Not anymore.

Dammit, but he'd sneaked past her well-constructed walls and made her trust him. Love him even. Her chest constricted with the painful reminder that she shouldn't be loving anyone. Not when she lacked answers for how long she had in this world. Not while he didn't even know what was coming.

Violet eyed Mios as he stretched, looking around the place with cautious eyes. How had last night's meeting with the alpha gone for him? Had they spoken about the locals in Scoria and their demands for a shifter to be killed in response to the attacks?

It wasn't like Mios knew all that much about the city since he'd been a captive the entire time he was there. Unless, of course, he was lying, and this was all a ruse... Perhaps he'd worked with Julius all alon—no!

There she was, doing it again. After everything that had happened with Harry and Laura, and how wrong she'd been then. She should try to open up to strangers instead of being so defensive and driving them away. And so she swallowed any cynical remarks and allowed her body to adjust to the uncomfortable churn of embarrassment until it trickled away.

She stepped to the street as the sound of familiar footsteps came from behind them, followed by Gavin's hand settling on her lower back. "Is your leg still bothering you? You're walking funny."

"It's not her leg, man." Mios' snort turned into a quiet laughter.

Gavin's cheeks flushed. "In that case, we should go back into the room and..."

She side-eyed him, crossing her arms. "If you say you'll heal me from the inside or something equally ridiculous, I will hurt you."

"It's not ridiculous. That's how healers work." Gavin shut the door behind himself.

He trotted in front of her in that carefree manner of his, not showing the slightest trace of soreness or tiredness. Damn him. Then again, he'd not been the one getting fucked all night long... Not that she was complaining.

"So what happens if someone—anyone—is internally bleeding? Would you also stick your fingers in all of their holes to heal them?"

"Goddess, let his answer be no," Mios muttered from the street. He was already walking away to give them some privacy. Or to give himself some peace.

"What if I said yes?" Gavin whispered. His breath teased the side of her neck as he stepped close to her. "Would you allow me to? I'm willing."

Violet battled the need to press her hand over his rakish smirk and smother him. The memories from last night returned in full force, warming her cheeks and turning her insides over with a pleasant flutter.

"Continue," she said. "I dare you..."

He chuckled. "Have I ever told you I love a challenge?"

It wasn't surprising. So far, he'd taken every difficulty that life had thrown at him and faced it with a smile. It only spurred on her growing affection for him. "No, but the real question is... do you enjoy getting hurt? Because you are purposely egging me on."

"I find it sexy when you're mean," he answered, and his fingers trapped her chin before he kissed her roughly on the lips. "That should be enough of an answer for you."

Her pulse throbbed in her neck. Maybe she wasn't hungry for food, and maybe having him heal her from the inside wouldn't be so bad. "That's a lie. You want me to stop every time I'm mean to anyone."

Gavin's brown eyes darted toward the street. Mios was far enough now that he'd turned into a black shape against the wide expanse of land around them. "It's not a lie," he whispered in her ear. "It drives me mad and makes me want to throw you over my knees and teach you some manners. Then I would do things to you that would make you come apart in my hand."

"Gavin!" She gasped, half expecting to see Mios gaping in horror at them. Still, her heart and her sex quivered at his words. It was always the ones you suspected the least that surprised you the most.

"So be mean, Violet, and let's settle the rest in the bedroom."

Her lips parted. Was he saying what she thought he was saying? Did he want to spank her? Now? Oh, fuck. Was she into it?

She grabbed his arm and pulled him back toward the cabin. "Food can wait."

"Did I catch you at the wrong time?"

Gavin cursed as they turned to see the alpha strutting down the wide set steps of the home next to theirs. He joined them on the street, casually fixing a leather strap that held back his long locs. He rolled his shoulders, and then straightened to his full, impressive height.

"I didn't think you would still be in Tulahn this late in the morning."

Late? The sun peeked out from over the tall pine trees, still painted with the orange shades of sunrise. The day had just begun. These shifters had some strange ways of looking at things. She was eager to leave them behind.

"We were going to go for some breakfast before leaving," Gavin said. It wasn't often that she saw a flare of annoyance flash through his features, but there it was. The thought alone made her smile.

"Where is Mios?" the alpha asked.

"He went ahead of us." She pointed at their friend's silhouette. He was a block away and easy to spot.

"We have a tavern that serves food. You may take some with you for your travels. It's going to snow within a day." While the alpha's tone was far from friendly, his animosity seemed to have dulled somewhat. "I didn't catch your names yesterday."

"I'm Gavin."

"Cora," Violet said and hoped this wouldn't lead to tedious small talk. She wasn't interested in the weather —not unless it came attached to an emissary's arrival.

"Lyall," the alpha grunted.

They caught up with Mios in the center of town. The air was warmer this morning, and the devastation of whatever beast had raged through Tulahn was a lot more evident in the bright light of day.

A passing farmer led a cart pulled by oxen, and the crates of milk bottles clinked as it wobbled over the rough, uneven street. It had been a long time since Violet had been in such a rural place. The pungent smell of livestock reminded her of her childhood. Of home—minus the sea breeze.

Gavin's brows lowered over his eyes as he, too, studied the damaged buildings around them. "What has been happening around here?"

"Those damn Sídhes," Lyall said. "They set their evil minds on our village a few months ago. Not sure why, since this land has been ours for centuries… But their new queen claims this is their sacred dirt. Too bad for her. We won't go without a fight."

"So what's their plan? Are they deliberately attacking Scoria so its citizens grow restless? Do you think they're trying to get the humans to attack you? Do they think they can force you out of here if you're targeted from two sides?" Gavin's concern was thick in his voice and clear in the way his face twisted.

"You didn't tell them what we discussed in our meeting last night?" Lyall turned to Mios, who shrugged noncommittally.

"They were quite busy. Besides, I doubt they care about the shifter's troubles, much like you don't want to know theirs."

True—Violet had enough trouble on her shoulders without being roped into this mess. Gavin, however, seemed more inclined to help. Damn him and his wonderful nature. He was bound to get killed one day.

Lyall grunted, dragging a hand over his tired face. "I suppose you're right. To answer your question, Gavin, the governor of Scoria refuses to work with me. He doesn't believe it's the fae. They aren't great at using their brains in that city, and the fae are difficult to see—even for us."

They walked past muddy fields that probably burst with tall grain crops during summer. The center of town was full of life today. The clanging of a hammer in the forge echoed in all directions as people sat on the rooftops, fixing the fallen shingles.

Violet studied the place. She couldn't see children playing anywhere. That was probably to be expected this early in the day, but then again, she didn't recall seeing many outside when they'd arrived here, either. Did shifters have the same problems reproducing as magic-wielders?

A woman on a rooftop was ordering about a few men working alongside her. She stood out, not because of her size, but because she was the only female around. Whatever she was screaming was in a language Violet didn't know, but she didn't sound happy. Her words were growing more clipped as a crack of mortar and stone echoed down the street. The woman stumbled, a scream torn from her lips as the roof gave way beneath her.

She fell from two floors above them, tumbling fast with the weight of her massive body. Gavin's voice rang somewhere in the distance, but Violet was already running toward the building, her hands prickling as she called on her magic. She raised both arms and a wave of hot air bloomed from every finger. The spell softened the wolf's fall. She rolled over it before landing on the ground with a grunt.

"Are you hurt?" Violet leaned against the column of the building and coughed loudly from the dust that rose around them. Whatever energy she'd replenished with a good night's sleep and a decent meal the night before had vanished within an instant, leaving her exhausted.

The woman blinked, staring at the open gap where the roof had been a minute ago. She turned her stunned, dirty face to Violet and her shaky voice broke through the surrounding murmurs. "Yeah. Thanks to you." She sat, dusting her pants off before getting to her feet. She extended her hand to Violet, who took it after a moment of hesitation.

"Violet," she introduced herself.

"Was that an air spell? I've never seen anyone use it like that before. You never cease to amaze me, wife."

Her lips twitched into a smile, and her cheeks grew hot as she avoided Gavin's gaze. Compliments always made her uncomfortable. The deeper, sinister side of her own insecurities sprang to life, making her wonder about the sincerity of it all. "It's not that special."

Air wasn't easy to master, and while she didn't particularly excel at it, it was not the first time the spell had come in handy.

"Ellie?" Lyall cut in. His massive hands grabbed the woman's chin, turning it to inspect her face before he let out a deep breath. "Thank you for that. Saving a wolf from my pack gives you our eternal gratitude, especially since it was my Elliana."

His—like some sort of mate? The woman also had dark skin, albeit multiple shades lighter than Lyall's, but they shared the same copper-toned eyes. His daughter, perhaps?

They headed to the tavern as soon as Lyall had reassured himself that Ellie was unharmed. It was the largest building in town, with two swinging doors and boarded-up windows. Even though its exterior looked tired and desolate, the moment they crossed the threshold the roar of drunken laughter and the clink of glasses welcomed them.

The place was dark, lit by oil lanterns on top of long wooden tables. The potent scent of sweat and wet dog hair pierced her nose. The further inside they got, the more she could smell the yeast from the freshly baked bread. It wafted across from the clay oven at the end of the room, where an older lady worked the bar.

Everyone fell silent at their entrance. Was it because of their presence, or simply a sign of respect toward Lyall? Perhaps a bit of both.

Holding onto Violet's shoulder, Ellie pointed at an open table. "Let's get you all something to eat."

They met the curious—albeit slightly standoffish— gazes of the surrounding shifters as they sat alongside Elliana and Lyall. And soon the chatter, singing, and rolling laughter resumed.

An out of tune piano was playing in the background, its melody interrupted by the screech of tables being dragged across the room. Two robust women placed a large pitcher with bubbling ale, roasted venison, and buttered potatoes on the table. And in the far corner, a group threw knives at a massive target board stuck to the wall.

"Neal told us what you did for Ellie. Please enjoy all the brew you want. It's on me," the woman added with a warm smile, her skin shining with sweat as she patted Violet's shoulder.

"Neal is our second in command," Ellie said, answering Violet's unspoken question. "He was on the roof with me."

"Do you always eat like this for breakfast?" Gavin asked while spooning some potatoes onto his plate.

"Is there anything else that's worth eating?"

Violet could think of few options. She was done with cheese and stale bread, so potatoes and meat sounded great.

They chatted casually as they ate, sidestepping the heavier topics of what had brought them here or any further mention of the Sídhes. Violet's mind kept drifting back to last night, replaying memories until a fist slammed on the table, startling her out of them. Ellie was holding Mios' hand between her own, her nose nearly touching his wrist where a few swirls of ink peeked out from underneath his sleeve.

He pulled away with a grimace, just as a whistle left Ellie's lips. "Pops, it seems we've got royalty amongst us commoners today." She flopped her head forward in an exaggerated mock-bow, almost knocking her beer across the table. "Your Excellence—or whatever we are supposed to call you—you honor us with your magnificent presence."

"Stop that," Mios growled, and looked around the room with worry etched in his eyes.

"What does she mean?" Lyall asked, his gaze fixed on Mios' sleeve.

"He has the marking of the Lionborn. I thought I spotted it last night at the meeting. Happy to know my eyesight isn't deteriorating like yours, old man."

"I would prefer that my lineage is not spoken about out in the open. I'm fine if people just think I'm a lion shifter and not part of my family."

Lyall cursed and rose from his considerably larger and more comfortable seat. "You. Take my chair."

Mios adjusted his sleeve to fully cover his tattooed arm. "I will keep mine and allow the alpha of his pack to stay in his damn seat."

"You should have mentioned you were one of the Lionborn yesterday when I almost kicked you out of the village. I don't want issues with your family."

"I thought you said we'd fallen out of favor."

Violet exchanged a loaded glance with Gavin.

"Still—"

"There's no issue," Mios assured Lyall. "This is good food and even better ale. The beds were nice, and we will be on our way after this meal." He looked to Violet and Gavin for confirmation, and she nodded. They had agreed to travel through the mountains together, after all.

"A powerful storm is brewing in the sky. You might all get stuck in the mountains, and I don't want the royal guards to come sniffing about in my town. I insist you stay a few more days."

What big storm? Hadn't today seemed brighter than the day before?

Lyall relaxed in his chair when no one refused his offer. To be fair, it sounded a lot like an order. Violet would have told him to shove his commands somewhere dark and private, but she wasn't a fool. The deep line in the alpha's brow smoothed. "When we spoke last night, I assumed you were a rascal lion. What brings a Lionborn all the way here?"

"I prefer to be considered a rogue. It grants me a freedom I can seldom afford. As you know, the commander of the King's army found me before I'd even made my decision to come here." Mios shrugged. "I was still weighing my options then. It was between the Tulahn cave or another one down south. I guess things do work out since I ended up here, so close to where I intended to go in the first place."

A cave? He hadn't mentioned anything about that last night.

"Are you talking about the mine?" Ellie asked.

The lion frowned. "I thought it was a cave? My map said it's on your lands."

Lyall appeared to mull it over, popping a chunk of potatoes into his mouth. Their buttery coating lingered on his fingertips which he promptly sucked clean. "It's partially on our land. The entrance to the cavern used to be in the next town over. The humans were mining some precious gems from there... They paid us a cut from their earnings while the endeavor lasted—not that it was that long."

"What gems?" Violet asked, leaning forward with a heavy feeling in her chest. Did they mean god stones? It made sense now that Mios was looking for this cave. Would she be able to find one herself while in this part of the kingdom?

The alpha shrugged, draining the last drops of his drink. "We don't cherish precious rocks, especially not the magical ones. They call for trouble... and they did. The Crows came five years ago. They usually travel in pairs. However, this time the Society sent several of its most senior members."

"The Corvus?" Gavin whispered.

"Don't know." Violet got the impression that Lyall couldn't care less about the hierarchy in the Society of Crows. "Twenty Crows showed up, demanding that we take them to the mines. When we told them no, they burned down our school and crops and left. A little while later we learned that they blew up the mine and buried everyone inside."

Violet swallowed. "How many did they kill?"

"We don't know." Ellie pressed the words through tight lips. "We tried to break them out from the back entrance. But the fuckers blocked that one as well."

"There is no mine or cave to go to," Lyall said. "Just a large graveyard crawling with spirits."

Silence descended as the reality of what had happened to those poor people sank in. The Crows swooping in and murdering non-magical humans wasn't unheard of. It was one of their favorite ways to punish those that sought a way to escape the drafts. And of course, a stone that could hide potentially magical children from their grimy hands needed to be destroyed.

Had the miners even meant to look for god stones in the first place? Or had they stumbled across them by accident?

Mios' shoulders slumped, and he buried his face inside his palms. His frustration equaled Violet's own. For a night she'd held some hope. But if Mios knew where these stone caves were, it was likely that the Crows also had a similar map. Those other caves were likely long gone as well.

"So now that's out of the way, shall we play a throwing game?" Ellie pointed at the boards to the side. Clearly, she was trying to lift everyone's spirits. "They say lions have the best reflexes, but I bet I can kick your ass. Fair and square."

Mios laughed against his hands and let them fall away from his face, all devastation wiped clean off his features. "It will be like taking candy from a child."

"That's it, take that back. Whoever gets the most bullseyes out of five pays four gold coins to the winner."

Violet's beer stuck in her throat. Four coins for a knife throwing game? Surely no one would ever do that...

"All right, little wolf. No changing your mind once I've taken all your gold off you."

... apparently someone would. Damn those rich folk.

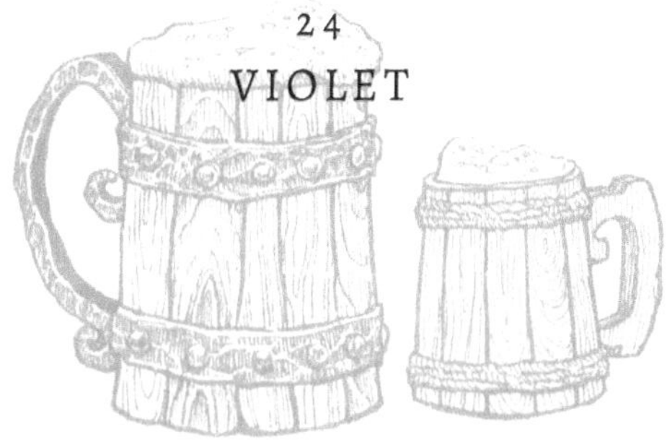

24
VIOLET

Ellie headed toward the boards and picked up a leather roll that held ten hand-sized blades. They played five rounds before Ellie had lost all her coin. While none of her knives hit the bullseye, Mios managed to get most of them and won every time. After her failure, they changed their bets to beer drinking. The wolf shifter downed an entire pint after each loss. By the tenth game, she was absolutely wasted. Ellie had transitioned from cocky to bartering away her services in an attempt to recover her gold. Violet had seen this kind of desperation only too often with gamblers when they'd lost everything.

"I'll be your guide to the cave if you still wanna go..." She hiccoughed and stabbed the table with one of the unused knives. "You need someone who knows the terrain!"

Lyall had made himself scarce once the game had begun. He probably wouldn't be happy to know that his daughter was trying to leave the pack for a random adventure across the Iron Kingdom.

"Let the alcohol wear off before you sell your soul away, little wolf," Mios said.

"Little? Have you seen me?"

"Ellie has a point," Gavin said, stepping to the table where the knives lay spread out. It was his turn to play.

"She's small to me." Mios shrugged. His pleased smile had the wolf grunting in displeasure, not that he was wrong. While Ellie must be at least six feet tall, the lion shifter was one of the largest men she'd ever seen.

"Are all lions as massive as you?" Violet asked after taking a healthy swig of her beer.

"Every race has their own unique strengths. But my family, the Lionborn, are larger than most other lion shifters."

The first throws were exhilarating as people from around the bar started hovering around their table. They were placing bets on whether the lion or the sorcerer would win. Were all these people exchanging money from hand to hand in a vicious cycle that left them all poor?

Violet hated gambling. It was exactly what had got her into this mess with Dargan. Her ancestors had bartered her life away. They'd paid a price for a soul that it wasn't theirs to give.

Still, she had to admit to herself that seeing Gavin fire that knife with a precision that few people possessed dried up her throat, regardless of how much ale she drank. She clenched her thighs together to ease the ache that built with each thump of the blade hitting the wood. It sounded awfully similar to the way their bed had hit the wall last night while he was inside her, his entire body touching her own. She swallowed and placed her cool fingers over her feverish chest, tracking his moves.

He was good at throwing knives. She hadn't seen him do it before. He preferred to use a short sword while training or in battle—or sometimes a long one, which worked well for his stature.

He was a much better shot than the wolf and had already beaten Mios in a couple of games. The two rich boys didn't seem to care about risking their coin. She wondered if she should remind Gavin that he was now a fugitive, and that his family's money was likely off limits, and his funds couldn't be so easily replenished.

He took a sip of his drink, licking away the foam that stuck to his upper lip with his thick tongue, and met her gaze across the table. "Are you going to keep staring from all the way over there, or are you going to join in?"

"I don't play with throwing knives. I aim, and I kill, you know that." She sauntered over to him, plucking the blade from his fingertips.

"You're always so serious. Why don't you let loose today? Have fun for a change and show us—show me—what you've got." His hand snaked around her waist, and he pulled her close enough that the heat of his body burned through her clothes. Meanwhile, the tip of his nose trailed a path of fire across her neck to her ear.

"Or maybe she's afraid to lose," Ellie said. She was leaning against the wine barrel beside the table. She hiccoughed loudly and half collapsed on a chair, letting her narrow chin rest on her arm. "Come on, show us what you've got!"

Perhaps she should relax a bit. Enjoy herself for a change. She placed the blade in Gavin's open palm and stepped away. "Fine, I'll bite. You get one game with me."

Gavin's knife cut through the air and lodged halfway in the white circle near the center of the board. Howls erupted in the background, and Ellie's ale spilled over the rim of her cup and on top of her shoes as she clapped. He turned around with an uninhibited smile. "You think you can best that?"

In her assembly, Violet had been the master of knife throwing. But no one here needed to know that. She reached for her weapon, testing the weight of the handle in her hand without breaking their gaze. "What would I get if I did?"

His eyes sparkled. "Name your price."

"What a rich man's thing to say... What if I wanted something that can't be purchased with gold?" She ignored Elliana's guffaw and Mios' laughter and dragged her fingers over his chest. She breathed around the butterflies that took flight in her stomach.

Gavin's hand rested on top of hers, squeezing lightly. "Now I'm really curious to know what it might be..."

She lifted herself on tiptoes, close enough for her mouth to touch the shell of his ear. "I want all of you."

"Lame! That can be bought with gold!" Ellie shouted, and laughter surged through the room.

Gavin held his breath, and his eyes lit up as he drank her in. He understood what she truly meant. It was his heart that she was after, fully and unconditionally. With a smile, she turned away from him. Her knife flew across the room with precise strength, hissing through the air before it embedded itself in the center. The force of the impact knocked Gavin's knife from where it was half-lodged near the center, and it clattered to the floor.

Bullseye.

She turned to him, her smile widening as the room erupted with cheers and howls. Ellie banged her fist on the table, and her chair wobbled on the uneven floor. "Look at that. She has your ass now!"

Gavin's cheeks were tinged red. He gingerly placed his empty pint on the surface in front of him. Then his arms coiled underneath her hips, and he lifted her up in one fluid motion before his pillowy lips found hers. She rejoiced in the intoxicating taste of his tongue, whimpering when he broke the kiss far too early. "I'm already yours, Violet."

According to their laws, he was. After last night, the spell that had been cast upon them had been cemented, linking their magic together. They would always be able to find each other from this point on.

"Get out of here, you two!" Mios pushed Gavin with

his massive boot, and he stumbled forward, his fingers digging into Violet's ass as he sought some balance.

"Stay and show us how wild magic-wielders can be." Ellie cackled at Mios' face, a croaky sound more reminiscent of an old woman than a young one. The ambiance of the tavern reminded Violet of how things had been in her assembly, once upon a time. Back when she'd thought she had friends, before they'd betrayed her and sold her to the Crows. But the wolves wouldn't betray each other like that. They weren't like the sorcerers she'd known.

In this cheerful, wide room, not even the sudden nip of the cold could distract her from her joy. The scent of cooked pork wafted through the air, mixing with the warmer scent of Gavin's skin. Still, she shivered as a current snaked up from beneath her feet as soon as Gavin placed her on the ground.

The feeling of eyes burning through her prickled at the back of her head. She craned her neck up and around, searching the room for its origin, freezing when she spotted a man by the front door. Everyone's movements seemed too slow, their voices drowned out by the ringing inside her ears.

The warmth in the air leached from the room little by little, sucked away by the chill of his turbulent magic. His long white hair billowed around his head with a gust of wind. The red cape that hung beneath his large, mangled wings matched the color of Luelle's tunic. An emissary of the Shadow God.

He walked into the tavern with the confidence of

someone who was invisible to the world. Much like the last two emissaries that had visited her, no one but her seemed to see him.

"He's found me." Violet's heart drummed in her ears. A breath seeped through her lips.

They always did. And they always brought a tempest along with them. She stumbled back, colliding with the table and ignoring the wetness of a spilled drink that drenched her pants.

"Who is that?" Gavin stopped when his gaze fell on the emissary. Violet could see it: the moment the haze of the masking spell these undying fucks cast upon people lifted from his expression.

"Cora Elder..." The man was now close enough to make out his features. He looked young and old at the same time. What could have been a beautiful face carved from alabaster had turned into a nightmare. Covered in hairline cracks, it resembled an evil porcelain doll. The awful picture was completed by the misty, humanoid shapes that hovered around him, weaving in and out of his inky aura.

His voice sounded both close and like it came from far away at the same time. As if he wasn't truly here, although he stood right amongst the shifters. "Your ancestor called upon Dargan, the God of Shadows, for a soul to be spared. The price of that soul will be paid with another of your bloodline. He has commanded me to tell you to abandon your foolish attempts to withhold what is owed to him—or he shall take you instead."

The God of Shadows must have known that she was near the god stones. Even though Luelle had only just visited her, he'd sent his scariest henchman.

Perhaps she'd given up on the Stone of Clemency too soon...

"Fuck," Mios exclaimed behind them. The dark emissary sneered and disappeared before their eyes, vanishing with a flash and leaving behind a faint trace of burned wood.

25
VIOLET

SHE COULDN'T TELL HOW MUCH TIME HAD PASSED SINCE THE emissary had come to deliver his message and she'd escaped back to the cabin. A trail of frost crept up the glass like tiny claws, closing in on the reflection of her face. The front door clicked shut, breaking the absolute silence that had surrounded her until now. Her heart jolted at the sound, and she jumped, half expecting to see the black-clad fae once more. Instead, she met Gavin's warm eyes, which trailed down her body as if she was an illusion and he expected her to disappear at any moment.

"You didn't wait for us," he scolded, but his voice lacked any heat. The worry etched into his face deepened at the sight of her.

She turned toward the window and the complete white-out that raged outside. Her jaw ached from clenching her teeth too hard, and a bitter taste clung to the back of her throat. The emissary appearing today in a busy tavern shouldn't have surprised her. It seemed like the bastards loved to make an entrance in a crowded place—after all, Luelle had done the same.

The emissary appeared to have been invisible to most of the people there, and it was unclear how many of the shifters had actually seen him. In fact, the only people who had seemed shocked by the Dark One's presence were Gavin and Mios. Violet had said nothing before storming out. Irrespective of the truth, it had felt like all of her secrets were out in the open for everyone to dissect. Anyone who hadn't been drunk enough to miss that something had happened, at least.

Besides, Mios was still a stranger to her and could betray her.

"I needed time to think." Violet pushed down the traces of ugly thoughts that threatened to consume her whole.

Gavin dusted the snow off the messy waves of his hair and shrugged off his coat before tossing it aside. He stepped over the puddle beneath him and headed toward her. "I was worried you'd left town in the middle of the storm."

What he didn't say was written all over him. He'd thought she'd taken off without him. A month ago, she would have done so without looking back.

Oh, how things had changed.

"What happened out there, Violet? Why was the Dark One after you?" He stepped closer. But the knot in her throat only grew thicker, her inability to speak a true sign that something was wrong.

The Dark Ones were fae that preyed on pieces of a being's soul. A nightmare turned flesh, they made the Sídhe look like benevolent magical beings. Rumor had it that they were descendants of Dargan himself. Fuck them all. With their dwindling numbers, it was rare to see a Dark One outside the Copper Kingdom, where they reigned, and had become somewhat of a myth.

She'd never feared his race, however creepy they were. But that would change from now on. "That was an emissary. The undying bastards of my nightmares."

"An emissary..." His face lost the last of its color. He was silent before pressing his hand against the wooden walls of the cabin. A warding spell left his tight lips, clicking into place like an orange shield.

Mios, who stood unmoving in the living area, cursed softly. "Are you a second-born child from a royal family?" His eyes rested on her with a molten gold intensity that made her squirm.

"Do I look royal to you?" she deadpanned. Mios shrugged, and she continued, "I'm not even a second born." She let her face drop into her open, sweaty palms with a sigh. "He wants the second magical child in my bloodline. I'm the first in many generations, and I guess he got tired of waiting for one to be born. So he wants my future child instead."

Except for the fire crackling in the fireplace, there was no sound. The worry in Gavin's expression morphed into understanding. Perhaps her actions from last night made sense to him now. Would he leave her, now that he knew she couldn't give him children?

It hurt all the more because he'd make an excellent father. If she wasn't such a selfish bitch, she would let him go. Alas, Violet wasn't the good person here, and she wanted him too much to push him away like she should.

She wouldn't hold it against him if he walked out that door, though. She'd be happy for him. She would be. Eventually.

"The emissary said he will take you instead if you continue to withhold what you owe him." Gavin paced around the room, tugging at the collar of his shirt.

"I won't have a child for him to take. So I guess my days are numbered…"

"Why do I feel like you're giving up?" Gavin stepped towards her, his wild eyes searching her face. "No, you're a fighter, Violet. You won't be leaving me here without trying to get out of this. We will find a way."

"The first emissary came to me that day in the Hulten lake, Gavin. For three years I've been searching for a way out. I was hopeful when Mios mentioned the god stones—but now we know the mine is destroyed."

"The cave isn't gone." Mios' deep tone had them both turning toward him. "The wolves could not get inside—and I'm not saying we should. We are close to it, though."

"Where is the entrance? Do you have a map?"

"Julius took almost everything I had. I always have some gold sewn into hidden pockets for safekeeping, so I have that left… But unfortunately, the map wasn't in there when they ambushed me. So it's gone."

"But you were betting in the tavern like you had a castle of gold at your disposal." She knew she was sidetracking the conversation, but it was a welcome reprieve from her current dilemma.

"I don't bet unless I'm positive I will win." He shrugged. "Either way, Ellie did say she would take us there."

She'd promised a lot of things to get back her gold, admittedly.

"We can head there after the storm settles," Gavin said with a reassuring nod. Was he trying to calm her— or himself? He reached for the curve of her hip. "And if we don't find any stones there, we can head south with Mios. If the Crows were so worried about that mining operation, there must be a few of them out there. I'm sure we'll find one for each of you."

"There must be others circulating around the rest of the kingdom as well," Mios agreed. "I refuse to give up so easily."

Hope bloomed in her chest, and the air seemed to flow more easily through her lungs, filling her body with renewed energy. They were right. There was no reason for her to lose hope before even trying. She had a lead, and if that made Dargan squirm, then all the better. Let him watch as she got close to a way to escape him.

"I was told one more emissary has to come before the god collects me..." She exhaled, feeling her resolve strengthen.

Gavin's smile mirrored her own, a tentative tilt of lips that was tainted with fear.

"We will leave here soon. Try to get some actual rest." Mios nodded, before he walked away down the corridor to his room.

"Mios..." Violet called from where she stood. The lion paused and turned slowly.

"Yes?"

"How were you able to see him?" As far as she knew, no one but her had ever seen the bastards every time they had appeared. Not even Cullen, who stuck around for a while.

"All of us with true royal blood can see the emissaries," he muttered, scrapping his hair back from his forehead with one wide hand. "I wasn't sure they would grant me the honor to see, let alone speak to one. Not after the Lionborn fell out of favor..."

"Oh."

"That was a scary bastard in there. I'm sorry it happened to you, Violet." He tilted his head toward Gavin with a softening expression. "And you."

VIOLET

It took three days for the storm to pass. They left Tulahn on a clear morning, as soon as the starry night had faded to golden hues with the first appearance of the sun's rays. Ellie awaited them by the stables, tightening a worn saddle over her white mare, a large beauty whose name Violet had forgotten. Mios had bought his own horse from a farmer in town. The man was only too happy to get rid of his eighteen-year-old beast and welcomed the ten pieces of gold that would feed his family for at least a week.

She'd almost choked on her breakfast when she'd heard about the ridiculous price he'd paid. No person in their right mind should spend that much on a walking, half-mummified animal that might not wake up in the morning.

Twenty-one, her mare, seemed ecstatic to be reunited with her. She trotted along the messy paths of weeds and over fallen branches with ease as they traveled deeper into the forest.

Violet had grown up in this part of the world. With each passing day, the area became more familiar. But as they descended from the Obsidian mountains, something else gnawed at her thoughts.

Without a map, she wasn't sure where they were headed. Was this cave close to her family's home? What if the humans that died in the mine were from her village? The further down they went, the more unease settled in the pit of her stomach.

Maybe her father had been desperate enough for gold and had become a miner? Even if he'd been a fisherman his entire life, it wasn't entirely out of the question.

Surely not. While not in as good a shape as Mios, Gavin—or even herself—both of her parents could provide for their family. She remembered that much.

The trail they rode on opened to a wide field near the bottom of the mountain. It might have been a quarry of sorts, although with the trees growing everywhere it was hard to discern. "Here we are," Ellie said, jumping off her mare. "We will have to leave the horses here, as they spook easily as we approach the mines. If yours are prone to wandering, you can tie them, but I recommend you let them lose. There are wild wolves that might make a snack out of them."

Heading for the entrance by foot slowed them down. And yet, having beasts near an area where Neems haunted the grounds wasn't a good idea either.

They followed the clear path humans had carved out of the wilderness to allow them easy access to the mouth of the cave. The road was overgrown, like the mountain had been trying to reclaim it since the Society of Crows incident.

Empty carriages lay everywhere, broken into pieces of sun-bleached wood and rusted axles. Their remains were the only thing that was left of the mine. Well, not the only thing. Violet's skin pebbled with the magic that lay dormant in this place, buzzing with a fierce energy.

"The main entrance was over there." Ellie pointed to where evergreen bushes hid it from view. "The second one is around that outcropping of the mountain. They were both blocked when we tried to get the miners out."

"This is all cursed." Gavin shook his head with a growing frown. "I doubt we would even make it inside. Even if we could go in, it doesn't mean we should. I feel like my magic is dulled—the stones are probably underneath this very mountain, making it so we can't use our magic fully."

His words rang true for her as well. It wasn't like she couldn't feel her power, but it wasn't as vibrant as it should be.

But Violet had to try, or getting away from Dargan would be impossible. She hated to agree with Gavin. He was right, though—going into the cave without the full power of her magic would be suicide. "So what, then? We just turn around and leave?"

Maybe she could stuff her pockets with dirt and hope for the best.

Mios popped a handful of nuts in his mouth and chewed slowly as he peered over the tall shrubs. "If there is an opening, I vote we check it out. Maybe we will find a few stones within easy reach."

How cute. She wouldn't have expected him to be a dreamer.

"Whatever." She grunted and strolled toward the bushes that hid the cave. "Gavin and I can inspect the one over here. You two can check the other around the back. We reconvene in this spot by midday. We don't want to camp in this place, as Neems tend to come out more at nighttime."

Not waiting for their answer, Violet headed down the path, only vaguely listening to the sound of Gavin and Mios' voices as they ironed out the details of her half-baked plan. Her heart drummed in her ears, a perfect companion to the twisting of her gut.

Gavin caught up with her by the bushes that separated the main road from the meadow where the cavern's entrance was. When he crouched next to her, the soft earth squelched underneath his feet. "Ellie said it will be best if we meet in the town's inn, just in case they don't make it back here in time."

The air was warmer this far down the mountain, no longer burning her nostrils with each breath she took. However, the coldness in her body remained. She moved the branches aside, and thorns pricked her fingers. A wide entrance appeared behind the greenery, exposing a tunnel blocked by enormous boulders that must have come down as the ceiling of the mine collapsed.

The anger that bubbled in her gut mixed with sorrow. What had the Crows done? They'd killed innocent people, buried them inside a cave with no chance of escape. And all because they'd wanted to keep stealing their children, unchallenged.

She would do anything in her power to get justice... She'd bury the Society under the weight of their own broken laws.

The shape of a man lingered at the bottom of the tunnel, standing still in front of the boulders, as if waiting for them to open. A haunted moan echoed through the meadow, and all the warmth inside her left Violet at once.

One lonely Neem shouldn't be too difficult to dispel, even if their magic was dull at best. The spell was simple. The angry spirits were pure energy which hung around the remains of their corpse. Like magic-wielders, they borrowed more energy and matter from their surroundings to create their physical form and to avoid fading away in exhaustion. She only had to borrow enough energy herself so that the spirit would vanish. A complication would only arise if there were too many Neems to handle.

Dry branches cracked under her clumsy feet, calling to the Neem that hovered inside the cave. Its head jolted up, and it moved toward them, floating over the ground in a way that turned her blood to ice. It had once been a dark-skinned male with tightly cropped hair. A burgundy trail of blood was smeared across its forehead and over its thick brows, pooling in its wide, empty gaze.

Her breath escaped her all at once, and the magic that hovered over her extended hand stuttered into nothingness. She knew his face well. She'd dreamed about him for years, longing for the day she would see him again. Her father's spirit stood perfectly still, as if listening out for anything that would show him his prey was nearby. Then, when nothing happened, he moved back to the boulders.

She waited in quiet horror, trying to regain her breath. Neems were the souls and bodies of those who'd died in horrible ways over sacred magical lands. Those who'd been murdered. While he was still hovering close enough, she could make out the curve of his wide nose—but his jovial smile and sharp mind were gone.

"Why is this one outside the cave?" Gavin's words barely registered, and she couldn't speak around the prickling in the back of her throat. "Do you think he was patrolling the mines, and the Crows killed him before they closed the entrance?"

Tears clouded her vision. Her parents had provided for their family for years with what the sea brought them. He'd prided himself on that and taught her gold was a fleeting thing. That knowledge was the truest kind of wealth someone could possess.

"We won't be able to investigate further with him

blocking the way," Gavin said, and readied himself to strike. Magic pricked her nose with its spicy scent. She wanted to tell him to stop, but found herself paralyzed by her distress.

A sob escaped her dry throat in a noise that was only too similar to the moans of the spirit. From the corner of her eye, she saw Gavin stiffen beside her, his face twisting with worry. "What's going on?"

"That's my—"

Her father cried out, his mouth wide, a horrid sound that made the hair on the nape of her neck stand on edge. He turned their way, called by their voices, and a snarl left his pale lips. The image of his large teeth, broken with decay, and his hollow expression would forever haunt her if she survived this entire mess. Her heart stopped as he rushed at them, hungry for a revenge that would never be satiated.

There was no sign of recognition in his eyes. He was angry and very dead. Maybe this was her punishment for trying to defy a god's will. Or for seeking vengeance and leaving Julius to die a slow death, when she could have made it a quick one.

Gavin's dissipating spell hit the spirit before a word could leave her lips. Her father's body collapsed onto the ground in a pile of skin and bones that evaporated into nothing.

"No!" Had that been her voice? It sounded so much like her, but not at all at the same time. A shape plummeted down from the trees above, landing on Gavin in a blur of black cloth and the silver flash of a blade.

Panic clutched Violet's gut, and she rushed over to where Gavin was grappling with his assailant. A boot collided with her stomach, and her fingers slipped off the handle of her own knife as the air was punched from her lungs.

The petite shape clung to him with long arms that wrapped across his shoulders. It hissed at the burn of his magic but refused to let go. The hood of a dark tunic covered the attacker's face. The fabric wasn't black, as Violet had assumed at first, but a deep burgundy shade.

The woman screamed, her voice shaking with anger and sorrow. She lifted her blade to drive it into Gavin, but Violet's spell hit her full force, sending her flying a few meters back into a dry bush.

Gavin jumped to his feet and stood at Violet's side. With a fluid motion, he pulled his short sword off of his belt. They didn't know if this woman was a Crow, waiting for someone like them to show up here. Or she might be a thief.

More likely the second, to judge by her lack of wrestling skill. Her attack had been passionate, but far from that of a trained warrior. Violet drew her knife and waited as the hood slipped from the woman's head, revealing long black hair.

She looked up, and Violet stilled when she noticed the color of her irises. Lavender, the same tone as her own—if not a touch lighter. A gift she had inherited from her father, a family trait that marked her as part of what had once been a powerful bloodline of magic-wielders. The very reason Dargan, God of Shadows, was chasing her.

There were only two people she knew in the world who had the same eyes as her. One had died outside this cave. The other was her sister. "Thalea?"

Gavin lowered his sword. To judge by the change in his expression, Violet got the impression he was putting the pieces of the puzzle together. "Your sister?"

Now that she wasn't moving like a shadow hunting for vengeance, Violet could spot the familiarity of the features she remembered so fondly. The small nose and thick lips that were so similar to her own.

Her sister's brows rose to the edge of her hair. "Violet?"

"In the flesh." She put her knife away, slipping it back inside its leather casing and walked with long steps toward where Thalea sat by the bush, offering her a hand. "Sorry if I hurt you. Though in all fairness, you were trying to kill us."

Her sister ignored her hand and rose to her feet by herself, dusting her pants off with an angry huff of air. She narrowed her eyes at Gavin. "This bastard killed Dad!"

"That was your father?" Gavin's voice shook, his face paling further. "Violet, I'm sorry…"

She raised her hand and Gavin stopped. "Don't pity me. I know well what Neems are."

"I'm not," he said with a harsher tone than she expected. "I feel with you."

"I haven't seen him in a long time." Violet shrugged

one shoulder, trying to brush off the weight of how much this hurt. Gavin drew closer with a sad tilt to his brows, yet he didn't touch her. Oddly, just the fact that he was near her was comforting.

"Well, it's great to know that twelve years are enough for you to not give a shit about him being killed." Thalea's whole body shook, and maybe she wasn't past attacking them yet.

"She cares," Gavin barked, taking a step forward and shielding her from her sister's murderous glare.

"You don't get to talk to me. You were the one who killed him."

"Neems aren't alive, Thalea," Violet said. "They're angry echoes of who our loved ones were, nothing more. Father would have slain you without hesitation. He tried to do the same to us just a moment ago. He would have killed us, had Gavin not dissipated him."

"No. He wouldn't." Her sister crossed her arms and glowered at them both. "I have been coming here for years now. He hasn't hurt me once."

Violet mirrored her sister's pose and lifted her chin. "Has he ever seen you?"

Thalea opened her mouth and then shut it. "It doesn't matter. I let him be. Why did you come back here to take that away? It was the last I had of him."

Violet's sorrow for what had just happened deepened. The numbness in her body increased. She hadn't known her father while she was an adult, and all this time she'd wondered what he would think of her. She didn't want anyone to see her fall apart either way. Not Thalea, not even Gavin.

"I know it feels like he was alive, because he lingered here. I assume he's been dead for a while?" Violet strode closer to her sister. Gods, she'd grown up so much. She hadn't seen her in twelve years. She was a young adult now, aged twenty. Violet's junior by only three years.

It didn't matter though. Looking at her like this, all she could see was the little girl who'd chased after the carriage, screaming for Violet to stay when the Crows had taken her away.

Thalea wiped her eyes with the back of her hand and bared her teeth. "Why are you here? Shouldn't you be in the Iron City?"

"Because—"

"Are you a deserter?" Thalea asked, and the calm mask that had fallen over her features obscured her intentions. Would she scream insults at Violet, much like everyone she'd considered a friend had done?

She could lie... But then, her relationship with Thalea would become tainted by that. "Yes."

"And who is this?" Her sister's lilac gaze landed on Gavin.

"This is Gavin, my husband." Violet swallowed past the flutters that awoke in her stomach. This was it. Her old life and her new one colliding in today's horrid events. The two most important people in Violet's world. Would Thalea have liked him, had they met under different circumstances? Violet moved closer to him, drawn like metal to a magnet.

"Hmm. I wish I could say it was a pleasure." Thalea looked Gavin up and down, and her scowl softened somewhat. "I guess you pass. At least in terms of looks."

"Wow, it seems the charming personality runs in the family," Gavin said, but he didn't appear happy. Where both her sister and herself were masters at masking their emotions, Gavin clearly was not.

Thalea's gaze flashed across Violet's shoulder toward the cave's entrance, then settled on her. "Dad always maintained that you'd be back one day. I wish he'd been alive to see you home. At last." She exhaled, and a warm, bubbly feeling took over Violet's body at her sister's tentative smile.

Then her sister crossed the distance that separated them and wrapped her in a tight hug. "Welcome home, Violet," she whispered in her ear.

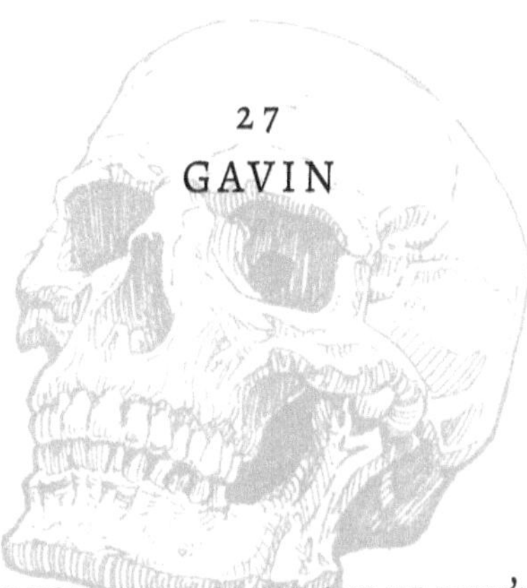

27
GAVIN

G UILT WAS AN UGLY FEELING, AND ONE HE DIDN'T EXPERIENCE often. He tried to swallow past the knot in his throat as the images of what had happened in the cave replayed in his mind. The spirit who'd come charging at them, and the light that dissipated from his vacant eyes when Gavin's spell had hit him full force.

They'd given Thalea Twenty-one to ride as they headed back to the coastal city of Sagewood. She'd mentioned that she enjoyed hiking up to the hills where the mine was at least once a month to speak to their father.

The horrifying reality of that statement lingered with Gavin for the better part of the three hours it took them to get to the town.

How lonely must she be? Why seek the company of an angry, murderous spirit instead of that of a living person? It also made him wonder how much education the non-magical people of the outer towns received on otherworldly creatures. Talking with a Neem wasn't only sad, but reckless. Her "father" would have killed her without a thought. Not that Neems had thoughts.

Violet had been suspiciously quiet as well, and the worry for her weighed on his chest. It clawed at his insides and was hard to shake. How would he act if something similar ever happened to him? He couldn't imagine.

"How are you really doing?" he probed, unable to stand the suffocating silence any longer. He gently wrapped his arms around her waist and tried to ignore the way his stomach clenched at the memories of her father's spirit, and what he had to do.

Violet's back curled forward, her shoulders hunching as if she couldn't keep her usual proud pose, and that alone wrecked him. "I'm fine." Lies. "I suspected I wouldn't ever see him again." She shrugged.

Her sister rode far away enough that it gave them the privacy they'd lacked around the shifters. "You know, it's a good thing to admit when you aren't feeling all right. You can't be strong all the time. I will lead by example." He cleared his throat. "I'm not fine, and I'm sorry."

"Why are you sorry?"

"Because I dissipated your dad's—Neem." His forehead scrunched as he replayed the awkward words in his mind, wishing he could take them back.

"I would have done the same, Gavin." Violet shook

her head and stared ahead, a sigh rippling through her shoulders. "He would've killed us all."

"Even if that's true, I'm sorry. Your turn."

But she didn't answer, and her body tensed under his arms. Maybe he shouldn't push this further. Perhaps a change of subject would help. "Do you think he would have liked me?"

"My father?" At his nod, she scoffed and looked back at him, a smirk almost breaking her serious expression. "No."

"No? But I'm very likable."

A grin. He would take that as a win.

"You would have had a hard time with him. He was the prickliest of us all."

Gavin hummed. This was working. The tense set of her shoulders had already eased. He dropped his nose to her neck, enjoying the way her skin reacted to his touch. The scent of warm vanilla that clung to her was intoxicating, mixing with the saltiness of the ocean air around them. "I got through to you, didn't I?"

"You barely did."

"True, but it doesn't change the fact that you let me in. Literally." At her surprised gasp, he chuckled. "I bet he would have warmed up to me eventually."

"You should stop betting. You're poor now." She batted his hand away from her hip, though the air lodging in her throat was enough of a signal that he had succeeded in his task. He'd distracted her, at least for a moment.

The buildings of a coastal city became visible

through the haze of the twilight. Behind the grayish rooftops, the shimmering ocean greeted the sky.

"I wish you'd had the chance to meet him when he was alive. I'm sure he would have loved you like I do." It was almost as if she whispered the words to herself and not for him to hear. His heart went into overdrive, regardless, making his pulse race.

Had she just admitted that she loved him?

One of his hands drifted over her stomach and settled on her hip bone. He cleared his throat. "I met the best part of him, in you," he whispered in her ear and felt the goosebumps which broke out over her neck and arms in response.

The trees changed in size and spacing, losing some of their thickness and vibrancy the further down they went. Winter was milder in this coastal town. The homes with thatched roofs and sun-bleached wood sidings squeezed tightly together. The hills lay at their back and a turquoise sea stretched out before them.

They crossed under a wooden archway, painted in blue tones and weathered by the unforgiving nature of salty air. The gold leaf that once had made the sign shine had cracked and come apart.

Gavin stared at the name he had seen for the first time when he'd accessed Violet's family records back in the Iron Kingdom. Sagewood. A town of fishermen—and, apparently, miners.

Thalea slowed down ahead of them and waited for them to catch up. "I bet it all looks different to you," she said, as if Gavin wasn't even there. Not that he could blame her for hating him right now. Not after what he'd done hours ago.

"There's no one out in the streets," Violet observed.

"The town has been struggling ever since the Crows sealed the mine. It's hard to keep a working city going when half of its population got wiped out." Thalea jumped off Twenty-one's back. She pointed at the lodge which stood tall next to them and dusted off the white fur that stuck to her black wool pants everywhere. "The inn is open, although you can always come home. Mom wouldn't mind it."

"I think we should stay here. It's been a while since she's seen me. Besides, I'm not alone."

"Ah, yes." Thalea's eyes were glazed with unshed tears as she looked at him. She forced a smile to her face. "Then why don't you join us for a meal tonight?"

"Tomorrow," Violet promised with a nod and slid off her horse. "We need to rest. I will see you both then."

"Don't tell mom you found me in the mines. Or that dad was there."

Violet tilted her head and nodded after a moment of silence. "All right."

The young woman hesitated where she stood. As if she thought that by turning around and leaving, she might cause Violet to disappear for good without another word. But eventually the silence grew so charged and uncomfortable that Thalea hugged Violet one last time and took off. His wife remained stiff throughout the embrace, her arms dangling limply at her sides, as if she didn't know what to do with them.

"You know, you can probably hug her back, right?" he said, once Thalea was gone.

"I'm not a hugger."

"You could have fooled me." His smile widened with her glare.

Seagulls mewed loudly above them, diving to pick at trash that littered the main road. The briny sea air carried the taste of seaweed. The winter breeze burned his cheeks and nostrils as he drew a deep breath, letting the horror of what had happened earlier that day wash away.

There weren't any people in the streets, even though the sun was still out and the weather was much more pleasant than it had been while they'd crossed the mountains. This felt like the wolf's village. Another town broken by the Crows.

A lone footman's steps interrupted them. The wooden flooring around the inn creaked beneath his feet as he walked over to them. Gavin gave him two gold coins for his trouble, and he promptly took their horses back to the stables behind the building.

"I thought I said you aren't rich anymore," Violet said as they trotted up the steps.

"Says who?"

"Me. You're now a fugitive of the law." She looked around as if a Crow would jump out of a dark corner to take them at any given moment. To be fair, they had no idea what had happened to the bounty hunters working with Julius back in Scoria. Whether they would continue their hunt was up in the air.

A problem for another day. "My family's funds aren't tied to any magical tracking. My parents made sure of that the moment I presented my healing gift. Because of our connections with the Crown, pockets of the money are protected and hidden throughout the kingdom." He tapped Violet's nose as he walked in front of her, rejoicing in the way her lips parted in shock. "Granted, I will need to find a larger city before too long to access it, but we should have enough to still pay people to feed our horses in the meantime."

He was thankful his parents couldn't track his whereabouts. After Julius' betrayal, Gavin wasn't sure who from his family's contacts to trust. It was safer for them if they just assumed he was dead... at least for now.

THEIR ROOM FACED THE BAY, AND THE GENTLE SLOSHING OF the waves crashing ashore in the distance welcomed them as they walked in. The cold winter breeze blew through the set of doors at the end, pushing his hair away from his face.

He closed the door behind him, and the tension in his shoulders eased. It was nice to be in a space where they could be on their own. Violet stood still, her stare fixed on him with an intensity that made him shift in his spot.

"Do you want to talk about what happ—?"

Her soft lips swallowed his words as she pinned him against the door. It was a demanding kiss that lit an instant fire in the center of his stomach. His desire pushed away any prior thought, flaring down to his groin and urging him to grab her.

She was the only woman that left him this hungry. That made him so hard he feared he might burst out of his clothes. The need to savor all of her flooded his mind.

He skimmed one hand down her body, over the curve of her breast, allowing it to settle in the center of her spine. He loved the play of her muscles underneath the fabric of her shirt. His other hand cradled the back of her neck as he devoured her lips. Her skin burned with a feverish heat. The nagging feeling that they needed to communicate about what had happened remained.

It was hard to forget his fear of losing her. What if she later decided she hadn't truly forgiven him? "H-hey." He pulled away between kisses. "We should talk."

"No. Talking." She pushed his coat off his shoulders and let her hands trace his pecs, making him tremble with need.

"But..."

"Gavin, I want you," she pleaded, still close enough that the warmth of her breath hit his well-kissed lips. "I need to feel good and make love to you without having to worry about everything else."

Damn, how could he deny her that?

She unlaced her white shirt, revealing the sheer layer of her chemise underneath which did little to hide her bare flesh. Then she pulled down her pants and stood naked—except for that delicious scrap of paper-thin fabric—in front of him.

Gavin's lips crashed into hers, and he was no longer holding back. Their tongues clashed in an urgent dance that took the desire that simmered under his skin and turned it into a raging fire. Violet dug her fingers into his hair as he picked her up swiftly, both hands beneath her ass. She wrapped her legs around his waist and kissed down the column of his throat.

He sat on the bed as she made swift work of removing his shirt and untied the strings of his pants. He let her ride him after. She smelled like everything he wanted, sweet, sexy, and his.

After a while, the intensity and need in her movements slowed as she looked him straight in the eye and dragged her finger over his jaw and mouth. His hands settled on the curve of her waist.

"I love you, Gavin," she said, and his heart thundered at her words. "I'm yours, angry and broken as I might be… for as long as I have."

"Shh," he whispered against her lips, swallowing the bitter taste of panic that flooded him. "No one is ever taking you from me."

She rolled her hips, and his cock slid deeper inside her. He took control of her movements, enjoying the warmth of her body as it received him.

They rocked into each other, again and again, until

the bed screeched over the floor, and hit the wall with soft thumps. Adrenaline pumped through his veins, and he burned with the need to touch every inch of her with his lips and tongue. Euphoria drove him to the brink. Her moans deepened as he flipped them over and pushed her into the mattress with more force. He kissed her soundly as she shivered underneath him. His pleasure almost brought him down as he struggled to not fall over the precipice.

But Violet didn't pull away when his rhythm stumbled. Nor did she push him away like she'd done the first time they'd made love. Her eyes blazed with defiance, but Gavin knew in the back of his heated mind that he couldn't come inside her. Even though he craved it like nothing else in this world.

He groaned, and his legs trembled as euphoria made his vision gray at the edges. He barely managed to pull out of her before his orgasm hit him and emptied himself over the apex of her thighs. That alone was hot enough that he wanted to do it again.

Then he collapsed on top of her.

"You're heavy." She grunted and attempted to push him away. He would not make it easy on her, either. Instead, he burrowed his nose in the crook of her neck and grinned against her skin when she squirmed under him. Who knew she would be so ticklish?

"I like it here. You aren't comfortable per se, but I enjoy being on top of you." His hands dragged over her sides, slipping under her hips and giving her ass a thorough squeeze. "I love these. I would love to try it from the back, next time."

She pushed him off her with all her might. "Who says there will be a next time?"

"Please," he huffed, a smile spreading over his face. "You jumped me at the door. I predict you'll be begging me to take you from behind later tonight."

"Shut up." She cuddled up next to him, and he enjoyed the peaceful quiet that followed. His body was tired and ached all over. It was almost shocking that he was still intact after the trip, Julius' betrayal, and the constant healing of others—and himself. Still, even though life had been far from easy as of late, there was nowhere else he'd rather be right now.

A sob broke through the distant thunder of the waves. Violet's shoulders were quaking as she finally gave in to her grief. His stomach clenched at the sound, and for a moment he wasn't sure what to do.

Then she drew closer to him, and it was enough of a signal that he enveloped her inside his arms, tracing soft patterns over her spine. "I'm sorry this happened," he repeated.

There were so many things he couldn't—wouldn't voice. Like all the things that had happened to her with her assembly, Julius, and her dad. But he wanted to say something—anything to make her feel better.

This time she didn't claim she was fine. Instead, she simply let him hold her until there were no more tears to shed.

"I drooled all over you," she said eventually, wiping her hands over the slobbery mess that was his chest.

He pulled her back into his embrace, then used his magic to pull the covers over them. "Do you want me to stay here while you meet with your family?"

Violet looked up at him from where she lay, her eyes still red and swollen. "Are you that afraid of facing Thalea and my mother?"

"I'd rather not have a knife thrown at me by another Elder." He shrugged. "I will come if you need me to. But I thought you might want some time alone with them. I can join you later on and get the awkward first meeting with the in-laws out of the way."

"It would be good to talk to them on my own. I haven't seen them in twelve years..." She sounded anything but happy about the prospect.

He dropped a kiss on her head. "They already love you."

"You say that because you are too nice."

"I love you as well. Just thought you should hear it from me."

"I know."

VIOLET

EVEN IN ITS CURRENT STATE OF DECAY, SAGEWOOD WAS THE most beautiful place she had ever been. On one side, the tar-colored rock shores met the striking waters of the Leona Sea. On the other, the tall mountains of Obsidian rose high like ribbons of trees and snow, obscured by the mist.

She fixed the collar of her coat, confident that it covered most of her skin, and tapped her boots against the board of the inn's entrance. The rhythm matched that of her quickened heartbeat. Gavin had insisted on walking with her to her family's home. He would explore the town and discover a way out of here by boat while she spoke to her family.

He was taking his sweet time getting ready. Did he really have to ask if the shifters had arrived last night? They couldn't be far. While the caves had been danger-ous, it seemed that Ellie knew what she was getting herself into... even if she had let herself get roped into this adventure while drunk.

Her nerves made her extra jumpy. Every creak or howl of the wind increased the crawling sensation over her skin. The early morning sun was peeking over the horizon. Violet adjusted her scarf over her head for what had to be the eleventh time and hoped it hid most of her features from anyone hunting for an out-of-place sorceress.

"They didn't come here last night." Gavin's voice made her jump. She assumed a defensive pose and pulled her blade from the belt that crossed diagonally between her breasts. "Woah." He chuckled, lifting both hands either side of his head. "It's just me, love. Are you feeling anxious?"

"I want to get this over with." The ache in her chest hadn't subsided. With each passing moment, it embedded itself deeper in her heart, making it hard to breathe around the image of her father's death. "I know you're worried about the shifters, but they both look tougher than you and I. They probably camped some-where overnight to avoid traveling while it was dark."

"Yeah... Neems do tend to come out at dusk." He scratched the back of his neck. "Should we call for the horses?"

"No. I'd prefer to walk there." She cleared her throat and softened her voice. "I haven't been here for a long time. I want to see what's changed."

She peered over Gavin's shoulder as she spotted several riders arriving at the front of the inn. Three men were handing their tack to the footman that Gavin and her had met last night. They wore black tunics with rich, furry lapels, a rare sight in this part of the world as it never usually got that cold. It could only mean they'd traveled here from far away.

Adrenaline rushed through her veins, warming her body just as Gavin's hand draped over her arms and he pushed her against the facade of the building. His lips devoured hers in a hungry, yet stiff kiss.

She wrapped her hands around his neck, swooning with the tender caresses of his tongue. He placed his arm over her head, invading her senses with his scent and the warmth of his body.

Someone was hovering nearby, casting a shadow over them. Gavin pulled away from her and shifted so that the bulk of his body shielded her from view. "May I help you?" he said, his voice ringing deep. He was shielding his face with his extended arm.

"You and your woman are blocking the bulletin board." She didn't like the sound of the man's voice. It had a slimy quality to it.

"It seems to me we've left you enough space, since there's nothing there to see. Move along."

Violet brought her hand down Gavin's torso and clutched the hilt of his sword, her heart pounding harder now, sweat prickling against her skin. Meanwhile, the other men were already climbing up the steps to the inn.

"Hilbert, why are you bugging these two? We aren't looking for a couple or trouble." The laughter of the second man gnawed at her nerves. She slid the blade from its sheath. Slowly.

"Of course." The man's eyes burned through her scarf as he joined the others, and they wandered into the inn.

Gavin's warm breath didn't move away from her face. The spicy scent of magic hung in the air. "Bounty hunters," he whispered.

"Why are they in the area?" She could feel him, still tense under her hand, although the men were out of sight.

"They travel around the kingdom to find work. A small group together like this is common. We have to be careful because it's only a matter of time before we are the ones being hunted. We must leave soon."

"Surely we can stay for a week or two?" she protested in a low voice. "I just found my sister. I need to understand what happened to my father. Make sure she's doing fine."

He clenched his jaw and backed away, pulling her with him down the steps and toward the street. She glanced at the bulletin board and the few papers pinned to it. Not enough to draw at least four bounty hunters. They were after someone, all right. She could only hope it wasn't them.

"Let's see your family, then we can find Ellie and Mios. I left a message with the innkeeper for them to meet us in the tavern for drinks." Gavin raked his fingers through his hair. "The army should have kept your records sealed. I should've been the only one able to access them. However, Julius clearly did as well. So we have to assume the Crows will send their people here, too."

Fuck. She hadn't thought about the Society for a while, but what Gavin said made sense. "We don't know how many bounty hunters Julius hired to get me. There were three with him when he took you. Did you recognize anyone here?"

"No. These weren't the same men. But that doesn't mean they won't come. Since Julius is dead, it's possible they'd continue to hunt us, hoping to sell us to the Crows back in the Iron City."

They rushed down the cobbled streets, which were poorly maintained. Any attempts to patch them up had already worn away, leaving behind large potholes that would prevent a carriage from going over them. The sea breeze grew stronger as they approached the coast.

Violet wished she could enjoy the salt in the air, and the way it made her battered heart flutter with a sense of belonging. But even here, everything had been tainted by the Crows.

Her childhood home appeared out of a layer of mist. It stood slightly away from the rest of the town, with its closest neighbors belonging to other fisher families. Her parents had whitewashed the wooden house with ivory stucco, but its facade was now cracked. A seafoam-green door that had seen better days hung crookedly in its frame, beaten down by the unforgiving conditions of this place. "That's the one."

"It's secluded," Gavin commented, looking around

the space. He wasn't wrong. While it was in a less affluent part of town, her family had owned this plot for generations. A piece of the beach and sea. The dilapidated front yard was new. Violet fondly remembered how her mother had taken great pride in her flowerbeds. But it didn't seem like there had been any flowers here for a while.

They walked past a few small boats which rested on the black sand in various states of disrepair.

"A fisherman's family. It makes sense now why you were so good at rescuing Elina that afternoon in the Hulten lake." His tone was infused with a healthy dose of awe.

"I thought you read my records. Didn't they go into my family's background?"

His cheeks bloomed red, and he cleared his throat, tapping his hand against his thigh. "I paged through it. It mentioned nothing about this. It just said that…"

"What?"

"Never mind. It's not important." He shook his head and earned himself a narrow-eyed glare.

Violet knocked on the door. Her fingertips felt cold and sweaty with anticipation. The air stuck in her throat when a skeleton opened. It took her a moment of panic to realize that the woman standing in front of her with a tentative grin was her mother.

29

VIOLET

Skin and bones. Unlike anything Violet had ever seen before. Her mother's mouth split into a wide smile as she recognized her. "Cora. I never thought I would see you again. I dreamed you'd be back." Her mom swung the door open and wrapped her in what should have been one of her signature, bone-crushing hugs—except that it lacked its normal energy.

Her eyes were filled with tears when she withdrew a little to take Violet in. "You look well. So beautiful."

"Thanks." She swallowed past the awkwardness settling in her stomach and held her mother close. The familiar scent of daisies washed over her, reminding her of the strong woman in her memories.

"And who is this?" She stepped back fully, giving them a clear view of the living area, and pulled her into the house with surprising strength.

"I'm her husband, Gavin."

"Husband?" Her mother's eyes widened as she

studied Gavin, and her smile became positively feline. "More to celebrate then."

Celebrate? No, there was little to be happy about here—other than being able to see her, Thalea, and to have Gavin by her side. Everything else was a wreck.

Her childhood home hadn't changed since she'd last been here. The same eggshell walls and wide wooden floorboards that creaked under her every step. Her father used to tell the story of how her mother and him had collected driftwood that washed in from the ocean and rebuilt parts of the house with it. It was all gray and smoothed down like a river stone.

The sea breeze howled past an open window at the side of the room.

"I'm sure you recognize little, Cora. I tried to keep it the same, just in case you ever came back. Is it still home to you?" Her mother's smile was as brittle as her appearance, and it ached too much to continue looking at her. It was too obvious that her days were numbered.

"Yes... I remember it all." Violet traced her fingers over the rough fabric of the side chair and shook herself out of the heavy feelings of belonging. Any happiness got squashed the instant she remembered that her father was missing.

"You came just in time for breakfast." Thalea's chipper tone sounded so different compared to yesterday. Was it an act? Now that she could see the state of her mother's health, Violet understood why Thalea would ask her not to mention the situation at the mine.

Her sister walked around the kitchen, wearing a

pretty, yet simple, blue dress, cinched with a corset. She held a steaming bowl of rice. "I caught fish for our meal. I'm happy you came early."

"We are meeting up with friends that are traveling with us, later. We need to find a ship to get out of this place. We were hoping you might be able to recommend someone."

"No... You only just got here." Her mother frowned. "You're already thinking of leaving?"

"We saw bounty hunters in town," Violet said, fidgeting. She was still waiting for her mother to realize she was a deserter and throw her out of here. Any moment now.

"If that's the case, then they won't come this way. You don't remember, dear, but no one ever comes to this place. It's going to be fine here."

Thalea dropped the dish towel into the cast-iron basin by the kitchen and looked away with a shimmer of tears in her eyes. She was clearly holding something back.

"We can't count on that. It will put you two in danger as well."

"Nah! We will be great! Let's have some food and not talk about doom and gloom. I want to know about the wedding." Her mother held on to the back of one of the dining chairs, most likely feeling too weak to stand without help. When had she become so frail? Would Violet see her again once they'd left?

Gavin's hand reached for hers and squeezed. He'd

watched every movement her mother made, and his frown only unsettled Violet further.

"The bounty hunters are looking for someone," she said to Thalea. "If it turns out it's me, and they've followed us here, then you take mother out of her bedroom window, all right? And don't look back."

Thalea sat down, her brows pinched together. "Wow, you are serious."

"Deadly."

"Then you know I can't leave you behind."

"They aren't here for either of you, but they will do harm to you in order to hurt me."

"If it comes to it, we can fight a group of bounty hunters so long as we know you two are okay," Gavin added, taking a seat next to her mother.

They served themselves, filling their plates with rice and fish in a charged silence. There was blackberry wine, too—a welcome balm to her frayed nerves. She wasn't usually one to drink alcohol so early, but on a day like today, she needed it.

"How many bounty hunters did you see?"

"Four," Gavin said. "Maybe five."

"Hmm. This isn't what I had imagined. Maybe we should change the subject?" Thalea cleared her throat, glancing around the table before taking a bite of her aromatic fish. "Father would have liked to be here to see you."

It wasn't how Violet had envisioned her return, either.

"Let's not talk about him right now." Her mother's

tense shoulders gave away her distress, although she tried to keep up a chipper tone.

"Mom, Violet hasn't seen either of us in over a decade."

Except that Violet had seen both Thalea and her father yesterday. If only she could forget the memory. But it was engraved in her mind.

"Where is he?" she asked.

The silence extended for longer than was comfortable, and her mother's eyes glazed before she spoke. "He died in the mines five years ago. Along with most of the town's young men." She took a tentative, far too small bite and chewed as if it tasted like chalk instead of buttery, salted fish.

"It has been just Lea and I for a while now. We are fine."

Ha! Her mother was a terrible actress. But Violet refused to let the lie fester further, and her need for answers trumped even the worry of being tracked down here. "Why was he working in the mines? He loved fishing and was proud of how you two supported our family."

"I don't want to talk about this!" her mother exclaimed. "What happened to your father is a tragedy we should've avoided. I wish not to be reminded of it at every turn."

Her bony grip tightened around the fork, and her now ill-fitting wedding band moved up her finger, clinking against the cup of wine in her other hand.

"I've been gone, but I remember him and who he

was," Violet insisted and looked at Thalea. She wanted to get the information that would fill the gaps in her knowledge. Her sister held her fork in the air, a bite of white fish flaking off it, but she said nothing.

Her mother shot from her seat like it was on fire and shuffled around the small kitchen table with a full plate of food still in her hands. Then she dropped it into the basin of dirty dishes.

"Mom, please leave that alone." Thalea's clenched jaw distorted her words. Was it the topic of conversation that had upset her, or the waste of a good meal?

Her mother's affectionate smile returned just as quickly, pulling up the folds of loose skin on her gaunt face but never reaching her empty gaze. "This day has wrung me dry!" She laughed, wrapping one arm across her stomach. "It was such a pleasure meeting you, Gavin. You're so handsome! I can't wait to hear about the wedding... I'm so tired now, though. I will retire to my room."

"You flatter me, Ms. Elder." Gavin's expression remained pleasant. The only thing that gave away his discomfort was the whitening of his knuckles as he pressed his hands against the table.

"Please, call me Cora, and before you ask. Yes, we do have the same name." Her mother's coffee-colored eyes met Violet's, softened with hope. "I quite like that we share that, every time someone called me by it, it reminded me of you. It's a connection that I cherish."

What on earth was she meant to say to that? What was this—another one of life's cruel jokes? She squirmed in her chair, feeling panic grip her anew. Gavin's polite smile spread across his face. Such a brilliant actor. And she'd thought him unable to mask his emotions before?

Both her mother and sister wanted to stay in this distorted reality, a broken pair hiding behind falsehoods. Violet knew she was bitter and angry—but she'd rather be that than lie to herself and pretend everything was all right when it was falling apart right in front of her face.

"Wait." She stumbled out of her seat, attempting to follow her mother, but Gavin grabbed her by the wrist.

"Not now," her mother said. "Tomorrow, we can talk some more then–if you don't want to stay in the inn, your room is still there." And she shuffled down the corridor, the soles of her shoes rasping across the rough wooden floors.

"Why did you hold me back?" Violet muttered under her breath. "I would very much like some answers."

"And I believe you're owed them, but I don't think that Cora can give us any in her current state." He frowned at her sister. "How long has your mother been starving herself? She is so badly nourished and sick. I doubt she'll make it a month if something doesn't change."

"I know that!" Thalea pushed away her own plate and grabbed the carafe of wine that stood in the middle of the table. "Who gave you the right to say anything about this either way?"

"Well, as your mother pointed out, I'm your family now. And I care about Violet. Even though there are bounty hunters in town, she came to see you. So you can drag it out and put us all in further danger, or you can tell us—why was your father in that mine? Why were you there? It's been years since he died."

Thalea paused with the cup touching her lips, her nostrils flaring. Her complexion had turned ashen with guilt. "Mom is living in this fantasy world that makes her feel less dead inside. She sleeps a lot, and I prefer for her to be happy instead of being angry or sad all the time. I have forced her to eat, and it didn't end up well. The last time I've successfully made her eat, she got so sick, she almost died. We've all been a mess since the Crows killed dad."

"I understand it's hard, maybe she needs to be hospitalized in a larger city, with magical healers. If she doesn't eat something, she won't live for much longer." Gavin's voice didn't waver, and his expression was stern yet remorseful.

Her sister wine spilled over her long, trembling fingers. "Last time I took her to the healer we used up the last of their savings. I don't have more gold to take her."

"At least you know people might show up searching for me here," Violet said. "My record has this place as my birthplace. It should've been sealed from anyone who isn't my family, but it's not." She leaned across the table and pushed past her own fear. "Gavin and I have to leave, which means we won't be able to help you—not unless you come with us."

A forced laugh flew from Thalea's full mouth. "Mom can only walk from her bedroom to here. We have no money left, and since I'm the only one working, I barely sell any fish. You know how people in this town feel about me."

Surely things had changed? It had been over a decade. There was no way the township still treated Thalea like she was a walking mad child.

"What do you mean, they won't buy from you?" Gavin's frown deepened. "Why not?"

"Because they think I'm crazy, all right? Or that I'm haunted by evil, or that I deal in black magic. They fear me or they hate me. You take your pick."

"You can do magic?" Gavin raised his eyebrows before he reached for his blackberry wine and drained the glass in one gulp. She couldn't blame him for only focusing on that aspect of her sister's words. Not when it was also all her simple mind heard.

"No, of course not. They've mocked me since I was little. I used to talk to my imaginary friends. Mom and Dad urged me to stop, to avoid any backlash from the people in town." Thalea shrugged.

The silence that followed was absolute. It settled heavily in the room, and a bitter taste built at the back of Violet's throat.

"Why was Father in the mines?" she asked for the second time this morning. Thalea pressed her palm to her chest, right over her heart. The movement called attention to the necklace that shimmered against her skin, half hidden beneath the folds of her dress. The glint of a dark gem peeked past the edge of the fabric. "Is that—Thalea, is that a god stone?"

"He was determined to get a magical stone for me. He assured me it wasn't because he was ashamed of my broken mind. He believed the Crows would take me, just like they did you."

Luelle's warning settled like a pile of rocks in her stomach. "Violet, you have been betrayed and betrothed, and you will escape Dargan's claim over you by the end of this journey, but it won't be what you hope for. You can find a way back to her in the old libraries of the world."

The room spun around her. She sank into her chair again, her knees weak with the news. If Violet's father had given her sister a god stone five years ago because he suspected she was a sorceress, that would mean Dargan hadn't been able to sense her.

Thalea was the second magical-born from her bloodline. The child promised to Dargan. Except that Violet would rather die than let that bastard take her sister with him.

"I told him I didn't need it because I can't use magic like you." Her eyes shimmered with tears. "It was the same as it has always been. The spirits visit me sometimes, mostly at night."

"That's what you meant by saying Father'd never hurt you. You were in the mines because you could talk to him, even though he was a Neem?" Gavin's skin had turned as white as the wall behind him. "I think I'm going to be sick."

"Father wasn't working there when he got killed. He bought my necklace from a miner weeks before the incident." Thalea wrung her hands, swallowing as tears streamed down her face. "I didn't know about the necklace then."

"Why was he there, then?" Violet's sore throat where a signal of her undoing. For once, she didn't wipe the tears away. No point hiding how all this broke her every bit as much as it did Thalea.

"The week the Crows sealed the mine, so many spirits visited our house. I must have been their only hope to communicate with their loved ones one last time. All the miners who perished right after the collapse requested my help. And I was so frazzled by the news, and was feeling so guilty that I still had my father when so many had lost theirs..."

"So I went to a few people and told them what the spirits had said to me. Some of the families were thankful, others too sad to even see me. Then there was one that hated me for it."

She sighed, brushing down her cheeks. "A few Crows stayed behind to make sure no one tried to open the cave back up. One family must have told them about what I did." She slumped forward, her chin wobbling. "They told me if I didn't show them my magic, they would kill Mom and Dad, and... I really tried to do what they asked of me."

"But they killed him." Violet felt hollowed out. Empty. Where was her anger when she needed it?

"I told them I might be a medium, able to see and talk to spirits but not able to do magic. They came here, and there were no Neems or ghosts to show them my gift—so they took us all to the mines. No spirit appeared there either. They hurt Mom and Dad so much... They must have known I couldn't do what they demanded.

"One of them killed Dad. Right where you found him yesterday. I'm so sorry, Violet. You have every right to hate me because I know it was my fault. I really tried to do something."

"It's not on you, Lea. What happened then?"

"They left. Father's spirit told me about the necklace afterwards. He'd hidden the necklace under my mattress. It was his way of shielding me from the spirits that used to visit me while I was in bed. I guessed it'd work."

"Did he speak to you when he was a Neem?"

"Yes, but it wasn't like when he was alive. It's different, they are jaded and come in and out of conscious thoughts. He did make me promise to never take the necklace off. He insisted the Crows would come back for me." Thalea pulled out the shiny green stone from underneath her simple dress. It caught the candlelight, casting a rainbow of colors on the table, and Violet's breath stuttered in her throat.

Right there was the key to her freedom. It would be so easy to reach out and take it from Thalea's hands.

The magic of the artifact buzzed like a void, distorting the air around it.

"Do you need this to escape the Crows?" Thalea moved to pull the necklace off her neck.

"No!" Violet launched herself across the table, sending food flying everywhere. "Never take that off!"

Thalea withdrew, her face twisting with shock and fear. "W-why not? When I go to the mines to talk with Dad, I've been removing it. I still have no magic. I feel nothing."

"You have magic, Thalea," Gavin said gently. "You have spoken to spirits, many times. That's not common."

"I have been able to do that since I can remember. Violet knows this. Yet when the Crows took her to join the army, they left me here. They didn't see any magic in me, not then—and not when they killed Dad."

"It's not the Society that's the problem," Violet blurted out. She sat back down, dusting the mess of food off her clothes. "One of our ancestors promised the God of Shadows the second magical-born of our bloodline. And if you have been speaking with spirits all this time—that's you."

"How do you know that?" Her sister rose and began to pace around the room.

"He's sent three of his emissaries to me, claiming that he owns my future child."

Thalea paused, twisting her hands together as she stared at the flames in the wood-stove. Then she burst out laughing. Gavin and Violet exchanged puzzled looks. "That's funny," she said. "You almost had me."

"Thalea…"

"No, don't mock me. I will take it from this town, but not from you." She trembled, and yet she stood taller, lifting her chin just like Violet did whenever she was feeling especially insecure. "I'm not magical, and my foolish attempt to pretend I was special, even for a second, was what got our dad killed."

"I would never tease you about this." They stared at each other for a long moment. Violet could have screamed at the top of her lungs about how unfair life was. The three people she loved the most were all inside this home, but she couldn't keep them safe. Her mother was only a shell of who she'd once been, and her father was dead.

Fate really had a way of knocking you down when you were already on the floor weeping.

"Do you still want me to come with you?" Thalea sniffed. "Even though I'm to blame for our father's demise?"

"If anyone is at fault, it's that bastard that sold you to the Crows five years ago. I wish I had more time." She'd show them what it meant to mess with the Elders. Slowly and painfully. "Do you know who it was?"

"Violet…"

"Theodore Nils," Thalea said, ignoring Gavin.

"We can't hunt this man when bounty hunters are all over Sagewood looking for you, love," Gavin insisted. "Even if we found him, we have to keep a low profile before we take off."

Gavin would always be the voice of reason. Unlike her, he didn't act first and think later. Violet had always found it easier to ask for forgiveness than permission. Clenching her fists, she exhaled through gritted teeth.

She knew what her impulsive actions had brought about before, on their wedding day. While she wanted revenge for her father, she also loved Gavin, and he'd already lost his family because of her. "You're right," she said. "I won't go hunting for Theo Nils."

They were a team, after all.

30
VIOLET

IT WAS COMMON KNOWLEDGE THAT THE SMUGGLERS THAT helped deserters out of the kingdom came to taverns at odd times. This was to avoid the watchful spies who worked for the Society of Crows.

Gavin, Thalea, and Violet arrived in the center of town before midday, leaving her mother at home sleeping.

Apart from the usual group of drunks at the far end of the room, it was just them. They found a place at the very back, away from the prying eyes of the bartender and the hairy old man who was tending the tables.

Gavin swung his coat over the hooks on the wall and rolled up his shirtsleeves, exposing his toned arms. "I'm going to get us something to drink. Do you want tea?"

"Yes," Violet replied, settling in one of the rickety chairs and searching the place for a potential threat.

"And you, Thalea?"

"I don't need anything," her sister said.

While Violet and Gavin had been on edge the entire way here, expecting a bounty hunter to jump out from every corner, Thalea had been asking questions about the Iron City and their journey here. But as soon as they entered the bar, she had lost all her words.

"You look like a rabbit caught in a viper's den." Violet dropped her hand over Thalea's and squeezed hard enough that her sister's wide eyes rose to meet hers. "Is everything all right?"

"I just don't come out very often. And last time I came here, it was a bit... unpleasant."

"How so?"

"I rarely get to speak to any people my age, and I'm awkward on the best day."

Well, that sounded pathetic. It almost made Violet want to slap her sister out of it. "Don't talk like that. Sit straighter. Bad individuals can smell how insecure you are from a mile away. It draws them in. You need to look confident to warn them off."

Why had her parents allowed her to become such a bundle of nerves and insecurities? Jumpy and ill-at ease inside her skin.

"I... I don't know how to do that."

"Lea, believe in yourself and how amazing you are. Even with what you perceive as weaknesses. Don't let anyone tell you otherwise."

"It's easy for you to say that. You don't have an ounce of insecurity within you. You've always been so confident."

Was she that good at fooling everyone? A laugh escaped Violet's lips. If only Gavin had returned with their drinks already. Instead of tea, she needed good whiskey to deal with this kind of conversation.

"Like everyone, I'm confident in myself when it comes to some things... but I struggle with others. I also push people away. Gavin has been teaching me how to stop doing that."

"I still don't like him, but he seems nice."

"Lies." Violet tightened her hand around Thalea's. "We don't have your ability to speak with spirits. Father's Neem would have killed us had Gavin not dissipated him, you know that, right?"

Her sister hung her head, hiding the sorrow painted in her features. "Do I? It's hard for me to let go of what my imagination tells me is real and to distinguish what's not, sometimes."

"Your gift with the spirits is not your imagination. Our parents should have known better than to let you believe that. Father did know better, I'm not sure why he didn't tell you."

"Because he thought I couldn't handle it." Her sister was quiet for a while, rasping her nails over the rough texture of the table. "Enough about me. Tell me about how you two met?"

"Gavin and I?" Thalea nodded, and Violet took a deep breath. How safe was it to go over all their history, out here in the open? "We met in the army. I used to see him from time to time, although we were in different assemblies."

"I bet you thought he was handsome."

"Well, yes. He wasn't my type." Or so she'd kept telling herself. "Either way, a couple of months ago, I confided in the wrong people. I was planning on leaving the Iron City because of what I told you back at the house."

"About Dargan?"

"Shh. Either way. Those bitches ratted me out, and the Crows matched us not long after."

Thalea seemed to mull it over, biting her thumbnail while staring at the bar, where Gavin was chatting to the bartender with a pleasant smile and deep dimples. "Well, if that's who you get matched to if you're in the army, it doesn't seem that bad."

"It's not like that all the time. I got lucky."

"I'd say so."

Violet smiled. "He got lucky too."

"Sure..." Her sister shrugged dismissively, then chuckled at Violet's open-mouthed glare. "I'm teasing you. Of course he did, but the better question is, do you love him?"

Her fingertips prickled with awakened nerves. The big words hung in between them. "I do, very much."

Thalea's lips turned into a warm, yet sad smile. "Then you should take the stone. I have no one but you and Mom."

Violet reached for thalea's other hand and it reached towards the silver chain that hung from her neck. "Don't take that off. Your life is far more valuable than mine, Lea."

"That's not true. No one wants to be with me, not even Mom. I weird everyone out."

"You've been hanging around where the dead rest, going to talk to them instead of heading here, where the living are."

Thalea pressed her lips together and crossed her arms. "That's unfair. Last time I was here, someone threw a drink at me and laughed as I tried to leave. You wouldn't come back if that had happened to you."

"Fair point." And the anger surging through her demanded that she show whoever had done that to Thalea a lesson. "Who did it?"

"You don't know Carter or Linus..."

Violet hummed and reached for her well-worn boot, and pulled out of it a small knife the size of her palm. She unwrapped the leather binding from it and revealed a polished handle and a sharp point.

She had borrowed it from the shifter tavern right before they left Tulahn. She doubted any of the shifters would miss it.

"Next time a cock like that does anything of the sort, you stab him with this knife, right in here." Violet poked Thalea right in the spot where the shoulder met the arm.

Thalea hesitated, but picked the knife from the table, examining it with a frown. "I'm not sure I can kill someone just for not liking me."

"You won't. It's small enough it won't hurt them that bad... that is, unless you stab them in the face."

"It seems rather aggressive..."

"Please. With the bounty hunters in town, it will make me feel better if you had it."

"All right."

"Hide it inside one of your boots. That way no one can see it," Violet said, and her throat closed in as she remembered her father gifting her the knife she used to escape her fate in the Iron City. That seemed like such a long time ago. Now he was gone, and so was that knife.

The sound of the swinging doors to the tavern opening made them turn around. A group of people entered, mere silhouettes against the bright daylight. Which reminded her...

"When Mios and Ellie get here, don't mention our father's Neem, or that you were there," Violet whispered, so low that she wasn't sure Thalea had heard her for a moment.

"I wasn't planning on it." Her sister looked at her with curiosity. "Why—aren't they your friends?"

"They are. However, Mios is also looking for a god stone. While I want to trust him, new as that is for me, I don't need him to get any ideas to take it from you."

They both tracked Gavin as he made his way over to their table, holding a tray with three clay cups. He placed them down and handed Thalea the one full of water, then gave Violet her own, filled to the brim with tea. "There are a lot of people here, given the time of the day."

Violet reached for her cup, bringing it to her lips. She took a big gulp as she turned toward the entrance to count the group. Five—no, six—men. They were locals, to judge by their old clothes, dressed like people who lived by the sea.

The leader of the gang was strangely familiar. Blond ringlets fell over his golden skin, right over bright blue eyes. He was the tallest of the group, and looked out over the patrons with a haughty air. Until he found her.

A grin split his face in two, revealing the yellowing teeth of someone who chewed too much tobacco. He appeared to have discovered a prize, and that made her stomach sink. Out of the corner of her eye, she saw her sister tense—another bad sign.

The man strolled toward their table with the confidence of a person who had five other men tailing after him.

"What do we have here? Crazy Lea. I thought I'd told you not to come back."

"Watch what you're saying, boy," Gavin said, as Violet shifted uneasily in her chair. The group drew closer, their hands on their belts.

How trained were they to attempt to tackle two magic-wielders? Did they even know they were sorcerers? Did they have weapons? Should she be worried— or were they just stupid?

"Imagine my surprise when I heard you are here, sheltering you deserter sister." The man smirked in a cocky way that reminded her of Julius. He lifted a piece of parchment. The black ink on it painted a portrait with Violet's features. The bold letters read, Runaway bride. Wanted for deserting the Crown. Thankfully, Gavin wasn't there.

"Go away, Theo," Thalea said, her hands balling into fists. Violet's blood ignited, sending her power surging through her veins. This was the one who was to blame for her father's demise. Her sister's fear and anger only confirmed it.

"Oh, fuck," Gavin said, and she registered the screech of his chair as he stood.

Theodore opened his mouth, unquestionably to threaten them further, but the words died on his lips as Violet threw her mug across the space. It shattered in his face, slashing skin, brows, and everything that had made him kind of pretty. She bolted from her seat like a madwoman hunting for vengeance, and the gasps of fear from his group only fueled her. Her magic gathered inside her, aiding her quick movements as she pulled two knives from her belt.

She kicked the man closest to her across the chest and threw a blade at another. Without pause, she danced away from one of their fists. They were too slow, all brawn and no brain, where she was magic and power.

Yes, she had told Gavin she would not seek out the bastard. But she'd made no promises about what she would do if he found her. They were fucked either way. The whole city now knew she was an outlaw. These small-town people needed to see what it meant to confront a trained soldier.

She jumped on the fourth man and plunged her blade into the place where his shoulder met his arm. His scream vibrated through the chaos in the tavern. Gavin's spell hit the fifth and last man, sending him flying across the room and into a mess of tables and chairs.

Their moans of pain filled the air. The bartender was hiding behind the counter, along with his waiter and a few terrified patrons. Violet's harsh breaths burned her throat as she looked down at the fallen men. Theodore was holding his face, crying like a babe while he rolled around on the ground.

Over by the table, Thalea stood frozen, pale, and with wide eyes. Was she afraid?

Gavin rushed to her sister's side, grabbing her arm and pulling her toward the back door. "Violet, let's go!"

Violet crouched next to Theo, plucking the bloodied wanted sign from his hands. "Judgment day came for you," she whispered in his ear. She pulled his knife from his belt and smiled as he curled into a ball, begging for forgiveness.

Let him think this would be the end of him—even if she wouldn't hurt him further. When it came to it, she was not as wicked as he had been with her family.

"Violet," Gavin urged, already near the door. He raised his hand, and his coat flew over from its hook on the wall. Magic was a novelty here, and any sense of fear could buy them time.

They left through the back door. Thankfully, most taverns were designed similarly, and she had trained herself to sit by the exit ever since she'd escaped the

Iron City. Unlike that night in Scoria, Gavin was no longer her enemy.

She looked at her sister when the alleyway spilled them out onto the city's main street. Her heart hammered in her throat. Thalea being here with her was dangerous. What had happened inside would come back to haunt her, without a doubt.

"Go home and get any gold you have saved. Pack a bag for both you and mother. You can take my mare out of this place. We will meet you later. If anything seems weird at all, you leave the house and find us at the piers." She pressed Theodore's knife to Thalea's chest. Her sister's eyes were still wide with fear.

"But, you already gave me a knife."

"That one is not the same. With this one you aim to hurt them enough, so you can escape."

"What about you?" she asked.

Another group of people turned the corner, more patrons on their way to the tavern. A suspiciously large group. Pushing Thalea in the opposite direction, Violet lowered her face to her ear. "I will be fine. I'm trained to survive, I promise. Now go."

IT WAS DIFFICULT TO RETURN TO THE INN IN THE MIDDLE OF the afternoon without being seen. They ran through the back alleyways, using magic to hide them when possible, even though their shielding spells were weak. Finding the shifters was imperative. They needed help, not only to bring their horses back to Violet's home so that Thalea and her mother could use them to escape, but also because they might need reinforcements.

Mercifully, they discovered them right outside the inn. Ellie was giving orders to the footman. Mios' mane looked messier than she had seen it before, ruffled by the wind after a long ride.

"He hasn't seen me yet." Gavin peered around the corner. "Fuck," he said. "This is a mess."

"I made it worse back in the tavern, but I just couldn't let that bastard get away with what he did," she muttered under her breath, leaning against the wall of the building. Now that the adrenaline had eased, she almost regretted her actions. The bounty hunters were here for her, and now it would be especially difficult to leave.

Gavin glanced back at her, and his expression softened. "He was looking for trouble, and what he got was less than what he deserved. I would have done something far less restrained than fracture his nose with a clay mug... and may I remind you that I find it sexy when you're mean?"

"Stop making me smile." She looked up at the darkening sky. "We need to go back home to help Thalea and mother."

"Yes. Wait—I think Mios spotted me. They are coming."

"Fancy seeing you here. Why are we hiding?" Ellie asked, stepping into the alleyway and shoving both hands inside her pockets.

Violet lifted the wanted flier she held in her grip and handed it to the wolf. Would the reward in gold sway Ellie? Never mind. It was too exhausting to mistrust everyone.

"Runaway bride? This is very scandalous. What an interesting turn of events." Ellie's copper gaze traced the picture before she handed it to Mios. "I thought you two were married?"

"We are," Gavin growled, resting his head against the wall. He eyed the few people passing by in the street with suspicion. "A few local men ambushed us in the tavern and tried to take Violet... You can imagine how well that went."

"You aren't in this flier, Gavin," Mios said.

"My parents are likely paying a fortune to keep me off. Or they haven't found out I'm here yet."

The lion nodded and handed the parchment back to Violet. "So, what now? Are you going to try to get the horses? I guess we can head south."

"I can't. We saw bounty hunters this morning." Her voice shook. She'd run out of time to find any god stones—in this part of the world, at least. "They must have my face plastered everywhere by now. I have to leave the Iron Kingdom. I take it you didn't get inside the mine?"

"A Sídhe ambushed us on the other side of the mine." Mios indicated his forearm, where a bloodied bandage covered him from wrist to elbow.

Oh. She'd almost forgotten about the Sídhes and their conflict with the shifters.

"I can look at that if you want to," Gavin offered, his eyes narrowing at the dried blood that spotted the dirty gauze.

"Here in the alleyway while you're being hunted down? No, I'll be fine. My nature will take care of it eventually."

"We have to go to my family's house and help my sister and mom," Violet cut in. "They can't stay here. Then we need to leave. Somehow."

"I can find us a boat out of here and meet you back at your place," Gavin said.

"You don't have to do it alone," Mios said. "I owe you my freedom, and Ellie owes Violet her ass. So we will find you a way out of here. You take care of your family."

Ellie glanced at Mios. "This might be a good time for me to tell you I saw another fancy horse, a stallion like yours, Gavin. Most regular people can't afford one of those. You wouldn't have one unless you're rich or—"

A chill ran up her spine. Or you were a member of the Society of Crows.

VIOLET

T HEY MADE HASTE TO THE OUTSKIRTS OF TOWN, THROUGH alleyways and small roads. The mist of the late afternoon gave them cover from the few people who went about their routines. Violet was thankful her house was so secluded. They didn't need any attention from strangers right now.

Hopefully Thalea had made it home safe without having to use the weapon Violet had given her outside the tavern. She took a calming breath. She was probably just being paranoid. Still, with the bounty hunters in town it was imperative her family left today.

"Tell me I didn't send Thalea to her death earlier, when I sent her home on her own." Violet strode quickly over the tan gravel that filled the pathway leading up to her house.

"She lives here," Gavin reassured. "No one would bat an eye at seeing her walk down the streets."

They kept their steps light, but the eerie silence

around them raised the hair on her arms. Her heart jolted when something crunched beneath the heel of her boot.

Violet looked down to see a green sliver of painted wood. A piece from what had once been the front door. She lifted her head slowly, her breathing impossibly loud. The porch hid most of the entrance from sight, but even here in the pathway, fragmented parts of it lay dotted about.

Someone was here. Her heart lodged in her throat, and both Gavin and her rushed toward the house, their magic buzzing around them in a thick air shield. They crossed the threshold and burst into the small living room. Her childhood home was a mess of shattered furniture with debris strewn all over the floor.

Gavin's sword sliding from its sheath broke the dead silence. The back doors swung against the walls, pushed by the wind.

The sea breeze had cooled the place so much that their breaths billowed in clouds before their faces. Violet's fingers were numb, stiff with the lack of blood as she tightened her fist. She stood frozen in her spot as she remembered her mother and sister. This morning they'd all sat at that table. Now it lay in pieces.

Gavin moved cautiously around the house, his sword drawn. She wasn't sure how long she stood there, staring at the remnants of what had once been her family's life, now scattered and broken. Destroyed by the Society of Crows. Blue flames hovered over her skin, feeding on the anger that boiled in her gut.

"Love, no one's here." Gavin pushed his hair out of his face. "It hasn't been gone that long. We can look for them in the streets, ask around. I'm not sure where they would take them."

Why leave this place empty? Why was the furniture destroyed? Her sister and mother wouldn't have put up a fight. Not against a member of the Society of Crows.

How many of them had been here?

Violet moved across the kitchen and toward the back doors, taking hold of one of them. She listened out for anything that wasn't normal. Steps, the creaking of floorboards, the grinding sound of sand that might alert her to someone walking on the beach. But her rapid heartbeats drowned out everything.

The boathouse. She'd almost forgotten about it. A dark building that had always given her the creeps since it smelled like death and critters lived in its the dark corners. Her dad used to keep his large fishing boat there.

"Violet, I didn't know you'd brought my satchel with you from Scoria. Did you leave it here earlier?"

His satchel? She turned to Gavin, her brows dipping low as she stared at the brown bag he was holding in one hand. She hadn't seen it since he'd given it to her right before Julius had arrested him.

Her blood ran cold, and she stopped breathing. No, that wasn't right. She'd last seen it when she'd broken into the governor's house—right before Julius had captured her in the tunnels.

"It still has most of my things—except for the

healing potion." Gavin met her eyes and paused, reading her face. "You weren't the one to bring it here."

It wasn't a question. She stumbled toward him like a newborn fawn. Gavin met her halfway, his expression shifting from confused to worried.

"Did you use the potion back in Scoria, in his room?"

"No."

Was Julius Coventry alive? She'd left him in that house to suffer a slow death, like the bastard deserved. He'd been at death's doorstep. There was no way he could have survived.

"Fuck, Violet. Did you actually kill him?"

"He was dying and unconscious." Or so she'd thought. "I locked the door so no one would help him." The words didn't ease the weight already settling within her. Of her massive mistake. One she'd repeated again.

Whenever she'd replayed that night in Scoria, she'd told herself that she'd wanted to protect Gavin from having to potentially kill Julius after his betrayal. Because he was good, unlike her. But now the truth slammed into her. It had been more than that. She hadn't trusted that he wouldn't heal Julius.

She hadn't wanted Gavin to kill his old commander and regret it, and yet she also hadn't wanted him to save the monster, either.

Lying to herself in retrospect had been easier. The closer she grew to Gavin, the happier she'd been that he hadn't been forced to make a choice that would burden him. But it had been her own uncertainties that had made her hide the truth that Julius wasn't dead in the first place.

She'd relied only on herself, just like she'd done her entire life. And now this massive mistake had come back around to hurt her family.

"He left the bag here to show us he was here," she said tonelessly.

She expected Gavin to berate her. For lying. For not trusting him.

"We will talk about this later." Gavin pulled her close, and his warmth seeped through the layers of her coat. "He's playing with us. He wants you to act irrationally. I know how he works, and he's overly confident. He would assume we're easy prey."

"Right now I feel like it."

Gavin's brows dipped as he peered outside, studying the gloomy sky. "Julius hired his own men back in Scoria. He might be alone or with them."

"Why weren't they waiting here, then?"

"He thinks he's already won. He's just toying with us. But I do think they are waiting. The question is where."

Unfortunately, Julius' approach was working. Violet knew how perverted his mind was—and now he had her sister. "I think they might be out there, in my father's boathouse." She pointed at the structure. For a moment they stood quietly, staring out at the pier which stretched toward it across the sands.

Then Gavin pressed his lips tightly together and

turned toward her. His hand traveled along her spine in a gentle caress and settled between her shoulder blades. "I'd say we get this over with. We don't want him to get his hands on Thalea."

Her heart slowed when his russet color eyes met hers. The warmth that flooded her wasn't the unpleasant despair that had been driving her mad this entire time, but a wholly different sensation that brought her ease. "You don't have to die here, Gavin. Not because of my stupidity. You should go back to your family."

"I have a family, and she is standing right next to me. Stop trying to save me, Violet. I make my own choices. I want to stay with the woman I love while she tries to rescue her people."

Tears blurred her vision, and she swallowed and took a shaky breath. Her nerves were strung too tight, and it left her dizzy. "I love you, and I'm sorry."

"If you think I blame you for making that choice, you're wrong. Not after Julius hurt you, and I had spent a few days before that defending the bastard." He shook his head and looked away, attempting to hide a deep frown. "I wish I'd had my eyes open before all of it happened."

They came up with a simple plan. She would run ahead of Gavin, hoping to draw any bounty hunters out of hiding. Then they would go into the boathouse together. If no one ambushed her, she would investigate the place alone while he inspected the surroundings.

The small backyard was cluttered with fishing gear, old and busted nets draped everywhere. Her house lay at the end of a natural lagoon, isolated because of the strong winds and storms which whipped it. The land had been in her family line for centuries, even though her parents had rebuilt the house when they'd moved here. Perhaps it was the magic in their blood that had protected it from the unforgiving weather. She steeled her spine as she crept over the uneven boards of the pier, her heart beating fast.

Violet hated the idea of walking into a trap. It would be so easy to leave now and forget that these last few days had ever happened. To put aside her love for her sister, who was almost a stranger.

But it was her fault that they were in this position. She wasn't going anywhere.

The waves crashed around her, thick droplets clinging to her skin and hair. She kept her body low and close to the planks, hoping her poor attempt at a shielding spell would mask her approach.

The water foamed as it retreated, the tide high and spilling on top of the uneven boards. The air around her tasted crisp and humid. A storm brewed in the distance, shaking the place with a strong wind.

No one jumped out at her from the boathouse. No bounty hunters or Crows. Yet, deep in her gut she knew that behind those doors was her enemy. The cocky bastard assumed she would bend to his will. But he didn't know that the God of Shadows himself was tied to her—and to Thalea.

32
VIOLET

THE INSIDE OF THE BOATHOUSE WASN'T ANYTHING LIKE SHE remembered. The building used to be beautiful. Its green paint had long since peeled away, revealing the silver wood underneath. The windows were cracked, shattered, or missing entirely, like they'd sunk into the water.

The floor was the same as the pier outside, forming a U-shape at its center that housed her father's proudest possession. Torn by the weather and the sea, a large fishing boat bobbed up and down. The ceiling had partially collapsed on top of it, and it creaked with every movement.

Drops of rain drenched her as she looked over the ruins of her past toward the three shapes on the other side.

Her mother and sister kneeled on the floor, with Julius standing between them. "Surprise, Cora," he said in a hoarse, rattling tone, then coughed. "I bet you didn't expect to see me here."

"No. I thought you were dead." She made her way toward him slowly. Keeping him talking would buy her family time. Make Julius focus his anger towards her, and give Thalea a chance to run.

"Ah. Not a step closer. Drop your blade. Now." He snarled the words, no longer pretending. His eyes never left Violet's swift movements as she stepped over a fallen board. The turquoise water beneath could have fooled anyone into thinking that this was some tropical beach. Beautiful, but dangerously cold. Especially during winter.

It gave her a sick joy. Julius was afraid of her talent with a knife. But not even her well-honed skills could convince her to throw her only physical weapon from this far. It was too much of a risk. In the best-case scenario, she risked it lodging itself somewhere on her father's fishing boat. Worst case, and it would end up on the seafloor.

"I said drop the blade!" His frown deepened. He looked considerably smaller than when she'd left him to die. Sick.

"Go fuck yourself, Julius." Violet pressed the words between tight lips, panic churning deep inside her. She wasn't under any delusion that he was planning on letting any of them live.

"I don't have to kill both of them," Julius bartered. "But if I have to repeat myself, I will, and rather swiftly." He yanked both her mother's and sister's heads back to further prove how much power he had over her. Their exposed throats bobbed with their cries.

Violet froze instantly.

"Don't do it, Violet!" Thalea's wavering voice broke the tense silence that had fallen on them. Her words had the opposite effect, and the prickle of tears stung Violet's eyes just as the knife dropped from her opened hand.

She swallowed at the sound of metal hitting the boards. Her mother's whimpers grew louder. "Let them go, Julius. Your problem is with me. They are innocent."

"Innocent?" His wild gaze widened as an ugly laugh burst from his thin, chapped lips. It sounded bitter and raw. "Cora Elder, the records of your family tree fill a whole tome in our library. What a waste of parchment. The Crows should have killed you the moment they learned you wanted to escape."

Violet couldn't even disagree with that.

"Aww, I feel special. Is that why you came all the way here? May I remind you how you ended up last time?" She flashed her eyes to her sister, her hands were tied in front of her, and too far away for her to reach the knife hidden in her shoe.

Thalea's eyes burned with determination, not fear. Violet knew they were thinking the same thing. Let the bastard believe he had it all figured out.

Calling his attention toward her was a dangerous plan, but unless Gavin came now with reinforcements, she wasn't sure what else to do. She kept her voice from shaking and said, "you're as pathetic as your cock."

Julius eyes burned, but his fists released their wicked hold on her family. Mission accomplished. His magic were gray swirls over his hands. This time, only her mother wailed in pain.

"Stop talking," Julius growled and walked toward Violet, dragging both her mother and Thalea along with him. "You know you won't leave here alive. It's up to you whether one of these two does or if they both die with you."

Dread twisted her stomach, pooling inside her like acid. She had little power here. Without her weapon, and with her magic only a fraction of Julius' strength, she would fail unless Gavin hurried up and helped her kill him. Together, just like they should have done back in Scoria.

"Why would you want to kill them? They've done nothing. You've won. Please let them go."

Julius laughed again. "Oh, Cora. I will hurt them because I enjoy seeing women cry—you especially. I must admit, you got me in Scoria, and that just made me want you more. But there's still that small matter of what you did to my cousin Morgan. So let's just say... your kin will pay for the blood of mine."

"Morgan wasn't an innocent. They are. People in town will ask questions." Violet swallowed, feeling sweat bead on her temple. She glanced through the broken window above them. The dark, stormy clouds were closing in.

Soon, the tide would flood this whole place. Why

was Gavin taking so long? She couldn't hear a thing from outside.

"Where's the boy?" Julius asked, as if he'd heard her thought. "Don't think you can surprise me today. I know he's with you. I'm not alone either."

"If you think that's news, then you're a dumb fuck." What else could she say to stall him further? "We aren't alone either. That shifter you pissed off will tear into you like you're made of butter."

Julius' face sharpened with anger. The scent of his magic grew even thicker, and the air became almost too spicy to breathe without coughing. Thalea curled in on herself, crying in pain, yet her bound hands dipped inside her boot and pulled out the knife with a white knuckle grasp.

"Let's not waste any more time. Pick who dies first, Cora. Your sister or your poor old ma?"

For a long moment, Violet stood still, frozen. Thalea wasn't crying anymore. Their eyes met, and she knew it was time. "Now, Lea!" Violet screamed.

Julius' shock bought them precious seconds as Thalea slammed her small three-inch blade into Julius' boot. He wailed and stepped back, his hold on both of them loosening.

"Run!"

But her sister hesitated by their mother's side. The attack didn't buy them enough time. His power, dark gray, came out in a spell that hit her sister in the back, sending her flying forward across the wooden floor.

Julius stepped over her mother's weak attempt at

holding him back, like she weighed nothing. His gloved hand wrapped around Thalea's neck, just as Violet picked her knife from the ground.

"No, no, no." The words echoed in her mind, and she knew she'd run out of time.

Julius pulled out a wavy dagger that caught the stormy light. Violet surged forward and aimed her blade at the man. Static crackled in the air as her sister struggled in his arms.

"I'll enjoy breaking you two." He used the curved tip of his knife to pull up the chain hanging over Thalea's neck. "Interesting. A god stone? Could this be hiding a magic-wielder from our King?" Julius clipped it off with the blade. "Death penalty to the guardian for such a crime."

The stone clinked over the wooden beams, shimmering in the distance.

A body came crashing through the windows, rolling to a stop on the uneven floorboards. Gavin? No. It was a man, but he looked nothing like him. As if called by her thoughts, Gavin stepped into the room a moment later. His stern features softened when he spotted her.

They must have ambushed him outside. His face was bloodied and swollen, and his thick gray coat hung in tatters over his shoulder.

Julius cursed and threw Thalea to the ground, dodging Violet's fire spell. Reinvigorated by the knowledge that Gavin was safe, she cast another across the boathouse, right at the bastard. He dissipated it with little effort, although his confident expression wavered.

He jumped away from her sister and landed next to her mother, his blade plunging into her without a moment of hesitation.

Violet's steps faltered, and a scream echoed through the place. Hers? She couldn't tell. Rain pelted down on them, followed by thunder. The surging sea crashed against the dilapidated remnants of her father's boat.

Her sister's screams joined hers. But it was her eyes that made Violet grind to a halt. They shone a milky, bright green. All the hairs on Violet's arms stood on end as the temperature dropped. Her mother's moan was barely audible in the background. Maybe Gavin could heal her. There was still time.

"Violet, get out of there!" Gavin called to her, sounding utterly panicked. A body rose from the center of the building, climbing out of the waters near the boat. Violet stumbled backward, away from her sister who seemed lost in her grief, tears dripping down her face. A green aura buzzed over her skin.

Magic. Thalea was calling on her own power, and spirits were answering her calls.

Neem after Neem crawled out of the water, missing limbs: a terrifying image of bones and rotting flesh. The scent alone left her gagging as she backed away, pressing herself against the wall.

But the Neems weren't interested in Violet or Gavin. They stalked toward Julius, closing in a circle before they descended on him. His cries of pain rang through the room.

A hand wrapped around her arm, making her jump, her own magic spiking.

"It's me. We have to leave." Gavin was pulling her toward the exit.

"No," Violet protested. "My mother and Thalea." She stared at the Neems which surrounded her sister.

"There have to be at least fifty of them. Once Julius is dead, we're next."

To be honest, Violet wasn't willing to gamble again on whether that cockroach of a man had actually died this time.

"What if she can't control them and they get Mom?" Violet struggled inside the cage of Gavin's arms.

"We will come back for her when the Neems are gone." But when she met his eyes, the clarity inside them only left her feeling sicker. He thought her mother was dead already.

Violet looked across his shoulder to her unmoving mother and the place where her sister sat. Thalea was staring at an empty spot in the distance, and the spirits hovered around her, a protective wall of maggots and flesh that would kill both Gavin and her if they dared to approach.

What if they left, and when they came back she was gone along with them?

The cold air was suddenly pungent with the scent of old magic. Violet held her breath, holding onto Gavin's arms as gooseflesh rolled over her skin. The storm shook the building with angry waves.

"My necromancer. At last." An icy voice slithered

out from nowhere and everywhere at once. Lightning flashed, blinding her for a moment.

She blinked and swallowed, trying to clear the buzzing in her ears. Before her stood a tall shape, wearing a black cloak that matched his long ebony hair. It contrasted with his milky skin.

His wide pink lips quirked, and the pools of his golden irises shone brightly as they drank in her sister like a prize that he desired. This was no man.

"Dargan," she whispered.

Gavin tensed as he, too, saw the god materialize in front of Thalea. When Dargan moved, all the spirits stood and turned to him in one motion, as though they'd been commanded to do so. The air grew thick and suffocating.

"Why are you bound and on the ground?" Dargan asked her sister. He glanced at Julius' broken body. His brows dipped low in a brief flash of anger.

Thalea rolled over and onto her feet. Her dress was tattered and stained with blood from her cheek. "Stay back, or I will ask them to hurt you!"

Dargan tilted his head, and a slow grin spread over his beautiful, deadly face. "Your ancestor called upon me. She asked for the last necromancer to be spared. You can only repay the price of one soul with another of the same kind. You are mine, Thalea Elder." And he took a step closer.

"I'm no one's!" Thalea shouted. Her hair, which had always been a deep black, suddenly looked bleached of all color. White, like that of all the other emissaries.

Luelle, Cullen, and the Dark One who had come to Violet in the shifter's village—they'd all had silver-toned locks. The mark of Dargan's claim.

Violet's anger churned hot. She fought her way out of Gavin's grasp and threw her blade through the air with the full force of her magic. It cut through the room with unmatched precision, past the spirits and the air poisoned with their rot. Her magic propelled it unerringly at the god's torso.

Fuck him.

He was so focused on Thalea he didn't see it coming. The knife embedded itself in his chest, right between his heart and shoulder blade. Everything stopped. Then Dargan turned, his eyes settling on Violet for the first time.

Did the gods feel pain? He pulled the knife from his body like it was nothing but an inconvenience. His nostrils flaring was the only reaction he gave her. "You can't kill me, pet."

Perhaps she could distract him long enough for Thalea to make whatever move she needed to make. The spirit's rotten, semi-corporeal shapes flung themselves onto Dargan all at once, stalling his forward momentum. Her little sister's lips tilted down as she fell back against the crumbling wall of the boathouse. One of her trembling hands lifted, her fingertips shining with green licks of flaring light.

"This deathtrap is about to collapse." Gavin grabbed Violet's hand, holding her back. He was right. The waves rose outside the windows, at least eight feet high and rocking the walls with a storm brought by the last emissary. The God of Shadows, himself.

Luelle had spoken the truth. Violet would be free of her curse, but she wouldn't be happy.

It had been Thalea all along. Her sister's imaginary friends, her talking to the spirit of their father back in the mines. Everything had led them to this moment.

"Call them off, now!" Dargan's growl pebbled Violet's skin with an icy cold touch, and her warmth breath turned to mist. The ground shook beneath her feet as she struggled to keep standing.

The moans of the spirits that swarmed around Thalea were awful, but they were holding the god back.

"Don't take her, Dargan." It was the second time she'd begged, and she would do it again and again if it meant keeping her sister safe. "We've come this far. Take me instead. I will do anything. Please."

She'd hated him and everyone who'd forced her into this mess, but it had been her own actions that had led them all into this moment. Violet would've sacrificed herself over and over again before she allowed her younger sister to live a life of never dying. It was unbearable to think of her becoming as jaded as Luelle had been.

Dargan didn't stop his approach, and although he was closer to Thalea than Violet and Gavin, she could see his face grow more frustrated by the minute, as more Neems piled on top of him. "I'm not interested in you anymore," he said. "Not when I have my necromancer." He turned his golden gaze upon her, and his eyes softened a fraction. "It's what you wanted all along, pet. Live, and be sure she'll be safe."

"No." Violet's voice was a pathetic whine.

Dargan reached Thalea, pulling her out of a wall of spirits that snapped their slack jaws at the god. They never harmed him, as every cut and bruise healed instantly before their eyes.

"Wait! Please, let me say goodbye. I will come with you without a fight if you do." Thalea struggled inside Dargan's grasp as he scooped her into his arms. The only remaining part of the roof collapsed on top of the boat, and it sank into the churning sea. Gavin dragged Violet closer to the door.

Dargan paused. Just when Violet thought he wouldn't respond, he placed Thalea back down. "Make haste. I'm not a patient man."

He was not a man, but a monster she couldn't kill. Violet ran toward her sister, swallowing the fear that spiked at being so close to the Shadow God and the surrounding Neems.

Then Thalea's arms held her tight, her lips hovering over Violet's ear. "I'm happy to do this for you."

"What?"

"You don't have to be taken." Thalea smiled. "Don't you see? You get to stay with Gavin. Have the family you desire. And for once, I'm not the crazy woman, feared and hated. I have a purpose."

A sob lodged in Violet's throat. "You shouldn't be taken to be exploited for your gift."

"No. But you wouldn't want me around you. I don't

even know what I'm doing. The spirits are always there, and they react when I'm overwhelmed. It's why Dad got the stone." Thalea stepped back and brought her small hand up to Violet's cheek. "I love you, even though I wish I'd gotten to know you better. I always have."

The floor beneath their feet trembled, and a board right beside them crumbled into the water.

"And I love you, Lea," Violet whispered.

"We have to go, Violet." Gavin pulled her back just as a piece of the building rained down on them.

"She's alive," Thalea screamed above the commotion, right as Dargan reached her, wrapped both arms around her waist, and disappeared them both from view. All the Neems vanished alongside them.

Her sister was gone. Violet's curse was broken, and yet... she had never been so sad.

"Who is alive?" Gavin asked and turned to where Julius' remains lay on the ground.

The commander's limbs were bent in weird directions. His blue eyes stared sightlessly at the ceiling. But Violet's gaze was fixed on the spot beside him. At the woman she'd avoided looking at since Julius had stabbed her.

"My mother," she said.

33

VIOLET

Lightning flashed behind black clouds that blocked out the sun. The heavy air still held a thick, rotten quality she could taste in her throat. This was the aftermath of being swarmed by death. Literally.

Violet closed the back door and followed Gavin across the mess of broken furniture and glass into her mother's room.

Gavin placed her over furs on the bed, which loomed twice as large in her memory. He straightened with a grimace and sank down next to her. He hadn't been able to hide the limp on their walk back here.

"How many bounty hunters were out there?" she asked.

Gavin undid her mother's nightgown and exposed the bloodied skin of her stomach. "Two."

Two bastards had caught him alone, while Violet was coming face to face with Julius inside. Probably the same ones they'd met at the inn. They'd left one body behind in the sea and the other in the boathouse.

She sighed and reached for his shoulder. "You're hurt. Tell me what I can do to help you."

"I'll be fine," he said through gritted teeth. "She's dying, Violet. If I don't heal her now, she won't make it."

She looked at her hands and recoiled. They were red with her mother's blood. When she lifted her face, she found his quivering smile. "I'll do everything I can to save her," Gavin said. "I promise."

"I know." She withdrew and rose. "I'll get the fire going and heat up some water for a bath."

She let Gavin do what he could for her mother and allowed herself to sleepwalk her way through the tasks. By the time the home was warm and the smell of stew was strong, night had fallen. Dargan's storm still raged.

Violet dug one of her hands into the pocket of her coat, pulling out the uneven green stone with rainbow highlights. She had found it right beside Julius' broken body when they'd picked up her mother before leaving the boathouse. Such a small, powerful thing, a sharp contrast against the lighter shade of her palm.

Even though Thalea had been seeing spirits since she was young, Dargan hadn't felt her before. Had her sister's magic gone unnoticed by everyone for a reason? Perhaps it was only palpable if she used it to its fullest extent, like she'd done today.

Perhaps he'd been so focused on Violet, he'd never thought of looking at Thalea. Or there were enough god stones to dull one's power underneath this town, like in the mountains. Come to think of it, hadn't the Crows only picked her up after she'd rowed out far, far to sea with father that one time?

Hadn't Violet once read of a non-magical town, Willowbrook?

What if it wasn't? God stones might be behind hiding innocents away from the Crows and the gods throughout the kingdom. The myth about them being so rare might be just that—a myth created to keep people in the dark. Maybe the Crows didn't want people to know that these natural deposits existed in the very soil they all trod on. After all, she had never found a spell that could dull magic for long with our being tracked.

These were all questions she would likely never get the answers to, but ones she would seek.

"She's stable for now." Gavin's voice jolted her out of her reverie, and she closed her hand around the jewel, half afraid it would fall between the cracks of the floor and vanish forever.

"Thank you."

He limped toward her, dragging his right leg behind him. He shrugged off his coat and tossed it over the only standing piece of furniture in the room, the bench which rested against the wall.

She waited for him. He was so handsome with his long, messy hair, his tanned skin, and his sharp jaw. He caged her body with both arms and leaned closer to her, his breath caressing her face. "That smells good."

Violet brought her hand to his cheek, stroking the raspy texture of his stubble. The fluttering in her stomach spread a subtle warmth through her that chased away the icy grip of sadness. "I get to keep you now. I guess I have to start being nice…"

Gavin grinned, although the gesture looked tired at best. If she closed her eyes, she could almost fool herself into thinking today was a joyful day to celebrate.

He pressed a kiss to her lips. "I like you just the way you are. What others think is their problem."

She might have to remind him of that later on, when he got annoyed at her snarky nature. They ate standing in the kitchen, watching the high waves that clashed too close to the house for comfort and rocked the pier beyond. The boathouse continued to fall apart in chunks, but the sounds of its demise didn't bring her much sorrow.

When night rolled around, they bathed and warded the building. Gavin discovered that he could fit into her dad's clothes and used his army coat as additional kindling for the fire, trading it for a light brown one instead.

"Do you think Mios and Ellie will come?" Violet asked. Even though they got rid of Julius and the bounty hunters, they couldn't stay in Sagewood long. Not only had the Commander found her family's property, but so had two of the bounty hunters. With the flyers still out there and offering a handsome reward for her capture, staying in her family home—or this town at all—was sheer idiocy.

"They'll come, but not tonight in this storm," Gavin said, and reached for her hand before pulling her towards her old room. "Let's get some sleep."

Morning arrived, though the darkness of the sky remained. Rain patted the clay rooftop. Her mother's odds of survival were small, and yet Gavin had spent most of the night caring for her, even knowing that she was probably too weak to handle this kind of trauma.

Violet was feeding a piece of the broken chair to the fire when there was a knock on the door. Or rather, on the wooden planks that Violet had used to board it up where Julius had smashed it. Gavin, who was already walking better, picked up his sword from the counter.

"It's us," Ellie screamed.

Mios and the wolf weren't alone. Next to them, a tall man with tanned skin and wide shoulders greeted her. His salt and pepper hair, oily from lack of washing, was tied back into a mess of braids.

She had seen him before. He was famous throughout the kingdom—a commander who had deserted the land years ago.

"This is Roman," Mios said.

"I know of you." Violet said.

Roman tipped his head as he walked into the house,

glancing around with a frown. "I see some trouble found you…"

"Julius Coventry and two bounty hunters, to be exact. You have a way out of this place?"

"I do, and I need some crew members. We are headed for The Gray Island, which is protected by treaties and difficult to find for the Society of Crows' scrying mirrors. I leave in two days, before sunrise. You're both welcome to join us. You will have to work to pay for your spot and food." Roman met Gavin's gaze as her husband walked into the middle of the room.

"Commander."

"Gavin Luna. I never expected to see you here." A smile lifted Roman's lips, and they shook hands like they were long-lost friends. "You're expected to do physical work… Have you ever done anything like that?"

A laugh bubbled out of Violet's lips. Oh, she already liked this man. Of course they knew each other. Gavin's rich network of connections never ceased to amaze her.

Gavin leveled her with a glare. "I can tell a mediocre joke and cook a half-decent meal if forced. Otherwise, I am pretty useless. But we can discuss payment for my services since I can heal people, perhaps?"

Roman pressed his lips together, hiding a smile. His eyes were calculating, like he knew well enough how rare the gift of a healer was. "I should have known the son of a rich merchant would know how to negotiate. A shark is always able to spot blood in the water."

"Indeed." Gavin's wide smile brought out those dimples she loved.

Gavin looked across Roman's shoulders at her, nodding almost imperceptibly. A man to trust, perhaps? She pushed away the instant urge to question it. Her old mistrust had crippled her and destroyed her life.

She could do this.

"So Mios said you killed Julius? It was about time someone did. Had they had not forced me to leave the way I did, I would have done it myself at some point."

She didn't want to talk about this. Not so soon. The ache in her jaw intensified, and she felt like her heart was breaking all over again. Tears pricked her eyes, and her strength to suppress them was wavering with every passing second. She gulped in air and looked away from the others. "Leaving in the morning is rather fast. My mother is badly hurt... I don't know if we can leave so soon."

"The place is crawling with bounty hunters. We saw at least three more by the docks," Mios said. "We weren't followed, and we can stay here with you for the time being. But more will come this way."

Whatever peace had come to her was already being dashed. "But..."

"Where is the rest of your family?" Ellie asked, her brows dipping as she sniffed the air. "It smells like old death here."

"Thalea is gone." Violet straightened her shoulders

and took a deep breath. If only their expressions of pity would go away.

She dug out the stone from her pocket and walked toward Mios, handing it to him.

"This thing is cursed," she warned, blinking tears out of her eyes. "Thanks to it, two of my family members are gone. Are you sure you want it?"

His golden cat irises widened when she revealed the shiny god stone in the center of her palm. His lips parted, then snapped shut again. He didn't reach for the stone. "What about you?" he asked instead. "Don't you also need it?"

"Not anymore."

"Is that why your sister is gone?"

Violet nodded, and Mios' lips pursed. For a moment, he hesitated. It really would be much better if he didn't take it—the thing would only bring him trouble.

But he did, and as soon as he took it, her magic buzzed freely through her body once again.

A moan came from her mother's room, and Gavin rushed down the corridor. Violet followed. Her mother was thrashing about on the furs, her skin shining with sweat as she cried, stuck in a nightmare of memories and pain.

The moment Gavin's hand settled on her mother's forehead, she stopped moving altogether. While her face gained some peace, Gavin's lost color.

"This would be much easier with all of my potions. I'm tired, and healing drains me."

Julius had brought along most of them when he'd dropped Gavin's satchel here, but what they really needed was the healing one. Exactly the one that bastard had taken to survive.

"We have to leave this place in two days, Violet. Your mother can't come with us."

She knew this, didn't she? "Thalea was the only one working to maintain this place. How is she going to survive here alone?"

"I can take her with me." Mios' voice came from the hall, right as he leaned against the doorframe. He crossed his massive arms over his chest, looking at Violet's mother. "We will stay here until she's stable, and then she can come with us to the Gold Kingdom. I'll take care of her until I see you again."

"You would do that?"

Mios' smile was a flash she might have imagined. "I don't have to travel across the kingdom to find the god atone for Lyra anymore. I'm heading back home."

He looked at Gavin.

"I can send a letter to your family as well. Explain all that happened with Julius in Scoria. You ran from your wedding night. Undoubtedly, the Society of Crows will try to blame you for Marrion's death."

"Morgan's," Gavin corrected with an amused smile.

"Her, yes. Either way, what they asked of you is against your laws. I'm going to guess your people can fight them, especially if they are friendly with the King."

Gavin's face cleared of all exhaustion, and his

expression filled with hope. He looked at Violet like a child who had just heard his wildest dreams might come true after all. It was enough to make her smile as well, even with everything that had happened.

"You are together, which is what they're claiming you escaped from." Mios shrugged. "But even if your King can't set things right, the Lionborn live outside your magic-wielder laws. If you're able to make it to my land—which I know is far away—you may see your family with no one bothering you. That I can promise you."

"Thank you," Gavin said, and the lion nodded, tapping the wood twice, before he turned around and walked back toward the living room. Violet could hear Roman's rough voice in the background.

"Do you think we can do it?" she asked Gavin. "See your family?"

"Our family," he corrected, and his words alone brought a rush of hope. She had no right to be feeling this way. "Yes."

"I didn't know you had met Roman."

"I was friendly with his partner, Mars." Gavin shrugged. "He was a well-known actor, and Mother loved him."

Violet looked down at her mother's sleeping form, and took a couple of sharp breaths. It was time to be strong and not fall apart, to forgive herself for all her wrongdoings. Because she'd tried her best, and learned so much.

She wasn't perfect, and this had taught her a lesson

she would never forget. She might still be mistrustful of strangers, but that didn't mean she had to work alone.

Gavin's hand landed on her shoulder, and he pulled her against him, reading her like she was an open book. She molded herself to his chest, enjoying the soft hints of her mother's lavender soap which clung to his skin. "Thalea is fine, Violet. Wherever she is going, she is alive. I trust that we will see her again."

"You don't know that for sure." Still, his words brought her a kind of peace.

"I don't, but I believe it to be true. It all happened too fast, but when Dargan saw her bound, he seemed upset."

For three years, Violet had been special. The God of Shadows had wanted her, and she'd hated every damn minute of it.

Her little sister had saved her from that fate. A family of women willing to sacrifice themselves for those they loved. Violet wished she could reverse the whole thing. Maybe a part of her would forever stay angry at life—and at her own choices. But today, as the sun rose behind the horizon of the silver ocean, she was grateful.

For once, she had a future. She'd had the chance to see Thalea again for a few days and met the wonderful, selfless woman she had grown up to be. These last few months had taught her many things. To be wary of false friendships. To fall in love and trust once again.

That power only corrupted people who let it—and wasn't Mios' offer the best proof of that.

But mostly, she now knew how lucky she was.

Most craved to be special, and yet all she'd ever wanted was to be normal. Whatever that was. The opportunity to have a life with Gavin was something Thalea had given her, and she would never take it for granted. She didn't want to be chosen ever again. Not unless the person making that choice was Gavin Luna.

Only then would she be fine with being the one.

**Gavin and Violet's story doesn't end here!
You can find them again in the first book of my
Wicked Kingdom series, and see what they are
up to:**

The Curse of the Crow,
Is an *action packed, sexy, fated mates Fantasy Romance!*

ABBEY FOX

The Curse of the Crow

THE WICKED KINGDOM

Book One

Destined to love each other. Determined to fight their fate.

Nava Forrest's brief meeting with a hooded stranger has forever bound her to her soulmate--a man she wants nothing to do with. Especially after her parents' forbidden love forced their family into hiding.

With her parents gone, Nava was left to raise her younger brother and sell potions to wary townsfolk to survive. When the Society of Crows finds Nava, intent on enslaving her, she is forced to flee to the forest, in search of the one person she was told can protect her.

Arkimedes is not what she expected, and her attraction to him is new and unnerving. As the chemistry between them grows, so does her power. With the Society closing in, they must learn to work together and create unexpected alliances to keep their freedom and save their destiny.

Escape to a new magical world in The Curse of the Crow! Action packed, sexy, and perfect for fans of Jennifer L. Armentrout and Sarah J. Mass

SIGN UP FOR MY NEWSLETTER!

For updates on future books, and to get extra scenes,
character art and more!

Go to

WWW.ABBEYFOX.COM

ACKNOWLEDGMENTS

Thank you to my critique partner Helen, for all your invaluable feedback.

To my beta reader, Jessica and Sara. Thank you for carving the time to check out the book during the holidays and help me make it better.

To my editor Amber, thank you for doing such a wonderful job and going above and beyond.

To my amazing ARC readers and street team that helped me hype up the book. Thank you for taking the time to read and review. It means the world to me.

To my friend Heather, thank you so much for making the wonderful ink illustrations in the book. Your skills never cease to amaze me!

FIND THE AUTHOR

facebook.com/abbeyfoxauthor

instagram.com/abbeyfoxauthor

tiktok.com/@Abbeyfoxauthor

pinterest.com/abbeyfoxauthor